The Queen of Sheba

Roberta Kells Dorr

MOODY PUBLISHERS

CHICAGO

Interior design: Ragont Design
Cover design: Brand Navigation, LLC
Cover images: iStock #9216951/14559153/453506, Fotalia #42310292, Shutterstock #74913688/93812500

Library of Congress Cataloging-in-Publication Data

Dorr, Roberta Kells.
   The Queen of Sheba : a novel / Roberta Kells Dorr.
      pages ; cm.
   Includes bibliographical references.
   ISBN 978-0-8024-0958-4
   1. Sheba, Queen of—Fiction. 2. Bible. O.T.—History of Biblical events—Fiction. 3. Queens—Sheba (Kingdom)—Fiction. I. Title.
PS3554.O694Q44 2013
813'.54—dc23

2013004373

We hope you enjoy this book from River North Fiction by Moody Publishers. Our goal is to provide high-quality, thought provoking books and products that connect truth to your real needs and challenges. For more information on other books and products written and produced from a biblical perspective, go to www. moodypublishers.com or write to:

River North Fiction
Imprint of Moody Publishers
820 N. LaSalle Boulevard
Chicago, IL 60610

1 3 5 7 9 10 8 6 4 2

Printed in the United States of America

Dedicated to my four splendid sons . . .

Philip

Paul

John

James

"No man is at all times wise."

— Pliny

Introduction

*T*hough the story of the Queen of Sheba's visit to Solomon has captured the imagination of artists, poets, and historians from time immemorial, there is little factual information available. Most of the story has to be drawn from the few lines in the Bible, the Jewish historian, Josephus, the Ethiopian history of its kings (Kebra Negast), the Qur'an, and from the Arab historian Ibn Ishaq, from which al Tabari gathered his information.

In both Yemen and Ethiopia there are numerous legends, some of which appear to be rather bizarre until one begins to peel away the fantasies to find the kernel of truth they undoubtedly hold. It is by putting together these legends with the factual information available and the customs of the people that I have attempted to discover this fascinating queen's story.

For instance, the Hoopoe bird mentioned in the Qur'an that carried messages back and forth from Marib to Jerusalem, must have been the nickname of a trader. Also in the Qur'an we are told that the queen worshiped idols, used the power of Jinns (demons) to work magic, and had her palace at Marib in Yemen.

From the Arab historian Tabari, we are told that she was thought by Solomon to have the feet of a donkey, that she married Solomon and was converted to his faith. It is from Arab legends that we also are told of the white Arabian horse named Zad el-Rukab that the queen brought as a gift to Solomon.

The Ethiopian legends found in the Kebra Negast give us more information. Tamrin is mentioned as a trader-emissary for the queen, and the guide for her caravan, which boasted seven hundred ninety-seven camels plus countless asses and mules all ladened with gifts. We are given the added bit of information that she stayed six months in Jerusalem.

It is from the Ethiopian legends that we learn how Solomon put the queen's bed in his room, ordered her food heavily salted, so he could claim her when she drank his water. We are also told in these legends that he gave the queen a ring for the son that would be born from their union and about the son's journey back to Jerusalem on a visit to his father.

We are told just where the son was born in Ethiopia and how the city of Axum on the coast was built as the queen's new capitol.

The references to the Egyptian princess and the worship of the cat god Bastet are based on Egyptian history. Shoshenk, the pharaoh during Solomon's reign was the first king of the 22nd dynasty. He belonged to a Libyan family. Their capitol was at Bubastis, in the Delta, and the cat god, Bastet, was the object of their worship. They had temples built to this god and all cats were sacred. The princess from Egypt who married Solomon would have been from this family and this part of Egypt.

The information dealing with Bilqis's long journey from Marib in Yemen to Jerusalem was gleaned from various sources plus my own travels in the Sinai. I have ridden through the narrow Siq leading into the fortress of Petra and have climbed the steps to the High altar. This altar, minus the golden platform, looks just as it must have looked centuries ago. The steps are still there winding up the face of the cliff and ending at the pinnacle of rock from which the altar was fashioned. Sheep and bullocks were the usual offerings, but in times of extreme crisis or when favors were requested of the gods, children or captives taken in battle were sacrificed.

Living in Yemen and visiting Ethiopia often, I was able to explore the new discoveries made by archaeologists at both Marib in Yemen and Axum in Ethiopia. I have seen the pillars of Bilqis's temple to the moon god Ilumquh, which now lies half buried in drifting sand. I have studied the layout of her city with its lovely palace and have walked on the impressive ruins of her dam. I have run my hand over the remains of an alabaster bull's head that to her would have been the earthly embodiment of the moon god she worshiped.

Most exciting of all, I came upon the remains of an alabaster throne in the Sanaa museum. There were only the armrests and the two front legs. Upon examining it closely, I discovered the legs terminated in the very realistic hooves of a bull. For me, the legend of the queen having the feet of a donkey suddenly became understandable. With long robes covering her feet, it is entirely possible that visitors might see only the hooves and imagined them to be her feet.

Bilqis began to take shape as I pieced together the bits of legend, studied the culture, and retraced her steps wherever possible. She was no longer a remote personage in a history book but a vital, intriguing woman who begged to have her story told.

The Queen of Sheba

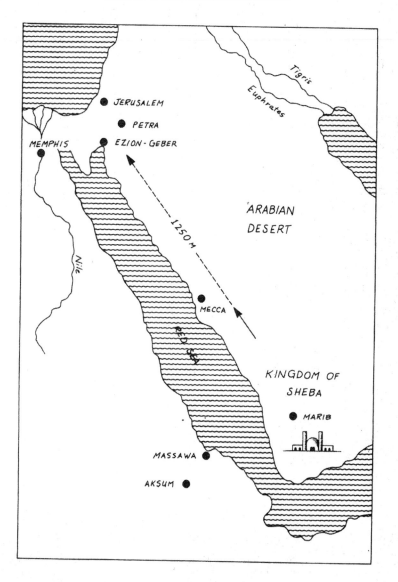

Bilqis

*I*t was the annual dry season and the first of the caravans had arrived in Jerusalem from the south. On hearing the news, Solomon with his son and a few of his friends retired to the more casual, tentlike quarters built on the roof of his new palace. This was an ideal place to view the varied assortment of bobbles and oddities with some real treasures brought from distant lands.

The traders would go on to Hazor and then Damascus, where they sold most of their wares, but in Jerusalem they had always found Solomon to be one of their best customers. He knew quality and was not reluctant to pay high prices for an item he happened to like. However, now that his ships had made a successful trip down the Red Sea to Punt, the traders were afraid he would no longer buy from them.

Old Badget, sometimes called "Hopoe" in jest, was the leader of this particular caravan. He was a Jew from Jericho who was known for his cunning and astute bargaining ability; more than that he seemed to have a penchant for finding real treasures.

When the king was finally seated on the golden pedestal with his newly acquired monkey perched on the armrest, Badget nodded to his men. "You see," Badget said, craftily keeping his eye on the king and waving his hand over the assortment that began to be piled on the plush red carpet, "I have brought you the best. You and your men shall have first choice."

Dust billowed from the trader's coarsely woven cloak as he quickly picked up first one unique treasure and then another for the king's approval. He had gained the name of Hopoe from just such bobbing up and down. It was true, he did resemble the bird in many ways and never more than when he was eagerly trying to find just that special buy that would interest his customers.

The king was his major challenge. He had such exquisite taste. He liked only the best. Any bit of shoddy workmanship or flaw was easily spotted and the piece discarded. Badget held his breath as the king's eyes traveled over the rich assortment and rested on a small box of ebony. Quickly old Badget pulled it from the pile. He blew the dust from it. Then he polished it with the end of his cloak before handing it to the king.

The king shook his head but passed it to the sallow-faced, rather bored young man on his right. "Here, my son," he said, "This is what our ships will bring us and we'll no longer be at the mercy of such pirates as old Hopoe here."

"My lord," Badget protested, "it's more than the ships you'll need. Not everyone can recognize a treasure."

Solomon laughed. He loved the wit of this man. In fact, he had learned much from just such men as Badget. They had drawn maps of the trade routes, pointed out the unique treasures of each country, and brought back the gossip of other kings and kingdoms.

"There, that polished horn," Solomon said, suddenly pointing to where the monkey had obviously spotted the gold band on the object and was struggling to get it lose.

Badget had known the king would be interested in this piece, and so he had carefully placed it where just the tip and glitter of the gold band could be seen. He took it from the monkey and handed it to the king then stood back, his feet planted wide apart, arms folded, and a gleam of triumph on his face. He was not disappointed.

The king's jeweled hands traveled over the smooth sides of the horn as he bent to look more closely at the decoration on its two gold bands. "I have seldom seen such delicate work. Is there a base?"

"No, my lord," Badget said. "It was made for a rich man who would always have a servant standing by to hold it."

"Where is this rich man who can commission such a cup?" the king demanded.

"Unfortunately the cup was never called for. The man who had ordered it died quite suddenly. I arrived at just the right time and was able to buy it."

"But who was the man? A craftsman works, but usually to the design of his master."

"He was a great king. He loved fine things as much as yourself."

"But, my wily Hopoe, who was this man?"

"Why, my lord, he was the king of Sheba."

"You are right. The king of Sheba is dead, and I hear that his youngest daughter now rules."

"He had no sons to inherit his throne."

"With such a rich country it won't be long until it is quickly swallowed by some of those vultures that live on either side."

"Maybe not. Bilqis, the old king's daughter, is as strong as any man, or so the gossip goes."

"How can a young girl hope to hold the throne of a rich country like Sheba? It's foolishness. I can't believe it's true." The king was definitely interested, and Badget loved to lead him on with a good story.

"My lord," Badget said, rolling his eyes, "you have never seen a woman like this. Before the old king's body was moved from his bed, one of his counselors seized the crown and had himself proclaimed king. But within the year the army with Bilqis at its head stormed the palace and slew the usurper. Then, without wasting time, she took the crown, placed it on her own head and had the priests formally recognize her as queen on the portico of the great temple of Ilumquh."

"It's easy to put the crown on one's own head, but to keep it there is another thing." Solomon put the horn cup down beside him on the cushions and the monkey immediately started examining it. "See? My new pet has the taste of a king," he said laughing.

Badget chuckled and then returned to the discussion of Sheba's queen. "She's held the throne for three years now and everyone's pressing her to marry. Her uncle's son has first right. He's an ambitious fellow who would aim to marry her just to get her throne. His father's behind it all. She's a brave one. They won't outsmart her if she has a chance."

"She may be more foolish than brave," Solomon observed.

"My lord," Badget leaned over and spoke in a confidential tone as though his words were meant for the king alone, "she's proven her bravery. Before becoming queen she took the virgin's place and rode in the Markab right into battle with the troops. It was a sight to see. The camel decorated with gold and jewels while she sat tall and proud with the side curtains pulled back and her hair black as a raven's wing and full . . ."

"I've heard of this custom. The Markab is like our Ark, only instead of tablets of stone and the ten commandments, it's one of their fairest maidens that rides in it. They say a whole army will die before they let the enemy capture their Markab. I would say it does take bravery. So she is brave? Is she also beautiful?"

Here Badget drew back and seemed to fidget with the hilt of the short dagger he wore in his belt. "My lord," he said, "it is not proper to carry tales, and if I hadn't seen it myself . . ."

Solomon knew that the old scoundrel was eager to tell any news, but lest he offend he had to play the role of being reluctant. It was this very kind of news Solomon liked best. Smiling, he looked around at his men to see that they also were intrigued. "Come, come Badget," he said. "Let's hear the scandal. It must be bad to have an old harpie like you hesitating."

"My lord, the woman is beautiful beyond anything I have ever seen, but she has one terrible flaw that spoils everything." Here again he paused as though dreading to tell what he knew.

"Come, come, we're waiting to hear it," Solomon urged while his son Rehoboam and the other men insistently joined in.

Badget, being a salesman first and a storyteller second, held up his hands for quiet. "First let me serve you. What do you wish to buy. When you have bought what you want, then I'll tell you of the flaw."

Knowing Badget, Solomon quickly declared his choice. "I'll take this goblet of horn. I'm sure there'll never be another quite like it."

Once the king had made his choice and declared that was all he wanted, the others quickly picked out items, and within the hour, Badget was waving to his men to pack up all that was left.

"Now, the Hopoe will tell us of the flaw in the beautiful new queen of Sheba." Solomon was absentmindedly twirling the glowing horn in his right hand and holding the monkey with his left so he couldn't reach it. Badget came and knelt before the king. "It's late, my lord, my camels are waiting at the Fountain Gate."

"Then tell it quickly." There was a note of impatience in the king's voice, and Badget was not one to trifle with such a tone.

"If I had not seen it with my own eyes, my lord . . ."

"Yes, yes, we have heard that before. What did you see, Badget?"

"My lord, I am just a poor merchant. I was brought before the queen because they said I had slipped by the guards without paying the usual tribute . . ."

"We don't need to hear all the details of how you saw the queen. I'm sure you would be one to slip by without paying tribute if you could. What is the flaw?"

"My lord, she was sitting on a throne of alabaster. Her hair fell down beneath her crown like the waterfall at Ein Geddi and her hands were like small jeweled fans, but as I raised myself from kneeling, her gown lifted slightly and I saw her feet. My lord, they were hooves like a donkey's feet. The queen has the feet of a donkey."

A loud gasp of astonishment went round the room, and in the confusion, Badget flung the last pack over his shoulder and disappeared.

$\mathcal{T}$he palace of Bilqis, the queen of Sheba, was nestled in among Tolok trees and palms. It rose out of this greenness with its stone walls and pillars whitewashed to a startling brilliance. The broad steps were of alabaster, as were its floors and rounded openings. Some called it the Alabaster Palace.

Formal gardens filled every space within the walls that surrounded the palace. These gardens were kept constantly green by the steady flowing of water through the irrigation ditches. The same water poured out of ornate fountains and spilled over into pools cut in the hard rock. Peacocks furled their plumes as they strutted picturesquely under the trees, and tigers and panthers glowered from cages fastened into the walls.

Inside the palace one was first impressed by the soft light pouring through the fretted openings of alabaster. It rested at various times of the day on different portions of the dusty old tapestries, gleamed from gold javelins and shields, and spilled out over worn rectangles of alabaster that formed the floors. This was made even more striking by the general darkness of the whole interior. The palace seemed to be filled with huge, unwieldy storage chests, screens, and oversized, rusted brass incense burners.

Even the throne was enormous and ugly. It was raised off the floor by a series of tiers covered in black ebony. Tradition said that it had been carved out of alabaster at some far distant time by workmen who first worshiped the bull-shaped moon god. A bull's head with red ruby eyes glared from its back while each armrest was the bull's foreleg and ended in crudely carved hooves.

In short, the palace still bore the firm imprint of the old king. It even smelled more of musk and stale beer than of the rose petals the queen had ordered strewn across the floors. Her own rooms and bed chamber were oppressive. The huge bed with its curtains, the carved chests for the royal robes, the old wooden stand with openings stuffed with documents, and the ever-present scribe's desk took up most of the space.

The Egyptian maid complained that she had only large baskets in which to store the queen's cosmetics, and the collection of gold shields that had been the old king's pride left no room for the silver mirrors that she had brought with her from Egypt.

The one redeeming feature was the bank of latticed windows that let in the fresh breeze and opened onto a balcony shaded by some ancient vines. On this day the shutters were open, giving a lovely view of the distant mountains and the stonework of the great dam that made the greenness of this valley possible. It was a lovely sight, but it was completely wasted on the queen.

"I'll not have him," Bilqis said as she impatiently snatched the carved ivory comb from her attendant and began pulling it through her thick hair with short quick strokes.

"Your highness," her Egyptian maid wailed, "you'll spoil the effect."

"You're making me look like a silly bride and I am not a bride. I am the ruler of Sheba." With both hands she grabbed up fistfuls of hair and pulled. "I may yet have this all shaved off like the queens of Egypt."

Immediately there were wild shrieks of dismay as all of her ladies fluttered around her pleading that she not do such a thing to her beautiful hair. The Egyptian maid began to cry, and at this crucial moment there was the sound of a door slamming and hurried footsteps along the outer hall.

"What's the trouble? I heard screaming." An old woman dressed in black with a red turban holding her gray hair in place stood like an avenging eagle viewing the scene.

"Now she's threatening to . . . to shave her head . . . cut her hair." The Egyptian beautician had fallen to her knees and tears were coursing down her cheeks while the young maidens were huddled together speechless.

Bilqis turned and smiled at the old woman. "Najja, they are trying to make me beautiful, and I must be like a vulture or no one will obey me." She let go of her hair and made her face as ugly as possible, all the time looking in the clouded brass mirror to see the effect.

The Egyptian turned to old Najja. "It's impossible for her to shave her head. In Egypt the crown is not like this. It fits the head and hair is not necessary."

"Of course the trouble is not the crown or the hair; it's the bride-groom that's waiting. Am I right?" Najja's voice was soft and tender and its effect on Bilqis was to melt her stiff facade.

"Go, all of you. Go and leave me with Najja." Bilqis said as she patted her hair back in place and held her mirror so it caught the image in the larger, highly polished brass tray now held by Najja.

"I haven't finished the hair," the Egyptian wailed, wringing her hands. "It'll be a disgrace."

"Don't worry," Bilqis said, as she impulsively handed her mirror to the Egyptian and turned to look in the larger mirror. "I'll pull a lock on each side like this, arrange the gold ornaments on my forehead spilling down the sides, then the crown will fit nicely around the top." All the time she was talking she was busy twisting, tying, and adjusting. "There, I am ready without all the fuss," she said finally. "Now go. All of you. I must see Najja for a few moments."

They backed from her presence, their eyes on the floor until they were a respectful distance, and then they turned and fled through the curtained doorway. They were still not used to a woman's being both king and queen.

"Go Najja. Follow them and see that no one remains listening at the door."

Najja pulled the heavy tapestry aside and nodded. Only the usual guards were there.

"Good, then we have a few minutes."

"You know your uncle is growing impatient. He has been waiting in the formal reception room all morning," Najja said.

"I'll not marry my cousin. They can't force me. I'm the ruler now."

"But my dear . . ."

"I know. They have all argued and pled. They say I've been queen for three years and it's time I think about a consort and an heir."

"Well, it is the usual thing."

"They have tried every argument imaginable. Some say I will anger the old earth gods, others warn that if I have no child, at my death the strongest man will take over. Already they are worrying about my death." Bilqis pulled back the jewels that dripped from her headdress. "Najja, I need my earrings," she said laughing.

"These?" Najja held a golden orb on each outstretched palm.

Bilqis nodded and went on explaining. "You should have seen our High Priest; he prophesied before all the wise men and counselors that if I didn't marry, my line would be like a desert well left untended until the sand blew over it and it became as though it had never existed."

"What he says is true. Do you find your cousin so repulsive then?"

"He's a braggart, a proud peacock with no understanding. He wants the throne of Sheba, the gold of her rich mines, the caravans and revenues. He pictures himself sitting on my golden throne wearing my ruby crown. He is no different from all the other kings and ambassadors that have come pledging their love and affection. They don't want me, they want my throne."

"He's handsome and he's from your family."

"If he were like my father it would be different, but he's a fool."

"Come, look through the peephole at him. See how fine he is." Najja went to the wall and pulled back a hanging to reveal a well-placed viewing hole. Bilqis saw her cousin Rydan. He was pacing the floor. Back and forth he went while all the time his jeweled hands held a rolled parchment that he thumped impatiently against his other hand.

It was obvious his turban was of the finest material and his beard carefully trimmed, but his eyes were like hard bits of flint. His mouth was set in a firm, defiant line.

The ornate reception room with its old swords and shields of brave men long dead decorating the wall and gathering dust was now full of the men from her family and tribe. They were all well dressed, perfumed, and sophisticated. Rydan's father, Hammed, was sitting bolt upright in the middle of a divan that stretched along the back wall. His large stomach filled the rich robe he wore and hid his belt completely. His eyes were wide open with that look of alertness that made one think he was very intelligent.

"See how eager they are to get their hands on my throne," Bilqis said as she let the hanging drop. "It must not happen. Another man I could divorce or banish, but a cousin never. He could do as he pleased and I would be at his mercy."

"But he is of your father's blood."

"He is not at all like my father. He is ambitious. I don't trust him."

"Is there anyone you do trust?"

Bilqis smiled and reached out to take the old nurse's hands.

"You. I trust you. You were the first person I remember. I held your finger to take my first step and you always tasted my food to be sure I wouldn't be poisoned. Then, the priests—I trust them also. They know very well that if a man were king he would insist on the priestly crown as well as the royal crown. All the old kings did."

Najja began to wring her hands nervously. "Be careful my dear. You are all alone. No father, no mother, and the whole tribe is plotting a marriage to your cousin. How can you stand against them?"

Bilqis motioned for Najja to hold the mirror again. She wet a finger and polished one of the jewels in the crown. "It is a bit big for me, but I'll wear it as my father would have wished. I'll be my father's son." With both hands she steadied it on her head, and then gathering up her robes, she told Najja to go alert the house guards. "I'll go surrounded by my own men and the priests. They'll not disappoint me."

Hours later she returned to the same room exhausted but with a glow of triumph about her. She had won a partial victory, and it was reflected in the new respect her maidens gave her. Their eyes looked at her with some of the awe usually reserved for images in the temple.

"My jewels, Nimba," she said holding out her arms and letting her bracelets slide into the girl's waiting hands. "My headpiece," she said motioning to the Egyptian as she sat down on the large cushion in the middle of the room. She reached up and took the crown from her head and held it lightly in her arms as the Egyptian removed the gold filigree with the coins.

Later as she lay within the gathered curtains on her bed, Najja came to take any last request. "You still have the crown?" she questioned, as she saw it cradled in her arms.

"The crown will sleep with me tonight. It's not fickle like a man."

"You have a very bad impression of men, I'm afraid."

"Not all men. But it was so obvious what my uncle wanted and what my cousin lusted for—not me. I assure you it was not me. I know that for all his nice talk once he has the agreement signed and I'm his, everything will change. He'll see that I have breasts and buttocks like any other woman and he'll set out to dominate me. I've been given a little more time and I'm determined to think of something."

"Then it's simple. Pick a weak man."

Bilqis sat up and hugged the crown more tightly. "I've heard that even the weakest sort of man becomes a strutting cock when he's had his way," she said. "Anyway, I'm not one to be taken by a weak man. I must give myself, and I can only give myself to one who's strong."

"Then it's impossible." Najja drew the fine linen sheet over her and backed away.

Bilqis lay in the darkness watching the evening breeze move the curtain that encircled her bed. She could hear the steady breathing of her maidens scattered on pallets in the adjoining room and the soft night noises coming from the garden that lay just outside her latticed window.

She knew this would not be the end. Her uncle was only appeased, not convinced. The priests had backed her but only by agreeing that she didn't have to marry her cousin right away. However, they still insisted she must marry. To escape their plots and plans would take every bit of cunning she possessed. She lay awake going over each aspect of the situation several times and finally turned over and fell into a troubled sleep.

This was not the only problem Bilqis was to face. The next morning as she sat in the council chamber with her wise men, she heard news that deeply disturbed her. "My queen," the young councilman said, bowing to the ground.

"Speak, we'll hear what you have to say," Bilqis said, touching his shoulder with her mace.

"Some moons ago a trader, a Jew from Jericho called Badget, or more often Hopoe, appeared before your highness."

"Yes, I remember the fellow well. He hadn't paid tribute and he tried to distract us by telling some strange story about his king building a fleet of ships on the Red Sea. I remember we laughed at the idea."

"It is no laughing matter, my queen. I sent a group of men down to the coast to spy out the situation, and I have stationed men at the city gate watching for this Jew when he comes this way again. We need to question him further."

"You have done all this without my orders?"

"My queen, you must pardon me. No one took this man seriously. I was afraid . . ."

"Yes, yes, we did laugh. What did you find?"

"I found it was true. This upstart king. This one who rules from the barren heights west of the King's Highway has indeed built a fleet of ships.

He has completely bypassed us."

There was a deadly silence, then an uproar broke out. Each one of her counselors had an opinion or a question and they all spoke at once.

"An impossible plan."

"It can't be true."

"They aren't seamen!"

"There's the monsoon. They can't have counted on that."

Bilqis had her chief councilman order their silence. "I can't imagine," she said, "that a king who knows nothing of the sea can manage such a thing unless he knows magic and has the Jinn working for him."

"That's the most frightening thing about all this," Tamrin, the queen's trader said. "This king has somehow tricked Hiram of Phoenicia into building the ships and has gotten the magicians to tell him where the treasures are. Monsoons are nothing to him. He simply orders the Jinn and they do his bidding through their magic."

Again questions and answers flew back and forth until the chief councilman signaled for silence; the queen had a question.

"How do we know the Jinn work their magic for this king?" she asked in a skeptical tone.

"There are more and more strange reports," Tamrin said. "For instance, when his father died, the palace was only a warren of old buildings and their temple was covered with badgerskins. Now, in this short time, without the sound of a hammer or tool of any kind, the king has erected the most beautiful temple in the world. It floats among the clouds and the gold of its walls blinds the eyes."

"And the palace?" Bilqis prodded.

"The palace rises like the temples of Egypt. Incense floats on the air so that one who enters the city gates finds he is greeted with the aroma of jasmine even in winter."

"And his wives? Does this king have wives?"

"His palace is bulging with wives and children."

"So the Jinn work their magic for this king and his wives?"

"His wives work a different magic. His queen is from Rabbath Amman. She brought him assured control of the King's Highway going from the Red Sea up the Jordan Valley to Damascus. His other queen is the sister of Pharaoh Shishak. She brought him the coastal city of Gezer and with it the trade route that goes from Egypt to Damascus. The rest of his seven hundred wives have other talents."

"And his favorite? Surely he has a favorite?"

"Ah yes. He had a favorite. I hear she was a simple country maiden from the north. He wrote songs praising her and grieved uncontrollably for her when she died. They say he has married all these women, even added three hundred concubines looking for another like her."

"Well," Bilqis said squaring her shoulders and standing, "what do you suggest we do?"

"It is obvious, my queen. We must fight."

At that all the counselors rose and began shouting and encouraging each other with the exciting prospects of planning a major battle.

"We must call the commanders and the captains."

"Assess our weapons."

"Gather our friends from neighboring countries."

"Send messengers."

"Buy supplies."

Bilqis waited until the turmoil died down and then she spoke in a quiet, commanding voice. "We don't need to fight. There are other ways."

"What other ways, my queen?" one old counselor dared to ask.

"If he can work magic with the Jinn, so can we," Bilqis said confidently. "We'll let the Jinn and their magic do the fighting for us. Undoubtedly our priests can summon stronger Jinn and magic than his can. They can stir up the winds or have his ships wrecked on the rocks. They'll finish his wonderful idea of a new trade route." Seeing that her counselors were all busy mulling over what she had said and not wanting to argue her point, she nodded to her attendants and swept from the room.

2

*T*he next morning Bilqis was wakened in the predawn darkness by one of her maidens. It was the day on which the last dim outline of the dying moon god, Ilumquh, could be seen in the morning sky. Today, as always at such times, there would be special sacrifices at the temple.

She stepped into the waiting palanquin and rode down the avenue of light to the great oval place of meeting. It was her custom to be present with her maidens for the morning ceremonies of incense and chanting. As she was carried through a thicket of oleanders to the marble steps that led up to the temple's entryway, she was conscious of the bubbling, trickling noise made by the water running through the irrigation ditches. "God willing," she thought, "the new moon will come again. But if anything should happen to the dam, this whole area would become desert. This is what we must fear."

That didn't mean that this monthly ceremony wasn't important because when Ilumquh left the sky and it was dark, then all the evil spirits and Jinn had an opportunity to work their mischief. Bilqis had always feared that the Jinn would someday destroy the dam, and at the dark of the moon this was most likely to take place. The dam must be guarded carefully at this dangerous time, and then by sacrifice, incense, and special offerings the moon god would be encouraged to return and they would all be safe.

Already inside the oval place of meeting, the chalk-faced black-robed priestesses, dedicated to the god Ilumquh, were chanting and weeping. Old women, toothless and haggard, sat in the shadowy comers under the sheltering pillars that circled the inner temple, drumming ominous rhythms on the deep-bellied drums of fate. Castanets rattled frantically as the wailing mounted and a band of temple priestesses came through the far door. Their faces were painted into grimaces of pain and they walked with a jerking, dipping motion that made their loose hair and mourning rags shudder with suppressed anguish.

21

The air reeked with the odor of burned hair and hot blood mingled with stale incense. It was the odor of Ilumquh, a god who could be gentle as moonbeams but fierce as a raging bull when aroused. There had been times in the past when only a human sacrifice calmed his destructive nature. But that had been before the dam had been built. They with their wits had outsmarted Ilumquh, and there were no more droughts.

In the center of the open courtyard, priests could be seen dimly through the rancid smoke stoking the altar fire. From time to time one would come with a golden vessel and pour clotted blood on the altar's horns. This was a signal for the priests to prostrate themselves or circle the altar chanting traditional songs of Ilumquh's death.

Ilumquh's earthly form was that of the bull, and there were carved alabaster bull's heads on the four sides of the massive altar. At the height of the ceremony the golden bull that lived in the small temple beside the pillared hall was brought out into the open court. It was hoped he would protect them with his own special magic while Ilumquh was gone from the night sky.

No marriages took place at this time, no seed was planted, and no business transacted. The moonless night that followed was a night in which the dreaded Jinn worked their worst charms. Witches and ghouls were abroad and evil deeds prospered.

Bilqis sat in the special enclosure reserved for royalty while the people stood in the open courtyard watching the faint wraith of a crescent that the sick moon had become. As it drifted over the edge of the temple wall, a great wailing and beating of breasts, even pulling of hair and loud chanting, erupted. Ilumquh had sickened and was dead.

As the ceremony came to an end, Bilqis moved toward her palanquin. She was eager to leave the stench and depressing air of Ilumquh's temple. Suddenly she noticed her maidens drawing back, even bowing, with a look of awe and fear on their faces. Bilqis turned and in the light of a waxed taper she saw the High Priest himself coming toward her. He made her feel uneasy. He wore the crown of Ilumquh with the dread eagle mask hanging by a cord around his neck. His ornate gold-encrusted robes were stained with blood, and there was the odor of burned flesh and singed hair that was stronger than the incense. His beard was clipped to a point and his eyes were cold.

Now as at other times in the past, it was his hands that bothered her the most. His fingers were long and tapered, always nervously plucking at things. He seemed to be constantly questioning, probing, and divining the worst in any situation.

Bilqis wished that her father had chosen another one of the priests for this office. Though he made an impressive sight before the great altar and his voice had power to make even brave men tremble, there was something almost sinister about Il Hamd. He was ambitious, even ruthless, where his interests were concerned. However, he needed her support and so she trusted him.

"My queen," the High Priest said, bowing only slightly and not waiting for her recognition before he continued, "since I am the great Ilumquh's high priest, it is my duty to warn you. If you don't choose a consort soon there will be much trouble."

"Trouble? Who will dare to cause trouble? It's a private matter."

"Nothing is private when one is a queen. It's been three years since you came to the throne and still there is no consort."

"Why now? Why are you bringing this up now?"

"The stars are in the right position for success. Your tribe demands it and the people are waiting. Who knows what evil will come upon us if there is no heir to the throne. At the time of the new moon, I will come for your answer."

"What do you mean, my answer?"

"Why, I will expect you to have chosen someone from your tribe or one of the noble sheiks that have come forward with offers of marriage."

Bilqis tossed her head defiantly. "I'll have none of them," she said emphatically.

"But you must not take the matter of the stars and their control so lightly. Think what it would mean to Sheba if there is no heir."

"The men you've mentioned are all greedy vultures plotting to wear the crown of Sheba."

"But you must understand. All the omens both in the stars and the sheep's liver, the flying bats, and the drawing of the chances point to this time as being right for your marriage. When the people hear . . ."

"Then tell the people that when someone comes that is not self-seeking and greedy, someone who is strong, someone I can admire, then I'll give myself, but not before."

"You are asking the impossible. Only a god would fit that description. Tomorrow I will come for your decision."

"You will have my decision right now. Until someone suitable is found, I will remain as I am."

"So you have rejected the son of your uncle and the finest princes of Sheba as well as the neighboring kings. There is no one left but the god himself, Ilumquh." His words were stern and harsh and Bilqis knew that he meant just what he said.

"And what if I choose the god Ilumquh?"

For a moment he seemed stunned. Then with a quick intake of breath he said, "Then you would come on the night of Ilumquh's full strength and spend the night in his pillared pavilion. Hopefully you would conceive."

"I would bring my maidens and . . ."

"You would have to come alone."

"I don't understand."

"I must have your answer at the rising of the new moon. If you want strength, what could be stronger than Ilumquh?" With that he bowed low and disappeared into the shadows as quickly as he had appeared.

Bilqis was first angry and then frustrated. She wondered which of her relatives had thought of this. It was a trick. If she didn't accept her cousin, then she would have to accept the strange ritual of coming to the temple as the bride of Ilumquh. It was impossible to refuse Ilumquh. The High Priest and her relatives were counting on this very thing. Of course they expected her to become what they called "reasonable" and marry her cousin. She would have to think about it. There must be some way out of this dilemma.

The torches had been extinguished and the great hall was almost clear of people. Only some old hags remained, and they were leisurely sweeping the marble floor with short brooms made of reeds. The fire on the altar was dying down and the golden calf stood gleaming on his pedestal. Bilqis paused to glance in his direction. Suddenly his ruby eyes flashed and glinted, emitting some strange power that seemed to paralyze her.

With a gasp of horror she turned from the fearful sight and hurried out the door and down the marble steps to her palanquin. Once inside she ordered the curtains closed tightly and the bearers to hurry. She had been badly shaken, but by the time she reached the palace she was composed and determined to block the whole episode from her mind.

* * *

The next morning when she came to the Hall of Judgment, she noticed it was more crowded than usual. She noticed there were some Egyptians of rank present and she wondered what they would propose. She must remember to save time for them after the usual business of the day.

As she entered, the people fell to the floor in waves, leaving a path down which she walked. Her eunuchs, great black Nubians given her by the Egyptian pharaoh, stood behind her throne while her counselors came and went among the people sorting out the most important cases. With a flourish of standards and the traditional shout of allegiance from the people, she mounted the six steps and seated herself on her throne.

Always at such times she felt the exhilaration of the challenge before her. Her counselors were cultured, learned men who were quick to notice any flaw in her judgment. She could see in their eyes the constant questioning of her ability to hold this exalted position. She could demand nothing of them. She must rule by her wits and she must never take anything for granted.

The morning went quickly and she was satisfied with the judgments she had made. She could see approval in the eyes of some of the older men, and she knew she had not disappointed them. Though her power was absolute and her decisions were final, still she needed this encouragement.

The last case was brought by one of her father's old counselors. He was loyal and helpful to her for her father's sake, but he was known as a man to be feared. The man with him was obviously wealthy. "Saiid Majd comes with a complaint against this young man and his mother," the counselor said.

The counselor had mounted the steps to the throne and was holding his voice to a low level so no one else could hear. "The young man has had the audacity to accuse Saiid Majd of moving the boundary stones at the edge of his property."

"Let the young man or his mother speak," Bilqis ordered.

The young man hung back, but his mother pushed him forward. He fell on his knees while everyone laughed at his confusion. "My father left the land to us," he managed to say before the counselor interrupted.

"You can see, my queen, that this young man is still a child. It's impossible

25

for him to care for the land, and his mother is incapable of hard labor."

At this the woman rushed forward and threw herself at the queen's feet. "Your majesty," she said, "we are poor people. This piece of land is all my son has as an inheritance. Both of us are willing to work from morning to night."

"It is better this woman goes back to her father's house," the counselor said in clipped tones.

"It is a small parcel of land," the wealthy man said, shrugging his shoulders.

"It is all my son has from his father. Never will he be able to get more land that is near the dam and well irrigated."

At this point Bilqis looked at the wealthy man and then at the crowd of her own counselors. It was obvious they cared nothing for the woman's problem. It had never been expedient to side with the poor. It was settled from the beginning. The woman should never have brought her son. She should never have complained. It was best that she go home to her father.

"It is settled," Bilqis said. "The marker remains."

She was pleased to see the instant approval on the faces of her counselors and the gloating look of triumph that passed over the wealthy man's face. She had made what they all considered a wise decision.

She hardly noticed the woman and her son leaving the hall of judgment as Saiid Hajd knelt before her in gratitude and her chief adviser, Aidel, leaned forward and whispered, "Very wise, my queen. The boy and his mother have no influence or position while this man can be of great service to you. Wisdom means using your power to gain the greatest advantage to yourself."

Bilqis did not answer but instead ordered her eunuchs to clear the audience chamber of everyone but her chief counselors. The cases that had not been dealt with would have to wait until the next day. She had other, more important business to tend to. It had been whispered that an Egyptian officer of rank waited in the vestibule with urgent news from the pharaoh.

In the confusion and turmoil that followed as the people were led from the hall, she found herself thinking again of her uncle and the tribesmen who were pressuring her to marry. "I'll never marry that weak, sniveling cousin. It'll serve them right if I surprise them and choose Ilumquh instead."

She saw that her uncle and cousin had remained with her counselors.

This was their right, but it irritated her. Her resolve was firming to meet the god himself. To bear a son by that god. What power that would give her son. She couldn't even imagine what such an encounter would be like. She ran her hand over the leopard-skin covering of the cushion she sat on. Here in Sheba their emblem was the leopard, and on festive occasions she wore the skin with the head fitted over one shoulder and the smooth, spotted hide draped down over her back. Leopards weren't afraid of anything, and neither was she. Even the god's lustful, ruby eyes were not going to frighten her.

Slowly she became aware of the silence that filled the room and realized her counselors were all assembled and waiting. With a nod of her head the trumpets were raised and the great doors opened, revealing a group of richly dressed men surrounding a fat, balding dignitary that was obviously the Egyptian ambassador.

As usual they prostrated themselves before the throne and had brought an array of elegant gifts from the pharaoh. Finally, as the pages and slaves moved back, Bilqis invited the ambassador to join her at the throne.

When he was at last settled and had delivered his pharaoh's greetings and small personal messages, he proceeded to pull a scroll of papyrus from an intricately decorated silver case hung on his girdle. With great deliberation he unrolled it and handed it to one of the scribes to read.

The message was more direct and less flowery than usual, and the whole assembly was impressed with the urgency of the pharaoh's concern. "A certain king named Solomon is planning to bypass the old trade routes," the scribe began and proceeded to read at length all that the pharaoh had gleaned from the threatening venture.

When the scribe had finished, Bilqis spoke slowly and deliberately. "I know of this king and have heard rumors of this venture. He is famous for his wisdom and rules in a mountainous area very far from the sea. I would think it impossible for him to find men to build the ships, master the monsoons, and find the merchandise."

"The pharaoh has definite proof that the ships have already been built and have made at least one voyage down the Red Sea."

"May I ask what proof he has?"

Here the ambassador leaned over so the court could not hear him as he whispered, "It is on the best authority. The pharaoh's sister is married to

Solomon and reports everything that happens to her brother."

"She is a spy."

"You might say so."

"Does Solomon know?"

"Of course not. He loves and trusts her."

"And what does the pharaoh suggest we do?"

"It is quite simple. If all of us along the various trade routes band together and hold firm, we can defeat him and bring his fancy plans to naught."

"And?"

"If it comes to war we will march together. He cannot stand against us."

"I would like to think there is a better way."

The ambassador looked puzzled. "It would be hard to find a better way, but we are always ready to listen."

"I have no plan right now. Now is the time to gather facts. We must find out all we can about the fleet of ships and even the king that has dared attempt such a thing. Perhaps nothing will come of it."

"And if no other way can be found?"

For a moment Bilqis was silent, studying his face. When she spoke it was with strength and determination. "Then we will cast our lot with Egypt. We have no other choice."

With a few other formalities she dismissed the ambassador and his men. They would be well entertained, and in the meantime she was determined to glean more information. Turning to one of the pages, she ordered, "I have been told the camel driver named Badget has again been seen at the gate. Go find him for me. I want to talk to him." With that she dismissed them with a wave of her hand.

The two sleek, well-groomed leopards were led out by their trainers, the banners were taken from their sockets by eunuchs, and the palace guards lowered their spears as they walked in front of the queen leaving the Nubians to march in formation behind her.

* * *

Late that night Badget was found sitting by the fire at the local inn talking to some of the other traders. He was at first frightened and then pleased to hear that the queen wanted to see him. "She wants to hear certain news of your king," he was told by the messenger. Badget was always ready to spread the news he gained on his travels and to be called by the queen would give him more to tell in the future.

The queen had decided to receive him in the informal atmosphere of her outdoor pavilion. Badget found her seated on a dais covered with leopard skins. A taster sipped from a silver goblet and then handed it to the queen.

Bilqis drank slowly from the goblet but kept her eyes on Badget, who had fallen prostrate on the ground before her with his head touching the ground. As she handed the goblet back to the servant, she motioned to Badget. "You may rise," she said.

Badget scrambled to his feet and took the seat she had prepared for him on the ground before the dais. "I am at your service," he said in his most contrite manner.

"I see that you are used to appearing before royalty."

"I've had my opportunities," he said, trying hard to keep from smiling his pleasure.

"Tell me, has this king of yours really sailed ships down the Red Sea?"

"They have made their first trip, your highness."

"But the storms and winds of the monsoons. Is he not afraid of them?"

Badget's eyes grew large. Here was an opportunity to brag. "Your highness, this is no problem to one such as Solomon. He controls the rains and keeps the four winds in bags under his throne."

"Come now. He is certainly a human being and not a god."

"Aye, he is not a god, but he knows the god's secrets and that is even better than being a god."

"Tell me, how does he rule his people?"

"I can't rightly say. It's a bit of a mystery. He doesn't need anyone to taste his food. That I do know." Badget nodded in the direction of the queen's taster.

The queen was immediately interested. "How can that be? Is he not afraid of poison? Does he have some medicine that is stronger than the poison?"

"No, it is not that. Though I'm sure he could do that too if he wanted to."

"Doesn't he have any enemies?"

"Oh yes. He has enemies, but not the kind your highness has."

"What do you mean?"

Badget hesitated and then explained. "I was in the palace today and saw the wealthy fellow who had moved the land marker. Solomon wouldn't have decided it that way."

Now Bilqis was leaning forward with real interest. "What would this perfect king have done?"

"Why, he would have decided for the boy and his mother. The ones who owned the land."

"I don't understand? Why would he have done that?"

"There are laws, rules, even the king has to obey them in my country."

Bilqis laughed a hearty, ringing laugh. "The king has to obey? I don't obey anyone." She ran her hand over the leopard skin and tossed her head defiantly.

"Well, the difference is the law. Some things are right and some wrong and the law tells you which are which."

Again Bilqis laughed. "How ridiculous. What I say is right. I am the queen."

"Well, all I can say is that he has no taster. If someone gets angry at a decision he makes, they blame the law not him."

"What a strange country and what a strange king. He is so powerful he controls the winds in bags under his throne and yet he must obey laws."

The queen seemed to be deep in thought. Badget shifted uneasily. He was no match for the queen. She spent a few moments with her fingers drumming on the arm of the chair and then stood up. "Badget," she said, "I believe your name is Badget, don't return home to your country until I give my permission. I am not through with you yet."

She left the pavilion trailing the three slaves and five Nubians in her wake. She left the Nubians at the door of her apartments and the slaves followed her to the door of the inner chamber. "Bring Najja to me," she ordered as she went to the balcony that overlooked the lush gardens of her private grounds.

Just as she had known, Ilumquh was totally gone from the sky. "Where did he go? Why must he always desert them?" She drew her robes tighter around her, a cool breeze had come up quite suddenly. It was the dark of the moon and on just such a breeze as this that the Afreet and Jinn traveled to work their evil magic on human beings.

With a bang she closed the shuttered doors and leaned against them. Only one lamp burned beside her couch. The corners of the room were dark, but through the open door came rays of light and the soft murmuring of her women. Her hands moved to clutch the jeweled scabbard of the short sword hanging from her girdle. It was made of iron, and the Jinn could not touch her as long as she wore it.

She had ordered a double watch at the dam and the priests would offer sacrifices and pray all night. The golden bull would stand in the midst of the temple and frighten away the evil spirits. "Najja," she called and immediately heard one of the outer doors slam.

"Tomorrow the high priest will come for his answer," she thought. "He wouldn't press me so if it weren't important. I must decide. There's no one who can help me. I must decide what I'll do. Surely it is only the Jinn and Afreet that would harm me, and Ilumquh can protect me from both."

3

*B*ilqis slept poorly that night. She had experienced two frightening nightmares in which the great dam that supplied all the water for her city had burst. Dreams were often prophetic, and she could not afford to ignore a dream that could spell such disaster to her whole kingdom. Long before morning, she was up getting ready to ride out and inspect it for herself.

The High Priest and her tribesmen would all expect her to be at the temple to chant and fast, encouraging the moon to rise again by their sacrifice and prayers. However, that was just where she didn't want to be.

The High Priest had said he would expect an answer today in regard to her marriage, and she hadn't decided yet just what she would do. She felt cornered, trapped. There were no choices she could accept and yet she knew the pressure would mount until she made some decision. She needed to get away, escape, if only for an hour.

The ride to the dam was out across the fertile valley and far enough to require riding in the regal howdah on the back of a camel. She liked that. In the howdah she was alone and could think without interruption.

Once on the way to the dam, she settled back into the cushions and breathed a sigh of relief. No one but her guards and a few of her servants knew she was going.

Of course they would miss her at the ceremonies. If it seemed necessary she could tell them about the dream. No one questioned the importance of the dam.

Before the dam was built, this valley was always subject to drought. There were stories almost hard to believe of the people's dependence on Ilumquh for every drop of water and even the food they ate. By their cunning her ancestors had built the dam and foiled the gods. She liked to think that in the same way she would triumph over this king who had set out to change the trade route.

This was her favorite hour of the day and her preferred way to travel. She loved to hear the jangling of the camel's bells and the creaking of leather against leather as the howdah shifted and settled on its base. The gentle swaying motion gave her a feeling of peace, and she could enjoy the fresh breeze that blew through the fragile curtains of the howdah.

Behind her towered the jagged, rose-colored mountains that led off to the ancient city of Sana while before her were the familiar humped mountains of Balak Al-Kibli and Balak Al-Ausat between which stretched the dam. It had at first been just a huge bank of earth eighteen hundred feet long. Later one of her ancestors had made it more secure by facing the upstream side with stones set in mortar. Spillways and sluice gates for irrigation had been out into the sides of the mountains long before the dam was built.

The water was channeled out into what was known as the North Garden and the South Garden. She wondered briefly where the plot of land owned by the boy and his mother had been. How strange of Badget to say that Solomon would have ruled in favor of the boy.

The more information she gathered about Solomon, the more she found herself disliking him, but on the other hand, the more interested she became. He seemed to have an insatiable desire for women. Seven hundred wives was more than any other king or pharaoh boasted.

His palace was supposed to be splendid and his gardens magnificent. Kings gave him their daughters to wed and even Pharaoh thought him important enough to marry his own sister. More surprising was the fact that Pharaoh had sent his army up to take the town of Gezer so that he could give it to Solomon as his sister's dowry.

No one said much about how Solomon actually looked. He was undoubtedly short and fat with a large semitic nose and puffy cheeks. Otherwise why would they talk all the time about his wealth, his wisdom, and his many wives but nothing really personal about him. "Solomon" meant "peace" and she had been told he loved peace. She had never heard of his fighting a war. He seemed more inclined to marry the enemy than fight him. She had to smile. If she were a man, that would also be her choice.

She was surprised to find that they had reached the dam so soon. She insisted on getting down and walking out on the rampart above the sluice gates. She loved this view from the dam with the early sunrise lighting the whole fertile valley below her. There were those who acclaimed the dam a feat as miraculous as the pyramids in Egypt. When anyone asked her how it had been built, she always told them it was the work of the Jinn and magic.

For just a short time she stood looking down at the valley. She loved this green oasis with its palms and fig trees bordered by hundreds of small irrigation ditches that circled off the Dahana River. Because of the dam, the river flowed all year and kept her valley green.

Down below her in the midst of her city she could see the great oval temple of Ilumquh, sometimes called the place of meeting, sitting like an open jewel box in the midst of oleanders and small bursts of bright flowers. Her eyes followed the royal avenue lined with palms up to the wall that almost surrounded her palace. From here the palace with its white-washed walls and tall pillars marking the entrance hall seemed small and of little consequence.

She sighed. She supposed she had been wrong to make so few changes. Everything was old and familiar but dusty and worn. It was still a man's palace with a man's rougher tastes. Even her own rooms contained the furnishings her father had chosen.

She noticed the market was now almost deserted and the huddled houses of her loyal subjects seemed lifeless and empty. Almost everyone was at the temple. In a few moments everything would change. The people would pour back into the market and the eight gates of the city would be opened for traders. The traders all came from the south and the west or even the north but almost never from the east. To the east lay the great empty quarter and the dam that proved a discouragement to caravans.

For one moment she felt free and invincible. She was the leopard goddess of Sheba and no one, not even the High Priest, dared dictate to her. Then suddenly the troubling matter of her marriage became oppressive as she realized that her uncle and cousin with all the tribesmen were undoubtedly back at the palace waiting for her answer. If she didn't agree willingly, they would manage to force her with omens, predictions, and foretellings that frightened the people. She was not as free and invincible as she had liked to believe and her time was short.

There was always the fearful alternative, marriage to the god Ilumquh.

She could not imagine what that would mean, but suddenly it seemed a fair alternative. It would be only for a night. Marriage to her cousin would never end. She shivered thinking of it.

The sun was now high in the sky, and its warm arms were reaching out to every living thing. Dhat Hamym was the sun's name. She was the lovely consort to the moon god, but they never seemed to meet. She wondered briefly if Dhat Hamym would be jealous to find Ilumquh had taken a human wife.

She raised her arms to Dhat Hamym and then bowed down before her. "Please don't be jealous if the leopard goddess of Sheba chooses Ilumquh rather than a mortal."

There was no answer. Dhat Hamym neither hid her shining face behind a cloud nor frowned. Instead there was the encouraging warmth of her rays. Bilqis waited, but there was no change and finally she said, "I'll choose the god Ilumquh. It's better I surrender to a god than to a man who will try to take my throne."

She motioned to her Nubian eunuchs and immediately the howdah was brought and she was helped into it. She was not happy about her decision, but she was determined to end the frustration and this seemed to be the only way.

Back at the palace she was told the High Priest was waiting for her in her private reception room. She turned toward her own rooms. "Let him wait," she said to the astonishment of those standing nearby. "It's he that is doing the fishing, not me."

"Bring the Egyptian," she ordered as she entered her rooms, snatched up a brass mirror, and sank down onto an ebony stool.

The Egyptian came and with her all the women of the bed chamber. They had heard that the High Priest was waiting, and they were curious to see what Bilqis would do. "I will go to the priest in mourning wearing no makeup and no jewelry," she said.

There was a gasp of astonishment that Bilqis enjoyed thoroughly. She tossed her head and glanced at them pleased to see that they were all cringing in awe of her.

When she finally appeared in the reception room, she was composed and sure of herself. She noticed with satisfaction that the High Priest could hardly recognize her. She saw his eyes travel over the black robes she wore and then linger on the lovely crown of Sheba. Again and again his eyes returned to her face, which was painted with the chalk white of mourning and to the veil that covered the lower part of her face leaving only her eyes free. This veil was worn usually when talking with foreigners or dignitaries of another tribe, and it was now meant as a quiet affront to the High Priest and her own tribesmen.

He, for his part, was dressed in his most ornate robes, and his long fingers were covered with rings. She noticed this because he kept fingering the fur trim on his robe and pulling at his short beard. His priestly turban sat well down on his forehead, making his nose seem enormous and his eyes protrude.

He was surrounded by dignitaries. Among them she immediately recognized her own chief counselor, her uncle, and her cousin Rydan, the young man they all wanted her to marry. She noticed that Rydan stood with his chin jutting out and a look of injured defiance about him. It was obvious they expected her to agree to marry him, and he was ready to accept her.

For a moment she stood with her head thrown back looking at the High Priest and he returned her gaze with an almost imperceptible smirk. There was no doubt that all of them had come to see how she would take defeat. They wanted to see her forced to choose the cousin she had rejected, and even the High Priest she had viewed as a friend was defiantly gloating over his power.

The High Priest raised both hands above his head and clapped for the scribes, who came running with their reeds, inks, and parchment. "We have the papers all drawn up your highness," he said, as he bowed slightly and picked up one of the parchment rolls. "We need only the royal seal here." The High Priest was pointing with one finger at a space near the bottom.

Bilqis looked down at the parchment and noticed only that the High Priest wore a ring on his finger fashioned like a snake with the eyes made of small red rubies. She was standing close enough to smell the heavy odor of stale incense that she always associated with the house of Ilumquh. She looked up into those intense, protruding eyes and realized he had not a doubt in the world that she would stamp the parchment with her seal and marry her cousin.

With one quick movement she reached out and snatched the parchment from the High Priest. then quickly rolling it into its original cylinder, dropped it into the scribe's lap. "We'll not need that," she said. "I've decided against it. For many reasons it isn't wise."

At first there was a shocked silence and then an uproar. Everyone tried to talk at once. The High Priest finally raised his hands again and clapped for attention. "But the stars and the goat's liver all agree. It is dangerous to go against such signs."

"I've no intention of going against such signs or of bringing needless hardship on my people." She paused for a moment to enjoy their look of puzzlement. They were obviously taken aback. Her uncle had wiped the sweat from his brow with his sleeve and her cousin no longer had the bored look on his face. Instead he had crossed his arms and lowered his head so that he looked at her through mere slits.

"I've decided to become the bride of Ilumquh."

She stepped back and watched their mouths drop open with surprise, and then a look of awe took its place as one by one they fell to their knees. Most of them were afraid of Ilumquh. To them he was the raging bull with bloodshot eyes, pawing the earth and snorting fire. None of them would dare go near his pillared dwelling place. It was all they could do to stand in the oval of the great assembly and observe the offerings and sometimes add to the chanting.

It was obvious they could hardly imagine a frail woman like their queen being strong enough and fearless enough to invite an encounter with the god. What would happen they couldn't imagine. She could lose her mind or be burned by his brightness.

Only the High Priest remained standing and showed no emotion. "The decision has been made," he said in sonorous tones. "At the height of Ilumquh's strength during the full moon, the queen will come to his pavilion. Let her make every preparation for her meeting with the great and terrible Ilumquh." With that he turned and walked from the room.

Bilqis had enjoyed the whole episode. Seeing the High Priest's puzzlement at her dress and then his sureness that she would stamp the parchment with her seal was exciting, but not half as exciting as seeing the horror and awe on her uncle's face when she had said she would marry the god Ilumquh. And her cousin, he had looked bored and impatient when she entered the room, but he had been one of the first to fall on his knees.

She didn't wait for them to recover their senses and rise, but lifted her skirt and hurried from the room with all of her women following behind. She had proposed something more daring than the bravest men of Sheba even imagined. There was no turning back now; she would have to go through with the venture.

4

*S*olomon had spent the hours after the early morning sacrifice sitting on the throne that projected from the eastern wall of the temple area out into the court of the women. The throne was originally built so he could watch the construction of first the temple and then his own house. It was a pleasant place with pigeons fluttering down to strut about on the pavement or settle on the king's arm. He loved the openness and had been known to summon a pet raven by a simple gesture.

Now it was rumored that he came here to be closer to his people and deal with disputes more casually than was possible in the great judgment hall.

He had just settled the last case for the morning when one of the pages came pushing his way through the crowd and fell at his feet.

"My lord, your servant the builder Jeroboam must speak with you."

"He knows where I am," Solomon said impatiently. "Why has he not come himself instead of sending this . . . this message?"

"There is trouble at the house of the Egyptian princess, my lord. He dares not leave."

"He is asking me to come to him?"

"There is trouble, my lord. It's the princess."

"And what does my builder have to do with the princess, my queen?"

"I don't know, my lord."

A look of frustration and then anger crossed Solomon's face. They all knew he dared not ignore any hint of trouble that involved the Egyptian princess. Though he had built a beautiful, small palace for her next to his own and had indulged her every whim, there always seemed to be some unfortunate problem involving this beautiful woman.

First there had been the difficulty of her dress. The people of Jerusalem made a show of hiding their faces when she appeared with her scanty robes that left one breast bare. "Harlot! An Egyptian harlot!" they whispered at first and then shouted as they threw stones or spit whenever they passed her house.

Then there had been the shrine for her cat god, Bastet. She'd had it built beside the steps that led up to Solomon's new temple. To make matters worse, she had insisted on bringing fifty priests to chant and sing, rattle sistrums, and beat drums just at sunrise when the men of Israel were gathered in the temple courtyard for the morning sacrifice.

Finally, when it was realized that her priests and she herself faced the rising sun greeting it as a god, while the priests and men of Israel stood with their backs to the sun facing the Lord Jehovah's sanctuary, there was almost a riot.

Solomon had been able to settle most of the disputes amicably. He loved this princess, with her dark twined hair and long fringed lashes framing the cool blue eyes that were so alien to her dark skin. He could refuse her nothing and took her side against all criticism.

"She's a spy for her brother Shishak," his brother Nathan had told him more than once. But he waved him aside impatiently. He found her both distracting and charming. He could not bring himself to believe she did not love him devotedly.

Now as he neared her small but exquisite palace he could hear screaming and crying as though not only the princess but all of her priests and servants were terribly upset. He quickened his pace. With such an uproar the princess herself must have somehow been hurt.

He hurried down the marble steps with his counselors, scribes, and pages following behind, all trying to keep up. Never had they seen Solomon so upset nor had they seen him throw aside his kingly dignity so easily. "He loves her more than all the others," they concluded.

He found Jeroboam, his tall, handsome foreman waiting in the doorway. "My lord, I thought I should warn you. A terrible thing has happened."

"Not the princess!" Solomon's eyes were dark and questioning.

"No, no, not the princess. It's the cat. Her sacred cat. The cat she and all her people worship as a god."

"I know, I know, but what has that to do with the princess?"

"My lord, the priests of Yahweh have killed the Egyptian cat."

"Killed her cat?" Solomon immediately realized the seriousness of the situation. "Why . . . How?"

"It was unfortunate. The cat escaped and ran to the temple area. The priests say he was running away with part of the holy sacrifice. There was nothing to do but kill him."

"And now?" Solomon wanted to learn as much as possible before he faced the accusations and recriminations he knew were inevitable.

"I knew at once the problem was serious. I quickly had the cat washed and wrapped in fine linen. I sent a messenger to warn her of the tragedy, then I myself brought her the cat."

"And?"

"It's as though her only child had died. She's sitting beside the lily pond rocking back and forth holding the cat and weeping."

"I must go to her," Solomon said as he grasped Jeroboam's arm in grateful approval.

"Stay here," he ordered his men as he turned and went through the ornate arches into the darkness of the fresco-decorated entryway. In spite of his agitation and concern, he was immediately aware of the delicate scent of jasmine in the air and the wailing seemed to be accompanied by the beating of great hollow drums that made the very air vibrate with some high tragedy.

The moment the princess had moved in, this palace had taken on the aspect of a small segment of Egypt. Everything he remembered from the trip he had made as a young man was captured here in miniature. The walls had been painted meticulously with hunting scenes of the delta and bordered with lotus blossoms. Her bed was of teakwood inlaid with ivory, while on a small tray sat a marvelous array of delicate boxes holding the secret beauty ointments she used to produce the eternal illusion of health and youth.

He paused for a moment at the doorway leading out into a court-yard. Here a fountain usually splashed and behind it fitted into the far wall rather unobtrusively was the shrine encasing the ebony cat goddess. Solomon looked through the gauze curtains and saw the doors of the shrine hanging open, and the great cat image seemed to glare down in anger at the scene around the pool.

The princess sat by the lily pool and clung to a swaddled bundle. Her cheek rested on it as though she were comforting a crying child, while her ornate wig of shoulder-length hair fell down on one side obscuring her face. It was impossible to tell if the princess was crying, as the noise of the drums and screams of her maidens and priests were deafening.

Solomon had never quite gotten used to the unabashed nakedness of her serving girls. Their breasts were always exposed, and now in their anguish some wore nothing but a woven girdle.

Solomon squared his shoulders and pulled aside the gauze curtain, and immediately the drums were silent. The frantic whirling of the priests slowed and stopped while the young serving girls froze in place as though they had seen an apparition. Only the princess didn't notice the king and now her sobs could be clearly heard.

"Leave us," Solomon ordered. "Leave us alone." Quickly the priests left through the side door to the shrine and the maidens vanished leaving only the sobbing princess and her linen-wrapped cat god.

"Come, my love," Solomon said, bending over her and speaking tenderly. "We'll bury your cat with full honors."

He got no further. The princess flashed him a look of scorn as she flung back the thick, black hair of the wig, revealing red, swollen eyes and full, parted lips. "Bury him, never! He is a god. He must be embalmed and the killer found and beheaded."

"Beheaded! A priest beheaded for killing a cat that steals the holy sacrifice?" Solomon was for the first time aware of the enormity of the problem. He had thought it could be simply solved with enough ceremony and a few nights of his undivided attention. Now it was evident much more would be required.

The immediate crisis was averted by Solomon's ordering Jeroboam to leave with the body of the cat the next morning for Egypt. He assigned him a division of his bravest soldiers and arranged for the cat to be carried in a golden box with silver trim. Jeroboam was instructed to take the cat to the temple at Bubastis, where it would be properly embalmed.

In the meantime the princess declared a month of fasting and mourning to be observed by her maidens and priests.

At first she had insisted that all Jerusalem fast and mourn, but Solomon had dissuaded her. However, he had not been able to divert her from the determination to have the head of the priest who killed the cat nailed to the temple gate. When Solomon procrastinated and made excuses, the princess regaled him. "How is it that my lord cares more for one of his priests than for the princess of Egypt?"

The month of mourning was at last over, and Jeroboam had returned with news of the cat's reception by the priests of Bubastis. The cat had been embalmed and after much ceremony was buried in the sacred cemetery. Jeroboam also brought gifts for the princess from her brother and some secret parchments sealed with the pharaoh's own seal.

* * *

It was evening several days later when Solomon accepted the princess's invitation for a meal cooked with her own hands beside the lotus pool and then a game of senit. He had loved these times of quiet relaxation. She always had some new delicacy to tempt his taste buds or an array of silly stories that made him laugh. Tonight there had been no laughing, and as she moved her conical pieces against his spool-shaped men on the rectangular board, he sensed some real hostility.

Finally he brushed his pieces off onto the floor and stood up. "Is there to be no end of this trouble over the cat?"

"My lord, it is the custom in my country . . ."

"I know, I know—if one of the sacred cats is killed the 'murderer' is beheaded. You have told me that, but this is Israel. The cat dared go into the sacred area of the temple and desecrated the holy sacrifice. You don't seem to understand the seriousness of what the cat did."

She stood up and with a look of hauteur drew from her girdle a parchment. "There, it is written by the pharaoh, my brother. He says the man must die."

Solomon took the parchment but didn't read it. "It has been a long time since a pharaoh could give orders to an Israelite," he said. "We are no longer slaves nor are we his vassals."

She snatched the parchment back and with tears of anger blinding her eyes proceeded to read the message. "The exalted pharaoh, son of the golden orb and ruler of sky and sea and land on which it shines, orders that his most honored sister and her cat god be avenged speedily. Apologies must be made for slights and injuries and the priest who killed the Bubastis cat beheaded. If this is not done speedily the princess will move to the city of Gezer and claim it as her own." She again handed the parchment to Solomon and stood glaring at him in a way he had never seen before.

Solomon was appalled. This was serious. He could see the great seal of Egypt hanging loosely at the bottom of the parchment. It was obvious that when she had to choose between a cat and him, she was quite ready to choose the cat. He thought fast. He couldn't execute the priest. He didn't want to execute the priest. In fact, the priest was at that very moment being honored for his quick action in the situation. "My dear Tipti," Solomon said gently, "remember all that has passed between us, the love, the laughter. Is this nothing to you? Does this cat mean more to you than my love?"

There was no softening in her stance. She simply glared at him. "If by tomorrow at this time the priest is not executed, I will leave for Gezer."

"You are my wife, my queen," Solomon said with sudden cool dignity.

"I am also sister of the great pharaoh and he has ordered me to take back the dowry his troops won for me when I became your bride."

Solomon hesitated. Despite his plans for a sea route, he still needed Gezer. It was not as essential as it had been in the past, but it was the key city in his trade route up the coast. He had been so proud of his agreement with the pharaoh that had given him this lovely, flowerlike woman and the city of Gezer. He must stall for time. With time anything could be accomplished.

"My dear," he said, "I will consult with my counselors. I can't endure the thought of losing you." He tried to take her in his arms as he had done many times before when she had been upset, but she resisted him and turned her head away. He knew his words had sounded dull and lifeless. There was no passion in them. He was once again doing what he had to do, and it sickened him.

He turned and walked through the sheer draperies and out into the moonlit night where his men were waiting for him. He hurried on ahead of them, not knowing where he was going, just wanting to be alone. He'd like to talk to his brother Nathan, but he knew just what he'd say and he didn't want to hear it tonight. Nathan really thought Tipti was a spy. He had even tried to prove it to him on several occasions.

Probably all his wives were spies. Certainly Naamah had been found guilty enough times. In spite of this she was his queen, the mother of Rehoboam, the son that would inherit the throne of Israel. He had known from the beginning that she was a manipulator. There was always some plan or plot afoot that disrupted the whole order of things. She kept the other wives in tears and even his mother, Bathsheba, intimidated. She was ruthless and everyone feared her.

He came to the marble steps that led up into the temple area, hesitated, and then on impulse walked up the steps and through the double arches into the court of the women. Ignoring the guards and his men, he walked briskly over to the pinnacle that looked down on the Kidron Valley.

The moon was high, and though the olive groves on Mount Olivet were dark and shadowed, the small villages gleamed mysteriously in the pale moonlight. Down at the end of the valley, where it turned and went up the Hinnon, he could see a dim light and figures moving back and forth in its glow.

So they were sacrificing again tonight. Hopefully it was a lamb. Too often these days the sacrifices were young children. He tried to shrug it off. It was difficult to ignore. Naamah's priests insisted that because of these sacrifices, Israel was protected by Moloch. "There have been no wars since the idol's altar was erected," they bragged.

Solomon cringed. Naamah had forced him into letting her erect the altar to Moloch. "I have promised my firstborn child to Moloch," she had insisted when the midwife placed the newborn babe, Rehoboam, in her arms. Her eyes had been hard and calculating. There was something almost sinister in her look, and he had realized the child was not safe even for a moment in her care.

He had told her that in Israel the firstborn was never sacrificed but instead a ransom was paid, but she wouldn't listen. "I have promised Moloch my firstborn and if I don't keep my promise great evil will come," she had said over and over again when he tried to reason with her.

Finally he had taken his son from her and had allowed the temple to Moloch to be built in exchange for him. He had paid dearly for his firstborn son, and it frustrated him to see that the boy was soft, easily influenced, and a lover of luxury. How he wished he had fathered a son like the young Jeroboam or Mattatha, his brother Nathan's son. He had often noticed how these young men stood tall, were courageous, and at the same time had a penchant for learning.

Now he saw that so much of what he had worked for and even struggled for was meaningless. "Even the things that are of value," he thought, "will pass to my son. Who knows what he will do with all I will leave him." A black feeling of hopelessness and despair engulfed him.

"It's late. What can be of such importance that my brother is out here alone?"

Solomon whirled to face Nathan. "How did you know I was here?"

"It is impossible for the king to go anyplace without a flock of followers." He pointed back toward the steps, where guards, counselors, and finally various relatives of Solomon's numerous wives stood waiting for the king. It was obvious they hoped to catch his attention as he passed back down the stairs.

"I was going to call for you," Solomon said.

"Then," interjected Nathan, "you decided against it because you don't like my answers and warnings."

Solomon smiled. How well this brother understood him. "You might know I have a problem. A serious problem."

"I can guess that it involves the Egyptian princess and her cat. Am I right?"

"You're quite right. She's demanding that I have the priest who killed her cat beheaded or she'll take back Gezer. She even threatens to move there."

Nathan drew in his breath sharply. "That's a real problem. Of course you can't have the priest beheaded nor can you afford to let Gezer go. Undoubtedly Pharaoh is using this as a ploy to get his hands on Gezer."

"Even more serious. Can you imagine what would happen if the pharaoh decided to march up and defend his sister's honor?"

"I wouldn't put it past him if it served his purpose."

"My chief builder, Jeroboam, has just come back from Egypt, and he reports that the pharaoh still encourages my enemies to take sanctuary in his palace. He loves to hear of my plans, my wealth, and sometimes of my wisdom."

"He is undoubtedly furious about your plans to bypass him altogether with ships on the Red Sea."

"I can't believe Tipti would side with him."

"Maybe it's not as bad as it looks. You have always had such a way with women. Somehow you'll manage to charm her."

"This time it's something different. She's no longer the soft, gentle Tipti I fell in love with. She's suddenly grown cold and distant. Short of some miracle, there's nothing I can do."

Nathan didn't answer. Solomon turned and without a glance at the golden altar with its glowing coals or the lovely temple with its glimmering doors, he walked with Nathan to the little knot of men that had been waiting for them. They went down the steps, past the darkened house of the Egyptian princess, and into the great Common Room of the palace. They would be up most of the night discussing their options and determining at length that this was indeed a crisis of growing proportions.

That night Solomon tossed restlessly and found he could not sleep. He pulled back the curtains of his bed. A soft glow splayed out onto the rough stones of the wall and the polished tiles of the floor from a single oil lamp left sputtering in the wall niche. A breeze sprang up from somewhere outside, setting one of the latticed shutters to banging softly against the wall.

In the dim light he could just make out the blanketed forms of his steward and dresser along with his guards, who slept in a far corner.

The door to his reception room was standing ajar and he could see two of his house guards sitting cross-legged on the floor playing some game to keep them awake.

A wave of gray loneliness swept over him. He'd not wanted anyone of his many wives tonight. They all seemed suddenly frivolous and impersonal. Most of them had some petition for a relative or some plan of their own to promote. Now suddenly he feared they only pretended an interest in him to gain their own ends.

He'd not wanted to sit with his friends either. They were too eager to please. His family was too critical and his children were so in awe they never spoke their minds.

He ran his fingers through his hair, rubbed his eyes, and searched around in his bed for one of the parchments he had been writing on earlier in the evening. Now as he thought of it his whole existence seemed to be an experiment. Other people seemed to live from day to day without trying to wring some meaning or profound wisdom from their experiences, but for him this was impossible. It had always been impossible. He wanted desperately to understand what life was all about and how it should best be lived. He had been on a quest of sorts. For a time he had lived by his father's rules, and then without entirely discarding them, he had determined to try everything, to drink deeply of every experience.

He ran his hand along the edge of the parchment, making it lie flat so he could see the words he himself had written. "Vanity, all is vanity." That was the last thing he had recorded. In all of his searching for happiness, there seemed to be nothing but emptiness. Once, only once, in his life had he felt whole, complete, and satisfied. Now looking back it was the only time he had been really happy. Strangely enough it had been when he was very young and in love with his little shepherdess, Shulamit.

Her death had marked the end of love and the end of real living. Later he had cluttered his life with women. Women from every country and from every prominent family. He had found most of them provocative and alluring for a time, but always he tired of their full pouting lips, their too-eager smiles, and their constant demands. He now realized that with each new bride he had hoped for a return of the heady effulgence he had experienced with Shulamit. It never happened. He was always disappointed.

"Vanity, all is vanity." The words burned in his brain and he pushed the parchment down into the folds of his fur cover. That was a statement of poetic melancholy. In the past there had been a strange pleasure derived from such anguish, but now it was all too real. Tipti with her demands had destroyed his peace of mind. For the first time he was willing to consider seriously that she might be a spy for her brother. If it were true, it would be devastating. He had come closer to loving her than anyone since Shulamit, and he could not endure the thought that she did not mean all the charming things she had told him.

He thought again of her eyes looking at him with adoration, her lips hungry for his kisses, and her eager, responsive young body. She had taught him to experiment with strong drink, to dance, and to laugh at the risqué jokes of her jugglers. She more than anyone had urged him to forget Israel's law and enjoy the freedom of fulfilling his own selfish desires.

He pulled the curtains of his bed closed, flung his arm up over his eyes, and deliberately tried to will himself to forget her. It was impossible. He couldn't sleep. He rose again and paced the floor until the first cock crowed announcing the dawn. Only then was he able to fall across his bed and sleep for a few troubled hours.

5

*A*ll during the early part of the month Bilqis spent time in preparation for the night of the full moon when she would be brought to the god's pavilion. At first she had enjoyed the look of awe on everyone's face, and then she had been excited by the mystery of Ilumquh. But now, as the day approached, she was apprehensive.

Ever since she had stood by her father's side as a little girl in the great oval place of meeting, she had been overwhelmed by the appearance of Ilumquh. He was all of alabaster. A soft, glowing alabaster that was transparent in the blaze of the altar fires. His head was held high, and his horns tipped with gold glistened in the flaring light. None of this frightened her. Only his eyes, the glistening ruby eyes that fixed themselves upon her— they terrified her.

She had told no one. Her father would have been disappointed and the priests would have used it against her.

Now that she had chosen the god in place of a human husband, she had asked many questions of the High Priest and he had seemed evasive.

"Will Ilumquh come as the image in alabaster?" she asked.

"He may."

"How can he father a normal son if he is of stone?"

"That is part of the great mystery. He is a god and can come in any form or shape he chooses."

"Then he could come as a bird or a fish?"

"He could."

"Will I see him?"

"It is more likely that you will hear him. The pavilion is dark."

"Then we will burn tapers and place torches in the wall so I can see this god that is to father my son."

"No, no, that is not allowed. He comes in thunder and smoke and you will be fortunate if you are not bruised by his horns."

At first this disturbed her. Then she decided the priest was angry and wanted to punish her for not accepting her uncle's son. She stiffened. "I'm not afraid of Ilumquh," she said. "I'll wear my short sword and breastplate I wore when riding in the Markab. Even Ilumquh cannot easily have his way with me then."

"You shall come to Ilumquh with neither sword, breastplate, nor crown." His voice was almost defiant. "You will come as a virgin princess and not the queen."

She had been ready to protest, and then she remembered the alternatives and decided to go along with all that the priest had planned.

Each night she followed the priest's instructions. First her maidens rubbed palm oil into her skin until it glistened. Then just as carefully they scraped it off with a rounded piece of conch shell. Next they bathed her in soured goat's milk. This was so rancid she had to hold her nose and beg for a bit of linen soaked in oil of jasmine before she would sit another minute in the rock-walled tub. Finally there was the rose water and the combing and plaiting of her hair that took hours from her duties in the palace.

The special diet was even more repulsive. She, who had never eaten anything she disliked, now found that she must eat strange roots and the testicles of goats, drink sour beer and bitter wine. Each night she was given the sacred ergot so she might have erotic dreams.

When she summoned the High Priest and complained or refused any of these ministrations, she was shamed by being reminded that it was for the great god Ilumquh she had been ordered to do this.

Each night after her maidens had pulled the curtains on her bed, she rose and went out onto the terrace, where she could see the growing strength of the new moon. At first only his horns had been visible and then gradually his face began to appear. It was round and glowing like the alabaster idols in the temple. There were no ruby red eyes and she began to feel a strange attraction to this god that could light the whole dark earth with his countenance.

"I have done all that you commanded," she whispered. She waited for some response, but when there was none, she tiptoed back to her bed and finally fell asleep.

The day before she was to be taken in to Ilumquh's pavilion, she was ordered to take only the ergot drug. She was to eat nothing else. That night she went to bed as usual but was soon wakened by a bright splash of moonlight falling across the floor. It played on the softly blowing curtains of her bed and somewhere out in the night she heard a sound as of footsteps on the terrace.

With every nerve tense and every fiber of her body alert she rose from her bed and fell to her knees. "Oh great Ilumquh, forgive me for thinking you were cruel and ruthless. I see now that you are both gentle and brilliant and I will be your humble servant."

She waited hoping to hear the footsteps again, but there was only the rustling of the wind in the palm fronds and the cry of one of the watchmen on the wall below the palace. She rose and walked out onto the terrace, where she felt instantly embraced by moonlight. In a sudden flood of some strange, new emotion, she raised her arms toward the moon. "Oh my beloved," she cried, "to you and you alone I give my heart and soul. Only you are grand enough to be trusted with my love."

* * *

When morning came, she was swept up in the last feverish preparations for the visit to Ilumquh's pavilion. She could feel an air of excitement permeating the palace and was told that out in the city of Marib, tumult over the evening's celebration had reached fever pitch.

The day passed quickly as she tried on various robes woven with gold threads or encrusted with precious stones and trimmed with golden embroidery. She patiently waited while some imported beauticians twined her hair with rare jewels and others decorated her hands with intricate, feather-like designs. This took the better part of the day, and all too soon it was time for her to ride down the avenue of light to Ilumquh's pavilion.

Out in the city, tension mounted as the sun set and torches were lighted. People hurried to line the avenue leading from the palace and crowded onto the rooftops and along the great wall.

* * *

It was at this moment that Badget entered the local inn near the western gate. He proceeded to order his servants to bed down the camels and store his merchandise in one of the sleeping rooms. He was well pleased with his bargains. He had gone down to the coast to trade dye from the murex shellfish for incense and spices and was now on his way home. He had just settled down on a carpet beside a small fire built in the dirt floor of the inn when he heard the news.

"That's ridiculous," he said laughing. "I don't know what the moon is, but it's a sure thing it's not going to come down for your queen or anyone else."

The little man he had been talking to glared his displeasure. "I didn't say he would come down. We have his image in the temple's pavilion."

Badget laughed all the harder. "The queen actually expects to mate with that alabaster idol. I don't believe it. She's too smart for that."

For the first time the man looked a bit bewildered, but he quickly recovered his poise. "It's a mystery. The idol only represents the god."

"The moon, the alabaster idol, or a real bull, it's all foolishness. A trick of some kind I'll wager."

At that a small band of men gathered around him and raised clenched fists in a threatening way and swore dark oaths. Badget was immediately apologetic. He took back everything he had said and agreed to go along with them to the city gate. There they could climb to the wall and observe the procession that was already forming before the great pillars of the palace.

Badget's curiosity knew no bounds as he saw the golden palanquin move down the street of light toward the large oval temple. He thought of the queen as he had seen her just a month ago and wondered why she was doing this. Could it be that he had really been right about her feet and no king or prince would have her? "So no one would marry your queen," he half stated and half asked the man standing to his right.

"That's not it at all. It is she who will have no one. At the last they pressured her to marry her cousin, but she'd not have him either."

By this time the drummers and the dancers had reached the temple. They were followed by the queen's own horsemen and after them came the golden palanquin carried by four strong, black Nubians. Amid a fanfare of trumpets and roll of drums, the queen stepped from the golden box and with great dignity mounted the steps of the small, delicately designed building. Badget noticed that she was alone and walked as though in a trance. Over her shoulder was thrown the leopard cape, but she didn't seem to be wearing the short sword or the breastplate.

Her maidens were not with her, and her counselors were left at the foot of the steps. The crowd grew deathly silent as she majestically stood in the torch light's glow before the great door of the small pavilion. Then, as though summoning her courage, she moved forward into the darkness of the sanctuary and was lost to sight. The crowd erupted with a roar of approval. They clapped and stamped and even danced until the cobblestones rang with their enthusiasm.

At sight of the full moon rising over the distant mountains all eyes were leveled on the door of the beautiful little marble pavilion through which the queen had disappeared. "This is where the alabaster idol is kept and where the queen will meet Ilumquh," the small man shouted over the uproar to Badget.

The processions were now forming and people who had been standing beside Badget began to scramble to get down from the wall. "Where are you going?" Badget demanded.

"To the place of meeting—the temple. We must dance and sing before the altar so Ilumquh's seed will grow within our queen and the curse will be lifted."

"Curse? What curse?" Badget was now totally caught up in all he was hearing and seeing.

"Never mind. You wouldn't understand. Come along with us and you'll see everything."

Badget didn't hesitate. He wanted to know more of what was happening and so he scrambled down from the wall and followed the crowd until he came to the great temple. He hesitated only a moment and then mounted the marble steps that led into the dimly lit sanctuary.

* * *

Bilqis stood for a moment in the doorway of Ilumquh's small pavilion listening to the deafening roar of the crowd. They strengthened her resolve. Her people expected her to be brave and fearless and she was determined not to disappoint them.

Gradually her eyes became accustomed to the darkness. The room contained nothing but a long, low slab of alabaster raised only slightly from the floor. There was a strange, unearthly glow emanating mysteriously from its entire length. Flung across its surface was a fur spread. There

53

was nothing else in what appeared to be a circular room.

Every nerve was alert and tense. Her ears were tuned to even the slightest sound. A vast silence surrounded her, broken only by the distant drumming and high, lilting voices of priestesses in the oval place of meeting.

Suddenly behind her the great doors through which she had entered closed with a resounding thud. There was a rush of stale air and then a sliding, clanging, metallic sound as a bolt fastened them shut. Voices of the mob outside faded.

For a moment panic seized her. Her hand flew to the leopardskin cape and she breathed a prayer, "God of the leopards, help your queen."

There was no other sound. Gradually she relaxed and looked with fascination at the alabaster slab. It was undoubtedly intended for an altar, but there was no fire, only the mysterious glowing of the stone. She reached out her hand and found it wasn't even warm, yet it continued to glow as though burning with some internal fire. "Come, Ilumquh must not be kept waiting." The voice seemed to come out of the wall and echo round and round the room. There was no one in sight and yet the voice was distinct as though whispering in her ear.

"You must do exactly as I say and nothing will harm you." A face, creased with wrinkles and outlined with gray wisps of hair materialized in the darkness. Bilqis saw that the old woman had evidently been there for some time, but she was completely dressed in black that melted into the darkness of the room. She held a lamp in one hand and a clay bowl in the other and it became obvious that the lamp had been covered by the bowl.

"This is your marriage bed." Her gnarled hand moved over the marble slab and her eyes fastened on Bilqis in an almost hypnotic fashion. She set the lamp down and lifted braided cords from around her neck.

Bilqis backed away, "What is that? I'll not be bound."

The old woman continued to run the cords through her gnarled hands undaunted by the queen's protest, "These are the cords of love that bind you to Ilumquh's altar. It is an honor to be bound with these cords."

"I am a queen, not just a woman. And I'll not be bound."

The old woman shrugged. "Ilumquh will not be pleased."

Bilqis sat down cross-legged on the glowing slab, "Let him come. I am ready."

The old woman seemed a bit taken aback by her daring. She picked up the lamp, put the clay piece over it, then hesitated. "Ilumquh does not speak. He will come with smoke and fire and you must not move or he will be displeased that you are not bound."

Bilqis was now less frightened. Her eyes had grown somewhat accustomed to the darkness. She saw that there was no furniture, only niches in the walls and a huge door in front of her. The idol's niche was empty.

The old woman headed for the door and then hesitated. She set the covered lamp on the floor and returned with the cords, "Here," she said laying the cords in Bilqis's lap, "let this be on your head not mine. It is no business of mine if you have untied the cords." With that she turned and fled from the room as though in a great fright.

No sooner was the old woman gone than Bilqis noticed a strange odor that seemed to rise and float around her. It was sickeningly sweet and made her feel groggy. She was just steeling herself to resist the lethargy when she heard a distant rumble. The slab she sat on trembled and smoke billowed in under the closed door. The rumble grew louder and closer. The door shook and the room seemed to tilt and fill with puffs of smoke.

Now in real fright Bilqis clung to the alabaster slab and watched the dark outline of the door. She gasped for breath. She tried to remember that she was the leopard queen and nothing could harm her, but it did little good. The door shook and bent under the blows that now rained down upon it.

Suddenly it burst open with a loud, resounding crash. Light flashed, smoke flared and billowed, and in the midst there appeared the face of a jackal. The eyes protruded and the hair of the brows was stiff and brittle, the nose sharp, and the teeth were terrible teeth that glistened in the flashing light.

Bilqis stifled a scream. Never had she imagined Ilumquh to take such a hideous shape. He wasn't the soft, glowing light she had worshiped but rather a raging bull of an animal, and she was terrified. Never before, even in the heat of battle as she rode in the Markab, had she been so frightened.

She felt the beast's claws grasp her arms in a tight grip and she smelled the stale, sickening odor of Ilumquh's sanctuary. She began to struggle with the beast, her terror lending her strength. For a moment the beast seemed to waver as she kicked the cords off to one side. She thought she heard a curse as the beast's head bent over her, his hot breath sickened her so that she thought she would vomit. She felt his body pinning her to the slab and she grew wild with terror.

With one awful wrench she tore at the beast's red, glaring eyes. There was a ripping, tearing sound. The beast's ugly face was in her hand and an angry, human face stared out at her from a fur hood.

With almost superhuman strength she pushed him from her and jumped to her feet. She towered over him for only a moment before snatching up the lamp left behind by the old woman. With a flick of her finger she sent the cover flying, and holding the lamp high she looked at the beast.

She gasped in surprise. She saw first the carefully clipped beard, then the cold eyes, and finally the serpent ring on his finger; it was none other than the High Priest. "You, you!" she panted. "You meant to fool me. You meant to fool your queen."

At that the creature seemed to wilt. He let the fur robe slide from his shoulders and sat before her stunned and submissive. The blood dripped from his cheek where she had scraped him with the mask. He reached up and felt his cheek then looked at his hand. "You have wounded me," he said with growing indignation.

"And you have deceived me. For a whole month you have had me bathing in sour goat's milk, eating bitter roots and testicles of goats." Her mouth grimaced in memory of the awful ordeal.

"You suffered no special affront. We ask that of everyone."

"Ohhhh! How could you? Why should you ask that of everyone? It's not Ilumquh; it's you. Everything is false. Everything's a trick. It's all the ergot drug and your clever manipulation. There's no Ilumquh. Admit it old man—there's no Ilumquh!"

For a moment the High Priest looked stunned and then he collected himself. "Who is wise enough to know if there is an Ilumquh. If there isn't, there should be. If he doesn't speak, he should speak. It's not our fault if we must at times speak and act for him."

"Stop! Stop! This is unbearable." Bilqis was walking back and forth pausing only now and then to glare at the old High Priest. "You were going to pass yourself off as Ilumquh and be the father of my child. How could you dare to be so bold with me?"

The High Priest rose to his feet and tugged at the skins he wore around his waist, "It was all for you, all for you. A little deception, but what does that matter? You would have had the heir you need and stopped the people's complaint but now . . . "

"A little deception you call it. It's a little thing that you have robbed me of my god. Cheated me, lied to me."

"But, but don't you see it was for a good cause?"

"Oh," Bilqis exploded, "truth means nothing to you."

"Nothing if it is inconvenient, my queen, and this was very inconvenient."

"Don't you think I would rather deal with the truth than to depend on a lie? Truth is everything. Without truth the whole world has gone mad."

The High Priest looked stunned. It was evident that he had no idea why she was so angry. "You are upset that I left you out of the plot to gain an heir for Sheba."

"Yes, yes but more. I am upset that you lied to me."

The High Priest fell to his knees and pleaded. "It was just a little deception and it would have solved all our problems."

Bilqis pulled her robes out of his hands and drew herself up to her full height. "To me truth is everything. I am the queen and I must know the truth at any cost. Now open the door. I must tell my people the truth."

The priest's eyes narrowed and he jumped to his feet. "My queen, I beg you, don't be so foolish. The people are ignorant. They believe in Ilumquh. They plant and harvest by his strength."

"And they are terrified that he will desert them. You're a scoundrel of the worst sort, and I intend to expose you to my people for what you are."

The priest adjusted the fur robe and stiffened as though resisting her harsh words. It was obvious he had regained some of his composure. "I doubt that you will do any such thing if you think about it."

"Why, why should I not tell my people the truth?" Her eyes were flashing as she backed toward the door.

"You'll not tell them because they won't believe you. They'd rather kill their queen than believe Ilumquh doesn't exist."

Bilqis hesitated. She knew he told the truth. The people were simple and couldn't understand something so alien to all they had been taught.

"Open the doors!" she said finally with quiet dignity.

"But . . ." the High Priest was again anxious.

"I'll not expose you now." Her tone was clipped and firm. "I need time to think. Now open the door."

The High Priest fell at her feet in obvious fright. "My queen, you must appear before the people waiting in the great temple. They have been praying and . . ."

"Get up and open the door," she ordered.

The High Priest stumbled to his feet, grabbed up the hideous mask, and adjusted it awkwardly. With a motion of his hand a door slid open revealing a passageway leading into the large temple area.

Bilqis swept past him and then turned. "Until I myself have found the truth, I'll not rob my people of their faith. It's for their sakes not yours I will be silent now."

6

*B*ilqis struggled to hide her agitation until she reached the safety of her rooms. She was so shaken she hadn't spoken a word to anyone. She barely noticed the curious, speculative looks of priests and priestesses, guards, tribesmen, and the crowds that had to be held back to let her pass.

As she ordered, her palanquin had been brought directly to her private garden. She wanted to be alone, but even here in her own rooms it was impossible. She found her maidens all gathered around the door, hoping to guess by her demeanor what had happened in the temple.

With an impatient wave of her hand she dismissed all of them. Only old Najja was allowed to remain. As she helped her remove the elaborate robes, Najja seemed startled to find blood on her mantle and a section of her robe torn. Out of the corner of her eye, Bilqis saw Najja's eyebrows shoot up and a frown cross her face.

For a moment Bilqis toyed with the idea of telling her everything. The moment passed, and she decided Najja would be only scandalized and bewildered by such a revelation. Najja was a firm believer in Ilumquh, as were all the people of Sheba. They swore by the moon's rising, measured days and nights by its appearance, and would only plant and harvest by the full moon. Ilumquh controlled everything of any importance to them. Il Hamd was right; they would not easily be shaken from their belief.

With a sigh she settled into her bed and let Najja draw the heavily embroidered curtains, then listened as the old woman shuffled from the room.

Now she wanted more than anything to be alone. She turned her head and put her hands over her eyes as she remembered the terrible odor and the horror of the apparition. She shuddered and ran her hand back and forth over the place on her arm where his fingernails had drawn blood as he clutched at her. She turned over and buried her head in her arms as she tried over and over again to shake the horrible defilement that she had experienced. She who had been feared, honored, acclaimed, and treated with such diffidence that no one dared approach without her permission, had suddenly been accosted and deceived in this shabby manner. It was unthinkable.

She had only this one night to come to terms with this monstrous affront to her honor and her dignity. Her old beliefs in the god of her people, her trust in his priests, her own sense of dignity and power had all been stripped away in this tawdry performance of Il Hamd's.

She would have liked to have had him executed, but knew almost as she thought of it that this was impossible. The people would have to know his crime. She herself had elevated him to a position of honor that would be hard to discredit. He would, of course, deny everything if confronted. Whatever she did it could not include removing or punishing Il Hamd at present.

Her mind quickly went over all the reasons he had given for deceiving her. It would solve the problem of an heir, he had argued. She shuddered to think of it. This old goat of a man would father her son! He would actually let everyone, including herself, think it was the moon god that had lain with her!

And what would have happened if by some chance she had not become pregnant? Would he have insisted she return to the temple? She sat up in bed and hid her face in her hands. It was too unthinkably horrible.

Toward morning she got out of bed, wrapped a warm woolen robe around her shoulders, and went out onto the balcony. It was the blackness before the dawn. The moon had gone down and she was glad not to be reminded of her own foolish response to the ergot drug and what she had thought was Ilumquh's wooing. She must somehow put this all behind her. Il Hamd was right about only one thing, and that was that now she was left with all of her problems and had no solutions and no hope of a solution.

If she said nothing of what had happened in the temple, didn't expose the priest for being a fake, then she had a few months while everyone waited to see if she was pregnant before the pressure would start all over again for her to marry.

The other immediate problem that would face her this morning was the trade route crisis. She would have to give the Egyptian ambassador some answer. Imagine the cleverness of the pharaoh to place his sister in Solomon's court. How had he known this small, upstart king would come to wield such power? In fact she wondered at the very idea of such a small country growing in such awesome power that it could shake the great kingdoms of the Nile and Sheba.

She was almost inclined to laugh at such a possibility. But then, if the pharaoh and her own spies were right, if this king really had built a fleet of ships to sail down the Red Sea, their worlds could be shattered. The old trade routes would be obsolete. The coming and going of the caravans that paid such rich tribute meant everything to their economy. Without them they would all become nomads roaming the desert, lucky to find a few dates and some camel's milk.

She would have to stop this morbid brooding. There was a little time before she would be forced to decide on a consort, but the problem of the trade route was immediate and urgent. The Egyptian ambassador would expect his answer today, and he wanted war.

The sky began to lighten in the east. The great humped mountains on each side of the dam lay against the graying horizon like sleeping giants. A slight breeze sprang up and rustled through the branches of the palm trees in her garden. Faint and silvery upon the crisp morning air, she heard the jingling of the ornaments on the camels' harnesses as the caravans began to form outside her gate, arranging themselves in formation for the long trip north.

For a moment she let her mind wander out past the wall to the north gate. There would be the usual excitement. The scolding of the camels that insisted stubbornly on remaining seated as if their loads were too heavy and the drivers irrational. This awful sound of complaint always seemed to come from some place way down in their throat. Their soft upper lip would snarl and their half-closed eyes stare off in space as though pondering some profound secret.

The other drivers would gather and give advice while the camel's owner would tug and pull and cajole, all to no effect. If it lasted long enough, all the drivers would shout obscenities at the beast and threaten to leave without him. At this point the obstinate animal would seem to sense the game was over. He'd rather meekly rise and follow his driver off into the mist.

She could see it all and envied them the excitement of leaving familiar surroundings and going off into the unknown. Her father had found short trips out into the desert for a day of hunting the perfect escape. No ambassadors could reach him, no disputes had to be settled, no formalities had to be observed.

Her feet were bare and the coldness of the alabaster flooring brought her back to the present. There was no such escape for her. She must stiffen her resolve. Let no one break through her composure. Above all she must say nothing of her experience at the temple or show any aversion to Il Hamd. Hopefully he would have the wit to stay out of her way.

She hurried back to her rooms and clapped for Najja and her maids. To her surprise they all came pushing and crowding into the room, looking self-conscious as their eyes studied her face and then traveled down to her feet and back as they tried to determine if she had been affected in any way by her experience of the night before.

They were silent. No one seemed able to think of anything to say. Finally Bilqis waved her hand in dismissal. "Go, go, all of you but Najja and the Egyptian. I must hurry. I have important matters to settle today."

They seemed to come to life at her words and turning, pushed and shoved to be the first to start the day's round of activities. Actually they were eager to get a safe distance from the queen to ponder all that had happened and to discuss and speculate as to what had really taken place in the small temple. Why had she said nothing? Why did she seem intent on picking up the usual routine with no visible change? They all wanted answers to their questions and each was determined to get them one way or another.

* * *

In the middle of the morning the Egyptian emissaries returned. Immediately the scheduled business of the day was canceled and Bilqis made preparations to receive them. As her pages came and fastened the thin veil over her face that she wore in the presence of strangers, Aidel, her chief counselor, hurried forward to advise her. "My queen," he said, "the Egyptians must leave early tomorrow. They must have an answer for the pharaoh."

"So soon? I've not even heard their proposal."

Aidel looked around the room to see that he was not being closely observed, then putting his hand to his mouth he whispered, "The pharaoh wants to wage a war against Israel. They want us to join them and as we march from here with as many men as we can gather, they will march from the delta."

"But..."

"Oh don't bother yourself over it. It's all planned. When we come to Edom we will be joined by more men."

"Men from Edom?" the queen questioned. "They are also ready to fight?"

"The men of Edom have an old score to settle. They have just been waiting for such an opportunity."

"And what is their complaint against this king, this king . . . what is his name?"

"Solomon. His name is Solomon. Their complaint goes back before his time. It was his father, a king named David, who sent his general down to Edom and had all the men killed. Only one of the princes, a mere child escaped. His name was Hadad."

"Yes I know of this Hadad. He has married the sister of the Egyptian queen Taphenes. So he's back in his own country now ready to fight. But where will he get his army?"

"He's very rich. They say he's hiring tribesmen from the desert and paying them handsomely."

"Hired mercenaries don't sound too dependable."

"Ah, but he is not the only one preparing to come against Solomon. There is another adversary. A man called Rezon. He was a citizen of Sobah and is now living in Damascus. These kings have now gathered armies and are waiting, ready to join us in fighting Solomon."

"Ready to join us fighting? You sound as though it has already been decided."

"Yes, my queen. A very clever pincer movement. Egypt will move from the south, Hadad with us from the east, and Rezon will come down from the north. We'll totally crush this king and bring his big plans to defeat."

"So, it has all been planned and I have not even been consulted." She was flushed with anger, though her voice was steady and calm.

"My queen, wars aren't something you're interested in, and we thought..."

"You thought you could manage everything behind my back."

"No, no, that isn't true. We have just contacted people and discussed plans and now it is time to give the Egyptians an answer."

"It's very obvious you thought by getting things all lined up I'd have no choice but to go along with your plans." She was stunned. It was evident that her trusted counselor Aidel had been hiding the true state of affairs from her for a long time.

Suddenly everything seemed out of control, at least out of her control. First it had been the High Priest Il Hamd and now it was Aidel. Both men wanted to manipulate and manage things for her own good. They didn't hate her, they just wanted to use her to get on with their own schemes.

Aidel stiffened. "My queen, I've done nothing but manage things for your own good. When the Egyptians come, all you must do is agree to join them in this venture and the trade route will be saved."

"All you have to do." The words had such a familiar ring. They no doubt had discussed it thoroughly and had decided everything. She was just to be a convenient tool in their hands. Fierce pride rose up within her. They would not have tricked her father this way, and she must not let them succeed, or she would totally lose control. If she only had time she could think of something. As it was, the Egyptian ambassador and his whole entourage were already standing in the great golden doorway. She must think fast. There was no time, and that was just what her counselors were counting on.

She stiffened and with a nod dismissed her counselor and at the same time raised the scepter that gave the Egyptians the signal they were waiting for. She could see Aidel smiling and nodding smugly to the other elders and she knew he was assuring them that she would go along with their decision.

With their usual riot of feathered fans and colorful banners, the Egyptians advanced to the foot of the throne and bowed with their foreheads to the cool alabaster tiles. As they rose Bilqis noticed Aidel and the Egyptian ambassador exchanged glances that clearly said they were in some agreement. It was evident they had talked and thought everything was all arranged. This meeting with the queen of Sheba was to them nothing but a formality.

It must have been at times like this that her father had escaped to the desert for a day or two. She wished it were possible for her to do the same. Given time she could find some solution.

"Your highness!" the Egyptian ambassador said, as he bowed again with a great show of respect and deference.

She motioned for him to rise. A plan had suddenly presented itself, a plan so daring, so ingenious she hardly dared broach it as a solution. She looked at the Egyptian, rising with such an air of superiority and then at Aidel. He stood feet wide apart, head thrown back, waiting for the words he expected her to say.

She ran her hand along the claw of the leopard skin that she had chosen to wear on this occasion. It reminded her again that she was the leopard queen and she must maintain her position at all costs.

"Your highness," the Egyptian said again, "we await your decision. Our men are ready to fight and our allies are ready to join us. The plans are all made." At this the Egyptian scribes came forward unrolling the parchment that contained the agreement. It was obvious, they had the wax ready and all they wanted from her was her signet pressed into the soft red mixture.

"These are the terms of the agreement?" she asked as she stretched out her hand for the scroll.

Quickly Aidel moved forward. "My queen," he said, "all that is needed is your signet stamped here." He took the scroll, unrolled it, and with one long, gnarled finger indicated the space at the bottom.

Indignation and anger flooded over her anew. She found it hard to maintain her cool dignity. They were all, Il Hamd, her counselors, and the Egyptians, all treating her as though she were of no consequence instead of the queen. "Protecting her" is how they would have described it. Even the veil she wore in the presence of these strangers was a symbol of her helplessness.

Still holding to the leopard skin with one hand, she reached up and tore the fragile veil from her face. She enjoyed for the moment the startled look of the Egyptian ambassador, who staggered back and almost tripped over a kneeling scribe. She ignored her counselor, who lowered the scroll and stood openmouthed in amazement.

Her voice was sweet but firm as she announced, "I have considered all the facts and have concluded there is a better way. We may not need to fight."

"Not fight?" The Egyptian ambassador seemed totally bewildered.

"The plans are made . . ." Aidel's look of shock replaced his usual smug expression.

"We have readied supplies," one of her army commanders added.

"We've gathered camels and drivers," another proffered.

Though she was seething with indignation, Bilqis rose and smiled. "Your efforts will not have been wasted. I can use the camels and all the supplies to carry out my plan."

"Your plan?" Again her chief counselor could not restrain himself.

"Yes, my plan. I intend to leave as soon as possible. I'm going to visit this king, this Solomon, and talk with him, and then we'll see what Sheba will do." With a regal look of hauteur she stood before them, a queen, completely in charge of her realm. Then with a slight lift of her scepter, her Nubian guard stepped forward, there was a blast from the ten silver trumpets, and the banners were lifted from their sockets. The counselors, tribesmen, and all the Egyptians bowed down to the floor and she walked out of the throne room with an unusual feeling of elation.

No sooner was she back in her rooms than she sent a messenger out to find the trader Badget. He was vital to the success of her plan. She must see that he rode on ahead to announce her visit to Solomon. She would not wait for a reply. She must leave as soon as possible if her plan was to succeed.

Given time, the priests and counselors would band together and find a way to put a stop to what they would consider her foolishness.

As Bilqis paced back and forth on her balcony, Najja came to the door and pulled aside the gauze curtain. Bilqis saw that she was afraid to speak, and though it irritated her to be interrupted, she stopped pacing and asked, "What is it now? Have all the vultures followed me here?"

Najja nodded. "Even Il Hamd has come with the counselors and the important men of your tribe."

Bilqis laughed. "Now they must wait while I make my plans. Tell them when I'm ready I will call them, but now I can't see any of them."

7

*B*adget had been surprised to find the queen was planning to visit Solomon. She proceeded to ask him a great many questions, such as, how long it would take, what supplies were needed, what difficulties would be encountered, and what kings and kingdoms must be dealt with on the way. She concluded by asking questions about Solomon himself.

In Badget's estimation, the strangest questions had involved the new temple and the God of Israel. Instead of being put off when told that the temple held no idols, she seemed to be even more interested. He had expected her to lecture him on the greatness of Ilumquh, a god who could at least be seen in the night sky. When she didn't, he was momentarily puzzled but encouraged enough to venture, "The God of Israel is the God who created both the moon and the sun."

Again he had expected to see the look of smug amusement such a remark usually called forth from the people he met on his trading trips. They couldn't imagine such a God. It seemed to stretch their minds beyond possibility. To his amazement the queen had simply nodded her head and then sat as though meditating on the whole thing.

The audience was finally concluded by the queen's giving him a document. "Take this to your king. It will explain everything. I will, of course, send messengers to report our progress."

Badget bowed low and backed from the audience chamber. His caravan would be traveling north in the morning and he had much packing left to do. He tucked the parchment in his belt and covered it with his cloak. He meant to protect this with his very life. Keeping it on his person was the surest way of guarding it from both curiosity seekers and thieves.

* * *

Word spread quickly in Marib that their queen was going to travel to Jerusalem. Since only the traders and ambassadors made such trips, this was truly an astonishing bit of news. Even more astounding was the realization that the queen was not asking for advice or permission of her counselors or tribesmen but had simply announced what she intended to do.

The Egyptian ambassador was pleasantly dismissed with the message that she would inform the pharaoh later of any plans. She also made it clear that she would visit the kingdom of the Edomites herself and talk with Hadad. She intended to listen to the king's grievances against Solomon, but she was determined to let nothing he said deter her from visiting Jerusalem and finding out the truth for herself.

All the time her plans were being formulated she refused to see any of the tribesmen or priests. Instead she called in Tamrin, her own foreign ambassador, and some experienced traders to give her advice on the best way to prepare for this long journey.

It would be best, they told her, to travel with sufficient guards and armed men. There were brigands who roamed the desert seeking to rob caravans. She was also warned to have someone well-versed in the movements of the stars and the signs of bad weather. Whole caravans had been lost in desert storms.

When finally all the preparations had been completed and the day of departure was set, she began to make plans for the gifts she would take to various rulers along the way and most especially gifts for the king in Jerusalem.

"He likes animals," Tamrin said. "I've taken sapphires, gold, and the rarest kinds of incense to trade, but for himself personally he usually seems to like animals or birds."

The queen was immediately excited. "What kind of animal do I have that he would find amusing?"

"There's only one animal he can't get with his gold, and that's the animal he covets, above all else."

"Of course. One of our rare horses," she said. "Has he ever mentioned that he would like such a gift?"

"Often, my queen. I've told him our horses are given as gifts, but we never sell them."

"You're right. I wouldn't sell one of the horses. They're like members of the family. I suppose we could consider taking one along to be given as a very special gift. Even at that I would have to be sure he would treasure it."

"There's no doubt he would treasure one of your white mares."

"One of the white mares?" Bilqis herself loved the rare white mares she owned and was reluctant to part with any of them. The one she loved most was a blue-white mare who ran like the wind and had large, luminous, intelligent eyes. Zad el-Rukab was the mare's name.

Tamrin saw that she was hesitating. "My queen, I would advise that you take the best you have. When you see Solomon, you will understand and be glad of my advice."

Bilqis gave him a puzzled look. She was known for her generosity, but the horses were not something she could easily part with. A picture of the horse flashed through her mind, the long body with the beautiful, tight muscles, slim legs with hooves that flew above the ground seeming to barely touch it, the small ears, high carriage of the tail, but above all else the intelligent eyes that seemed to understand everything.

Impulsively she decided to take her favorite. "I'll wait and see. I can give him the other gifts, but I'll only give Zad el-Rukab if he proves to be worthy of the best."

Finally, when everything was arranged, she called for her palanquin and set off for the royal treasury. The treasury was a building of formidable size and strength. Its great brass doors were guarded night and day by chained leopards and their Nubian caretakers. The only light in the building reached the interior from openings high up in the walls.

Bilqis had taken very little interest in the treasury. It contained such a variety of battle spoils and gifts from distant kings and eager traders that it of all places was most oppressive. Now she wanted to choose treasures that would impress this northern king. For the first time since she had come to the throne she entered the treasury with a light step and eager, searching gaze.

There were boxes of rings and bracelets, chests of cloth from lands far to the east, spices that made the air pungent with their fragrance. Quickly she had her officials spread the contents out before her and then she carefully picked the articles that were to be packed ready to be taken as gifts.

She had just held up a man's arm band to inspect the delicately drawn inscription when there was a slight commotion out in the portico. She could hear voices raised and then the sound of feet hitting hard on the polished marble as someone came running up the stairs and into the room.

A young man fell down at her feet and didn't rise until she ordered him.

"My queen," the young priest said, "my master has followed you here. He must see you. It's urgent."

Bilqis stood, turning the armband first one way and then another, not looking at the man but playing for time. She knew she would have to see Il Hamd sometime, but she was annoyed that he should be the one to choose the time and place. She hadn't decided what to do with him. If she left him behind while she went to Jerusalem, it was likely that he would steal the throne. With a sigh she tried the armband on her own arm and found it way too big. "Bring your master here," she said finally. "I have very little time, but I will see him."

Within minutes Il Hamd stood framed in the great doorway. He was obviously in his best robes and had worn not the eagle mask around his neck but rather the heavy eagle medallion given him by her father. On his head he wore a turban held in place by the coils of a snake that in the front reared its ugly golden head and seemed to hiss.

When his eyes were accustomed to the light, he came forward and knelt at her feet. For a moment she breathed in the fetid air that seemed always to linger in his garments. She noticed that in spite of their elegance they were hopelessly bloodstained and had a dustiness about them. "Please," he begged, "I must speak with you alone."

Reluctantly she waved her maidens and the Nubian guards back and motioned for Il Hamd to rise. "Why must you see me and what is the urgency?" she asked with a coldness to her voice that made Il Hamd visibly shrink back toward the shadows.

"I've heard that you have defied the pharaoh and all your counselors and are traveling to visit the king of Jerusalem."

"Your informants are correct." Her voice was even now sharp and stilted.

"My queen, let me suggest you take a convoy of the younger priests. They'll be indispensable to you. When there are difficult decisions to make, when you need the stars read or the future told, they'll be there ready to help."

Bilqis smiled as she deliberately put the bracelet into the hands of one of her servants. "And, my clever High Priest, what do you intend to be doing while I'm gone?"

Il Hamd shifted uneasily from one foot to the other. "I? Why, I shall take care of matters for you here at home."

Bilqis could see his small eyes glinting with anticipation. It was obviously he could hardly wait for her to leave. No telling what powers he intended to usurp.

"Well, my ingenious one, you have come at just the right time to hear my news personally. Unfortunately my cousin Rydan will hear it only by messenger."

Il Hamd kept rubbing his hands together and his eyes were darting here and there with obvious pleasure. "My queen, I regret all the unfortunate happenings between us. I wish to redeem myself, get back in your good favor. To serve you would be a great pleasure to me."

"Serve me you shall but not here at home." Bilqis turned with her back to him as she reached out for a golden collar made after the Egyptian style. She fingered the delicate workmanship and looked at Il Hamd sideways almost gleefully. "You, Il Hamd, and my cousin Rydan will have the honor of going with me to Jerusalem."

"To Jerusalem!" Il Hamd almost shouted. "Why would you want me to go?"

Bilqis had to stifle a laugh as she turned back and looked him in the eye. "Do you think I would leave two such rogues as yourself and Rydan here to steal the throne while I am gone?"

"Steal the throne!" Il Hamd's voice was choked with emotion. It was obvious that he was desperately disappointed.

Bilqis ignored his outburst. "Yes, the two of you will have to travel with me. I'm also taking my throne and my crown."

"Your throne, you're taking your throne?" Il Hamd couldn't contain his surprise. "Then, my queen, who will rule in your place?" Il Hamd's voice was suddenly subservient and had none of the condescension she had found so distasteful in the past.

"I don't mind telling you so you can spread the news. I'm choosing my old uncle. He's clever and wise and hopelessly lacking in ambition. He'll be terribly disappointed he can't go and will feel only anger and frustration that he must be burdened with my scepter."

Il Hamd bowed low and kissed the hem of her garment in a gesture that was most unlike him. It was obvious he was completely taken aback by her cunning. "You are your father's child and have more wisdom than becomes a woman."

With that he bowed himself from her presence and she could hardly wait for him to disappear before she laughed a hearty, ringing laugh. She held the jeweled collar up to her own neck. "And I'll choose this for myself," she said stooping so she could see her reflection in an old brass shield.

* * *

When Badget left the queen, he hurried through the maze of winding lanes out toward the market; he had other matters to tend to besides the usual packing. He made his way through the gathering dusk to the shop of a merchant named Pelli. Pelli always supplied him with the most valuable ornaments crafted in pure shining gold and usually for a good price. Pelli in turn had been impressed with Badget, so impressed in fact that he had given him one of his daughters, Terra. "It'll be a good thing for you to have a woman waiting for you here in Marib," Pelli had said.

Now as Badget came to the shop, he saw that Pelli was still sitting surrounded by his treasures. Like all the shops in Marib, it was small enough for Pelli to sit cross-legged among the colorful cushions and still reach anything a buyer might want to see. In front of him, spread out in grand array, were the less valuable brass and copper ornaments with the gold and silver hanging in profusion behind him.

Badget stepped up onto the narrow platform that brought him to eye level with Pelli. "I received your message," he said as he reached across the confusion of brass and copper to clasp Pelli's hand in both of his. "I was concerned. What's wrong with Terra? Is it a fever?"

"No, no, not really," Pelli said. "It's nothing that medicine can cure."

"Then she is ill?" Badget said leaning forward and in so doing dislodging some copper ornaments that hung around the opening to the shop.

Pelli put his finger to his lips and spoke softly. "Not here, we can't speak of it here. Go on up and I'll come as soon as I've closed the shop." Badget looked up and down the street of the merchants and could see what his friend meant. Merchants and buyers alike had paused, obviously interested in the conversation between these two.

Badget stepped down and walked quickly to the door that had now become familiar to him. It was opened even before he knocked by a servant who brought him into the dark hall. As was the custom, the servant removed Badget's sandals and washed his feet, then taking the lamp from one of the wall niches, led him up the dark stairway. They passed some storerooms before they came to the ample living quarters of Pelli's two wives and many daughters. "You are to wait here for my master," the servant said, motioning to the family room decked out with luxurious mats, silken armrests, and pillows.

This was a room in which Badget had spent many happy hours both with Pelli and with his daughter, the charming Terra. He looked around expecting to see Terra smiling at him from the doorway, but to his utter disappointment she was nowhere to be seen. "You're missing my daughter?" Pelli came forward and bowed his greeting over Badget's outstretched hand and then took his seat across the narrow room from him.

"I had expected to see her," Badget said. "Is she then so ill she can't be seen?"

Pelli smiled his most disarming smile. "You must understand. Her eyes are red from weeping and she has lost all interest in food of any kind. We're terribly disturbed."

"But that's so unlike her." Badget was now obviously concerned and almost impatient with his friend.

"Yes, yes, we have never seen her so upset. There's no way we could comfort her. I brought her choice nutmeats and some of our market's finest figs and dates, but she would have none of them." Pelli dabbed at his eyes as though he himself were now on the verge of despair.

Badget had liked Terra from the first for her soft roundness and her obviously healthy appetite. If what Pelli was telling him was not an exaggeration, then Terra was really ill. "We must do something. Call the herb woman, order some charms, go to the temple and make an offering." Badget noticed that his concern seemed to please Pelli.

"I assure you none of these will work. We've tried them all," said Pelli with downcast eyes.

"Surely it is not totally hopeless." Badget wasn't used to such frustrations.

"No, no, there's a cure, not a cure either her mother or I enjoy contemplating." Pelli became even more downcast.

Badget leaned forward eagerly. "Whatever it is, whatever it costs, I am ready to oblige. Anything to make my darling well again."

"Only you have it within your power to cure her. But . . ."

"I, I have it within my power? Tell me, and no matter what the cost, it'll be done."

"It seems the maiden is sick with love of you. She can't endure your leaving without her. In short, she's packed her things and will hear of nothing but that she be allowed to travel with you back to Jerusalem." Pelli had made his fingers into a pyramid and while he appeared to be studying his own hands he was actually darting quick glances at Badget.

Badget turned pale and coughed nervously. He'd been completely charmed by the girl and would have been delighted to take her with him, but he had one problem. In Jerusalem he already had a wife, a very jealous woman who had blocked every attempt he'd made to marry a second wife. All his friends had encouraged him to marry someone else since his wife was getting older and had given him no children. Knowing how rich Badget must be, some of them had even offered their daughters. The arrangement had always been canceled when his wife discovered the plans.

His wife was named Yasmit and had at one time been married to an old trader named Eon. Eon had taught Badget most of what he knew, and it seemed logical that when Eon died, Badget should marry his widow. At the time Badget was captivated by her spunk and charm and assumed that once married to a younger man like himself, she would have many sons.

This had not happened and now Badget had grown impatient. He had not planned to bring Terra home with him, but neither was he willing to give her up. "Yasmit will just have to face the inevitable," he muttered to himself.

He knew there would be a terrible scene. Yasmit was not one to accept competition without a struggle. She would threaten and scold, making life miserable for everyone. In the long run, she would have to give in and accept the fact that she was fortunate to be the first wife and in charge of his home and his kitchen if not first in his heart.

It would take three months of fast travel to reach Jerusalem. In the meantime he would have this delightful creature all to himself. He'd face the problem of Yasmit later. Wasn't he almost being forced to take her with him? He couldn't have this on his conscience that lovely, plump Terra had died of grief for love of him. He smiled. "My friend, tell your beautiful daughter to dry her eyes. I'll go right now and hire the very best howdah fitted onto one of my camels. A howdah with all the amenities for such a charming creature."

At the door Pelli kissed him on both cheeks, wishing him godspeed, and Badget urged him to have Terra ready just before dawn, when he would come for her.

Badget had done all that he promised and more and found to his amazement that Terra was indeed one of the best bargains he ever made. By day she rode among the colorful, scented cushions of the howdah but at night she shared his dinner and his tent. They lay in each other's arms and watched the majestic movement of the stars while Badget taught her the simple words she'd need to manage in Jerusalem. He was happier than he'd ever been, so happy he hesitated to tell her of Yasmit.

Each night he tried to bring himself to explain just what she would face in Jerusalem, but over and over again he found he couldn't risk losing this newfound happiness.

At times he rationalized and fantasized that Yasmit would have grown reasonable. Of course he knew it was impossible. She wasn't the kind of woman to accept anything in life she hadn't planned or could somehow manage to control.

In Jericho he experienced the supreme joy of finding Terra to be pregnant. At all costs he wanted to protect her. He yearned to keep her to himself. He had always been a man of action and now faced with this dilemma he found himself undecided. He thought of sending a messenger ahead to tell Yasmit of his marriage. Maybe if she heard the news she'd leave, go off with one of the men he'd heard she entertained while he was gone.

Instinctively he knew this wasn't possible. If she was warned, she might be angry enough to kill them both. It was better after all, he reasoned, to surprise her. Surely he was man enough to face this woman and tell her just as other husbands had done before him that he was married to a second wife. It was done and finished. What could she really do? Surely she would realize that this time the matter was out of her hands.

The next day as they prepared to travel the last few miles to Jerusalem, Badget wasn't as confident. He'd faced wild animals, hostile foreigners, and been known as a hard bargainer. But to face Yasmit with a new wife was entirely different. He found himself irritable and anxious. The day was overcast, and all the signs he depended on as a trader and traveler were ominous.

At the last minute he decided to leave Terra with the wife of the innkeeper. He paid handsomely for a whole floor in the inn and for servants to wait on her. When he realized how frightened Terra was, he gave the innkeeper more money to pay for runners who would come twice a day and report on her health.

Last of all he told Terra about Yasmit. "She is a difficult woman, not one to accept a second wife without a struggle," he said as he nervously paced the narrow hall between the upper rooms.

"A wife?" Terra burst into tears and could not be consoled. "I didn't know. You didn't tell me."

"I meant to keep you in Marib, then it wouldn't have mattered. You were the one who insisted on coming with me."

At that Terra threw herself down on the mat where they'd spent the last night together and burying her head in her hands wept bitterly. Badget was at a loss as to what he should do. He tried to reason with her and tell her that Yasmit had given him no children. "You'll be the one to give me a son," he said.

When he offered to let her live in her own house in Jericho where she would never see Yasmit, she seemed to regain her composure. She sat up and dabbed at her eyes with the corner of her mantle. "Do you truly love me as you have said?" she asked, looking away so as not to see his reaction.

"Oh, yes, yes, you know that I do," Badget said as he hurried to take her in his arms and proceeded to dry her eyes himself with her mantle. "Haven't you listened to what I've told you over and over again?"

"You're a man who has a way with words."

"Look at me. Look in my eyes," Badget said turning her head so she had to look at him. "I'll go to Jerusalem if that is your wish and I'll settle this thing so you can be with me there."

At that she smiled. "Don't worry. I have your child to think of. I can manage."

Badget spent another hour making sure the wife of the innkeeper would bend every effort to make Terra's stay pleasant, then he rounded up his caravan and headed up the road toward Jerusalem.

He tried to dismiss all thought of Yasmit. He had no idea what would happen when he told her of Terra, but it would do no good to try to anticipate her reaction. He decided to face the problem head-on when he encountered it.

He had the message to deliver to the king. He must do that as soon as possible. If Yasmit was very angry, he could stay at the guardhouse just outside the palace. Certainly she wouldn't stay angry for long.

*T*hat evening when Solomon had said goodnight to his friends at the pillared portico of the Hall of Judgment he walked slowly up the long marble stairs to a pavilion on the roof above the women's quarters. Most of his guards and retainers were left in the courtyard below with only his personal servants following at a discreet distance behind him.

He breathed a sigh of relief as the servant drew back the heavy goathair covering. Just inside he stopped and looked around at the colorful banks of cushions and softly billowing draperies that covered the walls. The roof of black woven goathair moved gently in the spring breeze causing the tent poles that held it in place to sway hypnotically.

There were no torches here, only the small lamps carved of alabaster with their bit of fire at the end of the twisted sheep's wool that curled down into the rich olive oil. The light was dim but magical, transforming the bright cushions into rubies and emeralds and the gold and silver goblets and trays into gleaming particles of captured light.

He was about to call for one of his favorite harpists when a small, bent figure seemed to emerge out of the shadows. "Your lordship," the voice was almost a whisper as the figure with rather slow, painful movements prostrated herself at his feet.

He wanted to laugh as he recognized one of his old nursemaids. She who had been so bold and had wielded a very effective switch on his bare young legs was now almost frightened to approach him. She who had fed him with her own fingers and told him funny stories to make him forget a skinned knee had become distant and formal as though his being king had wiped out all the past between them. It was obvious that to her he was now someone remote and unapproachable.

"What is it you wish to tell me?" He tried to say the words in a gentle way, hoping she would relax and be her normal, humorous self.

"Your lordship," she said again with a trembling voice.

"Come, come. Enough of this formality. Let me get a look at you. I haven't seen you all year." He reached down to help her to her feet and a servant rushed forward. "I can at least help this old one to her feet," he said as he motioned the servant away. "She helped me often enough when I was just a little fellow."

The old woman stood trembling before him, her eyes on the floor and her hands nervously twisting the tassel of her mantle. "Come," he said, "look at me. Have I grown so frightful?"

"Your lordship, your mother wishes to see you. I've only come at her bidding." Her eyes were still looking down at the floor as though she could not look at him.

"So it's my mother who's sent you. You didn't just come to see if your little charge is behaving himself." He looked at her and could hardly recognize the jolly, tender, caring woman she had been. She seemed so stiff and formal with no trace of the person she had been.

At his words she looked up and he saw just a flash of surprise that he had spoken so familiarly to her. Then just as suddenly the mask again descended and a look of fear and awe took its place. This was the thing he hated most. Almost everyone treated him as though he were some royal object. He could have been a golden idol in a Canaanite temple for all the human warmth anyone displayed.

"Where's my mother?" he again asked gently so as not to frighten her.

"She's waiting below in her sitting room." Her voice was low and he had to bend down to hear what she said. He was so frustrated, he was tempted to force her at least to look at him. To see the little boy he'd been still hiding behind the elaborate finery—if she could only see him.

With a sigh he called one of the scribes to him. "Write an order for the keeper of the king's treasury." He waited while the man did obeisance and then sat down and began fumbling with his parchments and reed pens. "This woman is to be given a golden ring and pendant from the king's own treasures."

At these words the old woman fell to her knees and wept, while Solomon, ignoring her, now pressed his seal into the soft red wax making the order official. "Come. It is little enough the king can do to honor the woman who dared whip his legs with an almond branch." Solomon lifted her to her feet himself and handed her the parchment. This time he was the one who looked away. He couldn't stand to think that he'd again find fear written in her eyes at his little joke.

He dismissed her and then stood for a moment pondering the whole episode. His father, David, had somehow been able to command the respect of his subjects and friends without this terrible alienation from them. How strange it was that men fought and struggled to gain power and prestige and then found it to be such empty isolation. Vanity, all is vanity. The words drummed in his head like an ominous knell summoning in the depression he suffered from so often lately.

He motioned to one of his pages. "Take this to the court of the queens and hand it to my mother personally." He handed his royal scepter to the page and knew that when his mother received it she would know that he was waiting for her.

* * *

Bathsheba had heard rumors of trouble with the Egyptian princess and her cat and then the threats Naamah the queen was making against her Egyptian rival, but she had kept the more serious trouble to herself until she was sure of all the details. Now it was time to speak if disaster was to be averted.

She took the jeweled scepter from the page and followed him back up the dark, winding stairs to the king's pavilion. It was part of Solomon's new palace; in fact, this was the only really comfortable, casually elegant part of Solomon's new quarters. The rest was such a mixture of stark Egyptian and Phoenician opulence that Bathsheba never felt at home in any of the rooms. Black ebony couches with actual heads and tails of wild animals carved into their sides, small tables of gleaming mother-of-pearl, and stools and chairs all richly carved but vastly uncomfortable were placed according to some unfamiliar pattern on the marble floors.

The curtain parted and she saw her son before he saw her. She was shocked to notice how dejected, even sad, he looked. His hair was closely cropped, his beard trimmed. His crown was glinting and gleaming in the dim light. He wore a tunic that seemed to be belted with huge jewels that made his short sword seem smaller than it actually was. His legs were laced with otter skin and the thongs of his sandals were washed in gold; he was the very image of health and success, all that she had imagined he might become and yet he was obviously far from happy.

She sighed. She had no good news to impart and she regretted having to tell him anything that would burden him further.

She cleared her throat so he would know she had arrived and then swept toward him holding the golden scepter in her right hand. He turned, and seeing her, smiled. He took the scepter and tossed it into the cushions beside the makeshift dais and throne. "My mother," he said, leading her to a seat on the low mats next to the dais, "is it good news or bad that brings you out at this time of night?"

She didn't answer at once but let the servant help arrange the pillows behind her and bring an armrest for both her and her son. He had dropped down rather informally beside her and she noticed with astonishment that his arm leaning on the rest was circled above the elbow with a large, jeweled serpent. She drew back and stared at the ugly thing with its gleaming eyes and golden fangs. "What's this that seems to have taken the place of your phylacteries?" she said, leaning away from the creature.

Solomon looked to see what she was pointing at. "Oh," he laughed, "it is a gift from Tipti. She said it would bring me untold power, help me to read the minds of my enemies, and make me irresistible to women."

"But, a serpent! An ugly serpent! You probably would eat the forbidden fruit if Tipti gave it to you."

"Don't be so worried. I wear my phylacteries at prayer time, but they depress Tipti. She can't understand why they have to be black and so, so ordinary."

"I wanted more than anything for you to be king and to marry a princess and now you have it all and . . ."

"And what?"

"This isn't the way I had imagined it would be."

Solomon grew serious. "I know. Nothing is ever the way we imagined it. Sometimes it's better, but most of the time it's worse."

"I hear you have been depressed and moody."

"You've talked to Nathan."

"Not only that. Everyone watches a king. If you should not eat as usual, if you want to be alone, if you have added beautiful girls to the harem and then haven't called them . . ."

Solomon raised his hand. "Enough. I know. I can imagine. I hate being watched all the time."

"You didn't used to mind it."

"I didn't used to have anything to hide. I didn't care what they said because I was busy and happy."

"And now you aren't?"

"Let's forget about me. I don't want to talk about it. What did you want to tell me?"

Bathsheba's face grew pensive. "There are several things, but the most serious involves your beloved Tipti."

"Tipti? Do you mean about the cat and the stolen sacrifice? I already know about that."

"No. This is something more subtle, more dangerous."

Solomon braced himself for whatever revelation his mother had come to bring. She came to see him at night only if there was need for secrecy. "You think she's a spy for the pharaoh."

"I know she's a spy. There's proof now, and it's more dangerous than even I had suspected."

Solomon looked away. His face seemed to harden as though he was preparing himself for the worst. "You know she's a spy?" he asked at last. "Tell me. I'm ready to hear whatever it is."

"It's not only Tipti, but your favorite young friend Jeroboam."

"Jeroboam!" Solomon exclaimed with utter disbelief. "He's like my right arm. He's organized the work crews, stood up to my enemies, even smoothed over the problem with Tipti and the cat."

"Exactly. He could smooth over the problem with Tipti because he is in league with her. He's one of the main sources of her information."

Solomon almost jumped to his feet. "He wouldn't do that. What benefit would it be to him?"

"Listen, my son. This is important. Jeroboam is of the tribe of Ephraim. Now think. The father of that tribe was Joseph and the mother of the tribe was an Egyptian woman named Asenath, the daughter of the priest of On. I am told that Tipti has been telling Jeroboam of the glories of Egypt and convincing him that he must not ignore his Egyptian blood. When he went to Egypt he visited On and enquired of the priests. They told him some amazing things that have made him proud and defiant. He now says he sees nothing wrong in worshiping the bull as a visible symbol of Yahweh."

"He's young and Tipti can be quite convincing."

"Solomon, it's not his faith I'm worried about."

"Then what are you worried about? I thought that was the concern."

"No. That's bad enough, but worse is that he's critical of you and is telling his friends of an Egyptian plot to rob your treasury and the temple, take over the country, and put him in charge."

"Impossible. Why would Shishak devise such a thing? Why Jeroboam?"

"Don't you see? Jeroboam is a good servant but not a leader. He would do just as Shishak ordered. If Shishak told him not to carry out plans for a trade route going down the Red Sea, Jeroboam would listen. You won't."

"So it's the trade route that has the pharaoh all stirred up. I did tell Tipti about it. A king can be ruined by the foolish use of his own tongue. I know that."

"It's not just the pharaoh. He's gathered all your neighbors. They're all coming to surprise you."

"Who?"

"Prince Hadad of Edom for one, Rezon of Damascus for another, and now it is rumored that they have joined with the new queen of Sheba. All of them are angry about your bypassing the old trade route and starting your own sea route."

"Why not attack my ships? Why come to Jerusalem?"

"My son, don't you see? They've heard of your wealth and the beauty of your new temple and the palace. Pharaoh is secretly telling them that it would take years of gathering tribute to glean as much gold as could be had in one raid on Jerusalem."

"The old goat. He's really jealous." Solomon threw back his head and laughed.

Bathsheba hadn't heard him laugh in a long time, but she didn't join him. Instead she clutched his arm. "It isn't funny. Of course he's jealous and he's also greedy. He'll do just what he's planned if you don't take quick action."

Solomon grew serious. He pushed his crown back on his head and locked his fingers around his short sword. "Are you sure this is right? Who told you?"

"I have a very clever maid who waits on Tipti. She hears everything and reports to me."

"I suppose she also reports on the visits of your son to the princess."

Bathsheba blushed and dropped her eyes. She was embarrassed. "Yes, yes, there have been times, but most of the time it is concerning her other contacts and activities."

"What interesting listening that must be. It must provide you with endless entertainment." Solomon's voice had that sharp edge to it that warned her of the dangerous ground she was treading.

"Not entertainment, my son. It's for you. I don't trust her."

"Well, it seems she can't be trusted. I don't know what I will do, but I assure you I will be guarded in my speech when I'm around her."

Bathsheba knew it was late and she had accomplished her purpose. She let him lead her back to the curtained doorway a short distance from his guards. He was looking down at her with an amused, almost puzzled look. "Were we to part and you have no bad news to report of Naamah, the queen of insults and dark, evil plots?"

"I wasn't going to bother you."

"Come, come, we must hear the latest."

"She's invoked a curse against Tipti. She says it's now in the hands of Chemosh, and Chemosh will defeat Bastet, Tipti's cat god and Tipti will die."

"She's serious?"

"Of course. She hates Tipti because she's seen that you love her. She claims Tipti's cat was killed by the priest because of her charm and Tipti will be next."

"I don't understand. The priest of Yahweh, not Chemosh, killed the cat."

"My dear," Bathsheba said lifting her skirt slightly so she could step down into the outer courtyard, "the harem has become a place of struggle for power and authority. In foreign languages they scream at each other with terrible threats and their maids and eunuchs are always thinking of ways to best themselves. In my day the harem was not the pleasantest place, but it definitely wasn't like this."

After she had gone Solomon moved to his dais and sank down among the cushions. He ignored the message that friends and tribesmen were waiting to see him. He had matters to ponder, decisions to make. So, his little Tipti was a tool of the pharaoh. He couldn't believe it had all been a game, a maneuver for power. She had loved him. Perhaps if there had been no other wives, no Naamah to torment her it would have been different.

In his heart, he knew it wasn't so. Her final loyalty would be to Egypt and to her brother. He'd been foolish to love her. To give her so much freedom. Now, if his mother was right, and she was always right, he was about to lose everything he had worked for since he had become king. Everything he prided himself on was about to be lost.

He drummed his fingers on the armrest. Pharaoh had heard of the golden vessels in the temple, the fine carvings in his palace, the horses and chariots he had ordered from Egypt that had been paid for in pure gold. He thought of how proud he had been of all his accomplishments. "Pride goes before destruction," he said at last getting up from the dais and pacing back and forth across the length of the tent.

So it was not just Egypt but Edom and Haddad, Damascus with the bitter Rezon leading the charge, and, joining them, the queen of Sheba, like an angry wasp whose nest has been disturbed, was undoubtedly ready to sting. He had no forces strong enough to battle such a coalition. They would surround him, rob him of his dearest treasures, clean out the lovely temple and leave it desolate.

Worse than all of this he began to realize they would no doubt take him prisoner, put out his eyes, torture his sons, and rape his wives. For a moment he couldn't resist a small thrill of pleasure at the thought of Naamah, the terror of his harem, his evil queen, being led off into captivity. She wouldn't be raped, she was too cross and sharp-tongued, but she would be made to stand and fan some Egyptian dignitary, or perhaps, if she was really difficult, clean their chamber pots.

He crossed his arms and stood thinking. Usually his quick mind could imagine some defense, some counteraction, but if his mother was right, this could be the one maneuver he couldn't surmount. In such a bind only the God of Abraham, Isaac, and Jacob cared what happened to him and the lovely temple. "Jerusalem is where I have put my name," the Lord had said.

He remembered the dream he had had in the tabernacle at Gibeon before he became king. The commitment he had made to Yahweh and the promise Yahweh had made to him. He deliberately called to mind the promise all Israel had made at Sinai and the assurance that Yahweh would fight for them and protect them.

His hand closed around the snake bracelet Tipti had given him. "Thou shalt have no other gods before me" seemed to thunder through his mind. He looked down at the bracelet and for the first time saw that it was an ugly, evil thing. A talisman of the devotees of Isis, the Egyptian goddess of love.

He pulled it from his arm and flung it from him as he buried his head in his hands. "O God of Israel, unless your strong right arm defends us, we can lose everything," he prayed.

In spite of his prayer and his good intentions, the bracelet had reminded him of Tipti. He picked up the scepter where it was lying under one of the pillows. He twirled it in his long jeweled fingers and thought of Tipti. In spite of everything, he still wanted her tonight. Wanted her desperately, and yet he knew she was a pagan, worshiping false gods and it seemed, was also a traitor, her love simply a ploy. He could not give her the satisfaction of making him seem a fool.

It had been his habit in the past to go to the balcony where he could look down on the courtyard of the harem below. The maidens newly chosen as wives or concubines could easily be seen as they sat clapping and taking turns dancing to the steady beat of drums and clanging of cymbals.

The courtyard was lighted with torches and the women looked beautiful and seductive. He could hardly imagine, looking on this charming scene, that there could be such strife as his mother had described. He looked from one to the other, trying to find someone that would make him forget Tipti for at least a night. They all looked rather dull and uninteresting until his eyes found a dark beauty that played the small finger drum with an extra vigor. Her bead was thrown back and she was singing the words with the same enthusiasm. "I want her," he thought. "If anyone can make me forget Tipti and all my troubles for a few hours perhaps she can."

"Simon," he called, as he drew the curtains together, "I would see the maiden who is playing the finger drum and singing." He handed the scepter to the young man and then walked back to where he could see the courtyard. In a few moments the music stopped and he could see one of the old women hobbling out into the middle of the dancers. They all stood still and expectant while she looked from one to the other and then slowly walked over to the girl who was still holding the drum and handed her the scepter.

He could see that the girl was excited. All the others rushed over to her and began talking and gesturing while she stood rather dazed, holding the golden scepter. One of the few eunuchs allowed in the harem brought a large scroll and some reeds, for it must be recorded in case a child should be born.

He sat cross-legged on the floor while the older women looked over his shoulder and the young girls giggled and talked among themselves. Solomon was momentarily amused as a small child reached for the reed pen and the eunuch spilled ink on the precious parchment. For a moment there were wild flailing of arms, accusations, and recriminations as the mother snatched up her child and the eunuch began to write again.

* * *

For all of his original interest in the girl, the evening didn't turn out well. The girl had been shy and frightened. She looked at him with the same awe and reverence with which one would look at the holy ark. He could not get her to talk. She watched him closely and began to make him nervous. Finally, in spite of the fact that he knew there would be talk and the girl would be disgraced, he called the evening to an end. She had done nothing but make him all the more depressed over his mother's bad news and more lonesome for Tipti.

He ordered that she be rewarded and was pleasant up until the moment the curtains closed behind her, and then he sank down on the dais and breathed a sigh of relief. He wondered if he was losing his charm. Was he getting too old for love? Had he become so formal and austere or so morose that he would only frighten women from now on?

He briefly wondered why he had always needed women so very much. It wasn't that he was abnormally preoccupied with sex. It was more that he found it difficult to have friends, really close friends; most of them were too much in awe of him. They acted stilted and formal around him. Most people had even grown careful in the way they worded things or what they would discuss around him.

With women everything was different. Pleasantries were exchanged. Hands reached out to hands and lips to lips. For a short time he would feel a sense of belonging, a wholeness. He would feel accepted, part of the normal world, not set aside and only envied or admired.

Now after this miserable experience, he felt only depression. Ashes were in his mouth and tears of frustration in his eyes. The whole world had turned to dust and he ruled a kingdom that could vanish with the new moon, a kingdom in which even the best of friends could turn out to be enemies.

He had pulled out the parchment he had been writing on and was reading it over when he heard the guard outside his door clear his throat. Then there was the sound of footsteps and voices. "I have permission to see the king. It's urgent!"

Solomon threw down the parchment and rose. He recognized Badget's voice and he knew he would see him. Badget with one of his stories could make him forget all the unpleasantness of the day. "Come in, come in," he said as a guard appeared with Badget close behind him.

9

adget had passed tribesmen and counselors in the lower courtyard who were all still hoping for a moment with the king. At the entrance to the roof pavilion, he encountered more guards and scribes, also a harpist with his harp under one arm and a trumpeter who stood ready should the king choose to leave and return to his own quarters.

As he followed the page into the dimly lit pavilion, he was surprised to find the king virtually alone except for his pet monkey. Upon seeing Badget the monkey jumped and went scrambling up the chain that held an incense burner. He sat perched on the rim and kept moving the chain so the burner swung back and forth.

Though Badget was amused, he didn't forget to prostrate himself before the king and rose only at his command. Solomon was sitting cross-legged on a low throne that rose from a dais covered with lion skins.

"My lord," Badget said as he accepted a tasseled cushion brought by one of the servants, "I bring important news." He looked around the room as though trying to determine whether there was enough privacy.

"News? Is it good news or bad news? I've had enough bad news for one night." The king looked uninterested, actually bored.

Badget pushed back his headpiece a bit nervously and then smiled. "Why, I would say it was good news. In fact the very best of news for a hospitable man like yourself."

"Then perhaps we are to have a visitor."

"Yes, yes. But such a visitor you can't imagine."

At this Solomon became interested. He leaned forward and his eyes studied Badget with an intensity that was very flattering to one such as the trader. "This visitor, I take it, is from some country where you've been trading."

"Yes, my lord. A country to the far south filled with gold and beautiful women." Badget's eyes expressed more than his words.

Solomon laughed despite his lingering tendency to be morose. "Gold and beautiful women. You must be speaking of paradise."

"No, my lord, it is a real country and you know it well, the land of Sheba. You are to have a royal visitor."

Solomon was immediately interested. Since receiving word that Sheba's queen was joining with the pharaoh to come against him, he had thought of little else.

"A royal visitor coming here?" He intended to be cautious and only draw Badget out without giving him any indication of his own knowledge of the situation.

"The queen herself is coming. See." He pulled out a tasseled golden case from a huge pocket in his dusty cloak. "She has sent this message with me. I was instructed to deliver it in person."

Solomon reached for the case, but his face was a mixture of curiosity and caution. "Then you saw the queen and talked with her."

"Yes," Badget said drawing himself up and nodding enthusiastically in the manner that had given him the name Hopoe. "She asked me many questions about you and our country. Then she told me she was coming to see for herself if all I had told her was true. She is probably already well on her way."

"Already left? What did you tell her?"

"Of your wisdom and wealth. Your palace of marble and gold and the temple with its carved doors and hidden ark with the golden cherubim guarding it . . ."

Solomon fingered his scepter nervously. He didn't like it. Badget of course had done it all innocently, but telling of all his wealth would only make someone like this queen greedy to get her hands on it. "She's leading an army?" he asked.

For the first time Badget looked startled. "No, my lord. She's only coming to see you, to talk and ask questions. That's what she said. Of course, I had to leave before she finished making her plans but . . ."

"Did she talk about gathering an army?"

"No, my lord, only about a friendly visit. You will see. The parchment will tell you everything."

Solomon dismissed Badget and then opened the gold case and pulled out the parchment. To his surprise it was written in the square, boxlike letters of his own language, and he could read it easily. It bore out all that Badget had said and no more. The queen of Sheba was indeed coming for a visit "to ask questions and see if all she had heard of his glory and greatness were really true."

Solomon rolled up the scroll and pushed it into the golden case, then leaned back to think what it must all mean. It seemed obvious that this was some trick. A ruse. The queen was undoubtedly coming with her army, wanting to be the first of the coalition to attack. He had heard of such maneuvers before. A dignitary arrived as a guest with an army disguised as servants and traders and then rose up to slaughter the unaware host when he was least suspecting. "Well," he thought, "I'm prepared. If she comes, I'll be ready to turn any trick to her disadvantage."

With that he tucked the golden case under one arm, called the monkey down from his perch, and waited for him to settle on his shoulder, then he summoned his guards. It was late and he was tired. Hopefully he'd get a few hours' sleep before he had to make some important decisions. The trumpeter blew the staccato blasts that let anyone still awake in Jerusalem know that the king was finally going to his own rooms and to bed.

As he walked down the moonlit marble stairs past his pages, scribes, and councilmen, he paused for a moment in the shadow of one of the taller palms that shaded the lower part of the stairs. "I have very little doubt," he thought, "about the purpose of this queen's visit. I fear the worst. However, I do have a real desire to find out if it is true that she has the feet of a donkey."

* * *

There was now nothing for Badget to do but go home. Somehow he would have to face Yasmit. He would have to tell her sooner or later that he had married another wife. Her anger would be terrible. She was an angel of light until she was offended, and then the darkest demons of hell could not equal her ability to make one suffer.

Most of his caravan was bedded down at his inn on Mount Olivet. He had ridden into the city on a camel loaded with gifts intended to appease Yasmit. He now hurried to reclaim the camel with its driver. He had left them just inside the great gate that led into the upper royal city and the temple area.

His own house, once owned by Eon the trader, stood behind a high wall with only the fronds of palm trees and the upper room visible from the street. There was a dim light burning in the one window and Badget shuddered. Yasmit's spies had undoubtedly told her he was home and she'd be waiting for him. He wondered if they might also have told her of the woman he had left in Jericho. He sincerely hoped not.

He squared his shoulders, pulled his turbaned headpiece low on his forehead, and hurried down the marble steps to his front door. At one time when the house belonged to Eon it had been right across from the gate leading into the palace. Now Solomon had changed everything. Marble steps led to the area of the palace complex that included the pillared Hall of Judgment, Solomon's private apartments, the palace of the queens, and that of the Egyptian princess. Beyond these rose the magnificent temple with its courts and gates opening in every direction.

In the city below his house everything was much as it had been all his life. Even the house called the House of Uriah across the open court from his own was left unchanged. Only now it housed members of the king's guard and Badget suspected that when he was gone, Yasmit entertained various officers quite regularly. Since she always welcomed him enthusiastically and managed his house well, he had not bothered to question her.

At Badget's bidding the camel boy knocked on the gate with his prod and in moments the small window in the door opened. There was the sound of orders given and bolts being undone before the heavy gate swung open. As usual Yasmit was nowhere in sight. "She's probably at the window in the upper room watching to see if it is indeed her husband and if he has come with gifts or empty-handed," Badget thought as he handed the reins to the boy and looked around the courtyard.

Everything was much as he had left it. The jars of rich-olive oil, bread wheat, and barley waiting for the right price before being brought out and sold. He was always fearful that Yasmit in a fit of ill temper would sell some of his hoard for bobbles and trinkets while he was gone. He breathed a sigh of relief. At least she had not taken revenge yet. Undoubtedly she had not heard of Terra's existence.

There was the pleasant tinkle of bracelets and the swish of linen as Yasmit appeared in the doorway. "My lord," she cried, as she hurried across the courtyard and graciously bent to kiss the hem of his garment.

"She has seen the camel laden with gifts for her and she is in a fine temper," Badget concluded. "I'll not tell her until tomorrow about Terra."

Yasmit insisted on unlatching his sandals herself and then ordered one of the maids to bring the golden bowl reserved for visiting dignitaries to wash his feet. He watched as she herself poured the water that was comfortably warm. He noticed that it wasn't cold as it would have been if he had really surprised her or if she had been angry.

He noticed everything as though for the first time. The deceptive, practiced sweetness of her voice when she wanted something. The heavy makeup that was artfully applied to disguise the wrinkles but only accented each line. Her eyes that squinted in the lamplight, making the kohl-darkened lids seem artificial and harsh.

With her jewelry jingling pleasantly she clutched at his sleeve and pulled him into the bed chamber. By the light of the lamp that she held in one hand he saw her plainly. "She's old and faded," he thought with surprise.

He had always seen her before as the temptress he had first fallen in love with when he was just one of Eon's boys. He found himself wanting to pull away, hurry from the encounter she had obviously been planning for his homecoming. He thought he would vomit if she removed her linen robe to reveal her sagging breasts, flat belly, and boney knees. He wondered if she had changed so much in such a short time or was it that the memory of Terra, plump as a sweet fig, smooth as a melon, had spoiled his taste for such as Yasmit.

The rich rosewater perfume with which the bed had been saturated stifled him. He knew what she expected. If he lacked in ardor or attention, she would know that someone had replaced her. It was all evident to him now. This was part of a careful plan to keep him in check, to ferret out any rivals or any loss of her own power over him. With a sigh he reached for the lamp and crushed the glowing wick between his thumb and forefinger. He would try to act the part she expected of him, but he could not manage it with any light.

* * *

The next morning he lay with eyes closed, trying to remember where he was and what had happened. He heard the pigeons cooing and the fa-

93

miliar call of hucksters outside the wall and slowly he began to remember everything. He was in his own bed and his own house in Jerusalem. Still with his eyes closed, he stretched and was relieved to find he was alone. Like a bad dream, all that had happened came back to him. He had succeeded in playing the part, in making Yasmit feel his ardor was as hot as ever, his yearning for her unquenched. But now he was in danger of her returning at any minute and starting the whole miserable business over again.

He leapt from the pallet and hurriedly donned his clothes, not waiting for the clean linen she surely had prepared for him. The dust billowed from his cloak as he pushed his arms through the armholes. He hoped she wouldn't insist on his changing. That too could be a ploy in her arsenal of tricks. He had to get out of here somehow; think of some business, something that needed his attention.

She met him leaving the room and he noticed that she was indeed carrying clean linen. "My lord," she said running her fingers down his arm in a seductive way. "I've ordered your servants to heat water and to alert the bathhouse that you will be there today for a few hours. Your accountants and managers for your storehouse will meet you there and conduct their business so you can be back and spend the rest of the day here with me."

Badget was appalled. He'd gone to the bathhouse in Jericho, and that was more scrubbing than he was used to in the ordinary run of things. He had stopped at his warehouse and had even checked with the merchants that were waiting for his wares so he would be free to return to Jericho as soon as possible.

He was hungry. He told Yasmit he had time for some fresh bread and a few dates and then he must be on his way.

He noticed that she drew back and bit her lower lip while her eyes grew pinched and calculating. He hated that look. It meant she suspected something, and when that happened he was in for a long harangue. He turned from her and strode out to the courtyard, where an old woman was squatting over an inverted clay bowl that was cleverly placed over some glowing coals so that bread could be baked on the top.

"Welcome, welcome home. The bread is here in the basket waiting for you." She pushed the basket out with her foot and continued to throw the soft dough back and forth from one hand to the other until it was large and round ready to fit over the clay dome.

Badget loved this bread that the old woman made fresh every morning. He snatched up a few rounds and tucked them under his arm. "Now all I need is some goat cheese and a flask of my best wine." Though he seemed to speak this out into the air, it was only minutes before three servants came bringing just what he had ordered. He started to sit down on some cushions under the palm tree but just at that moment he saw that Yasmit was still standing in the doorway holding the clean linen with the questioning look on her face.

"My lord, I had planned a lovely time alone with you on the roof. I wasn't going to send you off without something to eat." Her voice was sweet, and yet there was something about the way she watched him that still made him feel uncomfortable.

He shrugged and smiled. This was always his best defense with difficult customers. It was obvious he couldn't tell her about Terra here in front of all the servants. He would go with her to the roof and there he would tell her.

* * *

Badget loved food, and on the long caravan trips he felt deprived. Now he was determined to enjoy the bounty of his own house before he told Yasmit anything. He had almost forgotten how perfectly Yasmit managed everything. She had a way of getting the best and though she undoubtedly paid dearly for it, still Badget knew he often ate better than the king himself.

He lingered over the last of the dried fish and gulped down more wine as he tried to think of a way to break the news. It was going to be more difficult than he had imagined and finally he knew there was no easy way. He would just have to blurt it out and prepare for the storm that would follow. Even Yasmit couldn't stay angry forever. Surely she knew that sooner or later this would happen. Most of the other men of equal means had already taken several more wives.

He wiped his mouth on his sleeve and leaned back in the cushions. He noticed that Yasmit was impatiently running her fingers over the clean linen she still held in her lap. He knew she was anxious as always for him to finish and get on with her plans for the day. "Yasmit," he said, looking out over her head at the green, ripening grapes on the vine that covered this part of the roof, "I'm a man and . . ."

Yasmit hid a smile behind her jeweled hand. "Of that I am sure," she said rather coyly.

"I am not just an ordinary man but a man of some means."

"Everyone in Jerusalem knows that, my lord." She obviously thought he was simply wanting to brag a bit.

"A man of means can afford luxuries a poor man only dreams of."

"That's taken for granted, my lord. It's late. You must hurry to the bathhouse and we'll talk more of your adventures when you return."

Badget opened his mouth and closed it several times but found that he could say nothing more. He couldn't just tell her about Terra and then hope to leave. He would be in for days of recrimination and harangue. It was better to get one of his friends to break the news gently while he was gone. The friend could send a messenger to Jericho when she was ready to be reasonable. He would do as she had planned now but he would not return home. He'd go back to Jericho to wait it out.

He stood up and she clapped her hands for the serving boy. "Here, take your master's clothes to the bath and make sure everything is ready for him when he arrives." The boy nodded and darted off down the steps to the lower courtyard. Badget hesitated a minute. The whole scene was so peaceful and pleasant. He was a man who disliked heated arguments and accusations. He couldn't stand to look at Yasmit sitting so proud and confident knowing how furious she would be when she heard about Terra. She was one who had always had her way where men were involved and wouldn't adjust to competition peacefully.

At the last minute he found that he couldn't even tell her he wouldn't be home. He'd have to leave that for one of his friends. With one brief look around at the pleasant luxuries of his home and a glance at Yasmit, he turned, went down the steps and straight out the gate heading for the bathhouse. He breathed deeply of the morning air, laughed that a rooster should still crow after sunrise, gave a beggar the piece of bread he still had in his belt, and concentrated on how he could cut the bath and business short to get back to Terra.

There were only a few men left in the bathhouse, as most of them had hurried up to the temple for morning prayer. Badget had been gone so long he had gotten out of the habit of going to morning and evening prayers at the new temple. He resolved to start again, maybe even offer a sheep some morning to assure the health of the child Terra carried. A quick wave of fright passed over him as he remembered hearing his mother say that any child born to a woman who hadn't been to the Mikvah the month before she conceived would be cursed. "Yes," he muttered to himself, "I'll offer one of my sheep each month until the child is born." As he had hoped, he met one of his old friends just leaving the bathhouse. The man had a reputation of bringing people together, settling arguments over land and women and showing a good bit of wisdom in the process. Badget insisted on his coming with him into the large, steamy reception room. "My friend," he said, "I need your help. You'll be well paid." He proceeded to tell him that he had taken a new wife and his first wife must be told. The old man understood. He had officiated in such situations quite often. "You must remind her that she is still the first wife," Badget urged. "She will, of course, control the house and the new wife. Try to show her that this could even be quite pleasant."

The old man said little. Perhaps that was the secret of his success. He simply kept nodding and muttering, "I know. I know. I understand."

Finally, when Badget was sure he fully grasped just what was involved, he bade him good day and hurried on into the bath. It had occurred to him that if the old man went directly to his house Yasmit would have time to gather her relatives and accost him before he was able to leave for Jericho. Only when he rode out the southern gate and was on the road leading over Olivet to Jericho did he breathe a sigh of relief.

The reunion with Terra was all that he had imagined. The innkeeper's wife had been kind, but Terra had spent her days on the roof watching the Jerusalem road that wound up out of the valley into the mountains. It was obvious that she had been crying a lot, and Badget was immediately attentive and solicitous.

As they went to bed Badget knew he should tell her that Yasmit still didn't know about her, but he couldn't endure adding to her hurt. More than that, he didn't want to spoil this night he had been eagerly looking forward to.

Terra was soft and warm and clung to him possessively all night long. He couldn't remember ever being so happy before. He had tried to explain to her about the lambs he was going to offer for the child's well-being, but she understood nothing but that he loved her. "You'll always love me and only me?" she asked bending over him just as he was dozing off to sleep.

"Only you my little round fig," he said pulling her to him. Gradually his arm relaxed and he was sound asleep. Terra smiled. This was a good man, as her father had said. He would keep his promise.

10

*T*he morning finally came when the queen of Sheba's caravan was ready to leave. Drums were beaten, silver trumpets blown, banners unfurled on the turrets as though it were a feast day, while the walls of the city were quickly lined with people wanting to see the queen's departure. It was rumored, and most believed the rumor, that her caravan included 797 camels, plus countless asses and mules loaded with gifts.

They pointed out Tamrin with several traders who would guide the caravan across the long stretches of desert to the few cities and welcome oases. They were surprised to see Il Hamd mounted and riding with the priests who carried the star charts. But most astonishing was the sight of the queen's cousin Rydan leading what was said to be a thousand mercenaries who would guard the queen and her treasures.

Pulling aside one of the curtains and looking back at the city Bilqis was surprised to see her people, like small ants, crowded together, motionless, lining the walls. They were still there when the caravan entered a deep gorge that cut them off from the view of the city. It had been a strange sight, and Bilqis never thought of her city without remembering that scene. The banners flying, the people curious, almost envious, and her old uncle sitting in the seat of honor at the great gate holding her scepter.

At first the queen's caravan kept to the highlands, where it was comparatively cool. Traders habitually avoided the Red Sea coastal plain because of the terrible heat. The water of the sea looked deceptively cool, but it was always tepid and salty and the torrid air settled down over the lowland like the breath of Hades.

On the mountain stretches there were thorn, acacia, and Tolok trees for shade, while here and there were clear running streams in which they sometimes bathed and from which they were able to get additional water to fill their goatskins. It was spring. The rains had already begun and could be depended on for at least two hours of each afternoon.

Bilqis found every new phase of the trip exhilarating. She wanted to linger on the mountain passes to look out over her country, which stretched as far as the eye could see. When they camped near a village, as they often did, she yearned to be free to visit the well with the other women or see inside the houses that were sometimes of a different construction than any she had seen before. It was at the village of Saada on the northern border of her kingdom that she was the most tempted.

Here the houses were built entirely of mud, packed tight, making thick walls with large beams forming the roof or upper floor. The wall that ran around the entire village was also of thick layers of dry mud. There was even a walkway at the top, and she could see people crowded together, pushing and shoving to get a look at their queen.

She didn't pull the curtains of the howdah, as she was inclined to do, but tried to look as dignified as possible while all the time taking in every detail of this strange town. Finally, as the ancient wooden gate in the south section of the wall swung back to let them enter, a little girl standing on the ramparts tossed flowers down to her. She was entranced.

They would be entertained that night in the house of one of the rich merchants, and she found herself looking forward to being once again inside something more permanent than a tent. The merchant was handsome and had a ready wit. He informed her that fifty sheep had been slaughtered for the feast in her honor, and twenty bakers had been summoned to bake the bread and honey cakes.

The feast was held in the walled courtyard before his house, and Bilqis was shown where she was to sit under a linen canopy. "I'll sit upon my own throne," she said to her host's amazement. Without another word being said, four huge Nubians came carrying a covered object that was so heavy it had required two camels just to transport it.

When the throne was in place, she asked Najja to bring her crown and commanded one of the guards to summon the trainers with her leopards. In a remarkably short time her throne room back in Marib was reproduced in the courtyard of her astonished host. Standard bearers, guards, pages all took their places before she majestically invited her host to come sit beside her.

He was obviously impressed. With a clap and a nod he signaled his men to open the gates for the invited guests. They entered bowing and whispering words of respect and devotion, then settled on mats placed around the wall. Excitement mounted as they waited eagerly for the jugglers and musicians who were to perform before the meal would be served.

As the evening came to an end, Bilqis was suddenly shocked to find her host looking at her in a practiced, calculating manner that made her uncomfortable. She briefly wondered if she had been foolish to enter this man's home and put herself and her entire company at his mercy. She glanced around and saw that the lamps were now flickering and would be out if the oil was not renewed. The moon was bright and full and there was the fragrance of costly incense being burned. It was a magical night. She felt foolish to even suspect the motivation of her host.

"My queen."

She was startled to find that he was speaking to her.

"My queen," he said, and his voice was soft and enticing. "You are a beautiful woman. Far too beautiful, if I may be so bold to suggest, to be without a husband."

She saw that his eyes were no longer cold and businesslike as when she had first seen him. Now they were warm with a hypnotic quality that terrified her. She tensed and ran her fingers down the leopardskin cape she wore across her shoulders. "I have no need of a husband," she said. "I am not as other women. I have a kingdom that is husband and child, father and mother to me. I'll never marry."

She had expected her hauteur and crisp reply to silence him as it had others in the past, but he seemed not to notice. "My queen, I have footmen, camel boys, guides, camels, treasures beyond any of the kings that have asked for your hand. I have three beautiful wives, but I am ready to divorce them tonight if you'll have me as your consort."

She had become calm as his tone of voice lowered to a whisper but increased in intensity. She found it almost humorous that he should presume to think his small treasure would tempt her. She wanted to laugh. "Wealth has no appeal to me," she said with her chin in the air and her eyes suddenly hard as chiseled stone.

"But love. What of love? I am ready to offer you such love as you can't imagine. I'm not a man to brag, but women have been ready to die for my favor."

"Then let them die," she heard herself saying, "but I've no use for love.

I'm married to this, my throne and my crown." She firmly patted the armrest on her throne and motioned to her pages that she was ready to retire.

"I hope you are not offended," he said kneeling before her as she stood to leave.

Quickly she tapped him on the shoulder so that he looked up. "I have no need of love, but friends I'm ready to accept. A queen never has too many friends."

She swept from the courtyard and followed her page up the winding stairs to some rooms that were to be hers and her maidens'. They were outfitted in a garish display of wealth. Heavy sandalwood incense rose from an assortment of brass bowls trimmed in gold and fitted into oblong niches in the thick walls. Layers of strangely decorated carpets covered the hard mud floor. The one window set in the mud wall had shutters that had once been finely carved teak but now sagged and were ill fitting. Several chests stood against the wall with their lids open to display the wild assortment of bobbles and strange weapons mixed with lengths of cloth done in curious design. Worst of all the walls had been decorated with a crude imitation of Egyptian art.

She was tired and ready for bed, but Najja stood in the doorway waiting to be recognized. She obviously had come with some message that needed attention. "What is it now Najja? I'm tired and have no time to see anyone."

"But my queen, it is Il Hamd. He's very upset and insists he must see you immediately."

Bilqis took off her crown with great deliberation and stood holding it as her eyes became hard and her mouth firm. "I've no intention of seeing that man. He brings nothing but trouble."

"He says it's important. There's some bad omen. All the camel drivers are frightened and your own tribesmen are ready to turn back."

"Turn back!" she whirled and her eyes flashed their indignation. "Of course we'll not turn back. Bring my throne." she ordered as she put the crown back on her head. From out in the dark hallway the Nubians came carrying her throne and waited just inside the low door for her instructions. "Here," she said. "Put it here beneath the wall torches."

The Nubians backed from the room with their hands on their knees and their eyes down, just as Il Hamd appeared in the shadows beyond the door. Bilqis sat down on the throne and let Najja and her maidens arrange the folds of her robe. Then stiffening as for an attack, she nodded to one of the pages, who quickly went to usher Il Hamd into her presence.

"My queen." He bowed, keeping his eyes on the ground in an unusual show of humility. She noticed his white garments were soiled and brown with dust while his headpiece though tarnished was still ornate and impressive. The long, nervous fingers were clutching some parchments. She saw the hated snake ring and remembered the terrible night in the small pavilion.

Her voice was sharp and clipped. "You know that I'm not one to be frightened, so be careful, old one, and tell only what you know to be true."

She noticed that his hand tightened on the parchments as he looked up at her with wide, startled eyes. "My queen," he said, "I'd rather face the fiercest Jinn than your disapproval."

She could see that he'd grown thin, and it was obvious the news that brought him to her was at least in his mind urgent. "Then speak but make it short. The hour's late and we must be on our way at daybreak tomorrow."

"That's the problem," Il Hamd said, nervously twisting the parchments into a slender cylinder. "We must not go on. It's dangerous. We must turn back while there's time."

"Turn back!" Bilqis was suddenly tense and cautious. "Of course we'll not turn back," she said with a toss of her head. "Though all the stars in heaven warned against it, I'd not turn back."

Il Hamd was visibly shaken. But summoning his courage he leaned forward and hissed, "My queen, don't speak so easily of omens. It's the omens that have warned we must turn back."

"What omens, what signs?" she demanded. "Remember, I'm no ignorant peasant to be frightened into doing your bidding."

"It's not my bidding. There've been shadows crossing the night path of Ilumquh and the birds that followed us have all turned back; now only hawks and vultures fly overhead."

"What then do you read into these omens? What does it mean?"

"It's obvious, my queen. Ilumquh is shadowed because he is in mourning, while the vultures and hawks are waiting for our destruction that will take place as soon as we cross the line that divides your kingdom from that of the desert tribesmen. The tribesmen worship many gods at their temple in Mecca and once on their land we are in their power. Ilumquh can't help us."

"But the caravans pass all the time and the gods of the tribesmen don't harm them. We can pay the same price they pay. Surely the gods like gold." Her tone of voice was almost cynical and Il Hamd paled under her steady gaze.

"The opposition is more than usual," he said. "You're not just a trader; you're the queen of Sheba, Ilumquh's queen. The Jinn would love to capture such as you."

"How do you know all this? Have you talked to the Jinn?"

"Last night several stars fell from the sky. There was a strange wind that could be heard but not felt and then I myself had a dream so terrible I couldn't go back to sleep."

"And . . ." The queen was unmoved through this whole rendition.

"It is obvious that we are being warned. The Jinn are waiting for us, and the moment we pass from Ilumquh's protection, they will destroy us."

"How?"

"What do you mean, how?"

"How will they destroy us? If you truly know all of this, surely you can also find out what they plan to do and then we'll just plan to defeat them."

Il Hamd was speechless. He had obviously expected the queen to accept his evaluation of the situation.

Bilqis drummed her fingers on the throne's alabaster arm and studied Il Hamd. He was no longer the frightening dignitary she had known all her life. Now he was a man like any other and she could see that he really believed her life was being threatened. Her tone softened. "I know this is difficult. You have your training as a priest of Ilumquh, but it must be evident to you as it is to me that some things are true and certain and others are traditions. Tell me now what do you know for certain. What is true."

"True?" Il Hamd twisted the scroll and looked for a moment like a schoolboy that had forgotten the answer the teacher was requesting.

"Yes, what do you know for sure? What would you risk your life on?"

"Risk my life on?!" Il Hamd was obviously nervous. The queen could see he had never thought in this way before.

"Yes, for instance, would you be willing to wager your life on what you've told me? Are you willing to face execution if your prediction is wrong?"

Il Hamd cleared his throat, stared at the wall torch for a moment, and then looked at the queen and shrugged. "Who knows what is true and what is false. We can only be cautious and respect all omens."

"Then we are doomed never to try anything difficult. There are always evil omens and men who invent evil omens when faced with difficulties."

Il Hamd flushed red at her words. "My queen, I've not invented the omens. They're real."

"But you would like to end this adventure and return to Marib and the pleasant rituals and easy rewards."

"It's best for all of us to end this 'adventure' as you call it. No good can come of it. Most of us will die and be left for the vultures."

"Again you've obviously tried to manipulate me, to make me change my mind by frightening me with omens. After that shoddy business in the temple, I'm not so easily frightened. We're going on. If the Jinn attack, then it is proven that you were right, but if not, then again we've proved the omens wrong."

"It's not safe to go against so many omens." Il Hamd was trembling. His eyebrows were raised and his eyes were wide with astonishment.

"You must understand. It's more important to me now to know what is true than to be safe. We're going on."

"Then may I request that I, your humble servant, the most High Priest of Ilumquh, be allowed to turn back?"

Bilqis stood up so that she towered over him. "You, especially, must come. We'll learn about truth together." The audience was over, but Il Hamd was too stunned to move.

"My queen," he said as he bent to kiss the hem of her robe as a sign of his submission, "how are we to find this truth?"

"Why, we'll start tomorrow by defying the Jinn and the omens. Then if we learn nothing from that, there is Solomon. Everyone says he is wise. Perhaps he'll be able to sort truth from old wives' tales and tradition."

Without another word Il Hamd rose, and bowing left the room. Bilqis watched him go and noticed that he was trembling. He was really frightened. It was clear that he used his knowledge to frighten and control others, but it was also true that he himself had a solid respect for his own beliefs. The final fault she found with him was that he had no real desire for truth. He accepted things as they were and asked no questions. And if the gods or Jinn didn't act, then it was his business to help them out.

She realized that early the next day they would be back on the camels crossing out of Sheba's territory into the deserts supposedly controlled by the many gods that ruled in the Kabba at Mecca. Many gods she had heard, one for every day of the year at least and one for every problem. Il Hamd may have a point. At least she'd alert her guards and have them ride fully armed under their cloaks.

* * *

On the same evening in the ancient Khan in Jericho, Badget was sitting in the great court warming himself by a fire made with dung. He was talking to some of the other camel drivers and exchanging stories of their adventures in strange lands and unusual circumstances while he waited for Terra to ready herself for bed. The sun had gone down and the moon was up, which clearly signaled the end of any work or activity but drinking, talking, and enjoying one's wife.

When in the desert Badget had often risen early and traveled late because it was cool and pleasant and the stars kept them on track better than the sun, but at home he was in bed when the sun went down and ready to rise with the first cock crow.

He had put from his mind all business and the complexity of telling Yasmit about his new wife. All he thought about was holding the plump, fragrant Terra in his arms again. She was such an innocent at love and yet such a willing pupil that Badget found himself eagerly anticipating the next lesson. With Yasmit it had been she who had been the teacher and Badget the pupil. At the time he had thought it the best of arrangements, but now he knew better.

"It takes a good two months and a half to come from Sheba, eh Badget?" Badget hadn't been listening until he heard his name.

"What, what did you say?"

"Two and a half months for the queen you were telling us about to travel from Sheba."

"It takes me two and a half months," Badget said rolling his eyes as he tried to calculate. "They won't be pushing. They'll rise early and ride late, but they'll be stopping in the heat of the day. Then she has stops along the way."

"Where's she stopping?"

"I've been told she wants to visit the temple in Mecca, and some of the princes will no doubt entertain her. I know she'll stop to visit Prince Hadad of Edom. She once asked me about the Siq that leads into the hidden city."

There was silence as the men thought about the strange turn of events that induced a queen to travel the rugged road they made their living on.

The conversation ended for the night, and Badget was about to excuse himself and go to his rooms when there was a loud knocking heard on the great gate of the Khan. A man's voice, muffled and insistent, announced a traveler, a woman that needed lodging for the night.

The old gateman hurried to open the smaller gate within the closed larger one. He held his torch high with one hand and undid the huge bolt letting the door swing back on its leather hinges. Badget glanced up and to his utter horror saw framed in the doorway the angry face of Yasmit.

Her eyes darted around the area lighted by the fire until they settled on Badget. "You fiend from Sheol!" she screamed as she flew at him with fists flying. He dodged just in time, covering his head with his arms so that her blows rained down upon him with little effect. "Where is she? Where've you hidden her?" she screamed.

Badget kept backing away, but she followed him relentlessly. He tried to speak, but no sound came. He dodged behind some of the men now standing by the fire, and she tore at them and pushed them aside leaving Badget hopelessly pinned against the wall.

"Is it true?" she said choking him until his eyes bulged from his head. "Have you taken another wife? Have you brought this insult down on my head?"

"Yes, yes." Badget tried to explain but he got no further. Yasmit turned screaming and cursing to the astonished innkeeper, his wife, and the assembled traders. In a fit of fury she pulled off her mantle and began tearing at her hair, clawing at her face until the blood began to run in streaks like tears.

No one moved. They stood as though frozen in horror trying to understand what was happening. Suddenly Terra appeared in the doorway. She had seen all that happened from a window in her room. Before Yasmit's arrival, she had been watching Badget with fond affection as he commanded so easily the interest and respect of the other traders. Now she moved out across the courtyard and came to stand so the firelight

107

wove a golden wreath around her face and made her look ethereal and fragile. "You must be Yasmit," she said in a calm, musical voice with just the hint of an accent. "I'm sure we will be like sisters."

Her words were like cold water thrown on a fire. Yasmit jerked around and stared in unbelief at this friendly voice. She ran her sleeve across her mouth and was silent, studying intently this small, plump woman who had emerged so suddenly and seemed so in command.

Very much in control of things now, Terra moved to her side. "Come, you must be tired and hot. I've heard it's a long ride from Jerusalem."

There was a moment while everyone held their breath. Yasmit was still heaving and choking with emotion but the shock had silenced her and now she was concentrating on this strange apparition that had dared confront her with such calm. "Who are you?" she said finally regaining her breath and pulling back.

"My name is Terra. I'm sure we will become the best of friends." All the time she was talking, Terra was gently leading Yasmit toward the inn door. When they disappeared into the shadows beyond the door, everyone relaxed. Badget sank down by the fire, his head in his hands, the innkeeper and his wife shrugged and went back inside while the other traders again took their places around the fire.

"Did you see that?" one of the traders said. "I never in my life saw anything like it."

"She just walked out here as calm as anything," another trader said, shaking his head in disbelief.

"It's like our king's always saying, 'a soft answer turns away wrath.'"

At this Badget straightened up and ran his fingers through his hair. "I just wonder what's going on up there. If you don't mind I'll sleep down here with the camels tonight."

*E*arly the next morning when the queen's caravan was preparing to swing out onto the old trade route going north, there was an air of impending doom hanging over everyone. No one talked, and it was observed that even the camels were skittish and out of sorts. They refused to move and had to have their tails twisted, their lead ropes pulled, and their riders' heels dug in hard before they would stand. It was nothing new for the camels to complain in harsh, guttural sounds, but for them to engage in such total rebellion was noted as a very bad omen.

There had been one other bad omen that really disturbed Bilqis. When she had returned to the camp, she was told that a lamb and a ewe had been carried off just after dark by wolves. They had all heard the dogs barking but no other sound. Only in the morning did they discover the prints of a male wolf near where they had heard the dogs while a female's prints were on the opposite side of the tents. With the female prints was a clear marking in the sand of something having been dragged.

"There's the evidence," one of the bedouin drivers exclaimed pointing at the telltale marks.

"Surely you would have heard the bleating of the ewe," Bilqis interjected.

"My queen," the rough, unkempt bedouin offered respectfully, "it's well known that a sheep when frightened makes no sound at all; goats are different. If it had been a goat, there would have been a terrible ruckus. Wolves leave the goats alone."

With a sharp awareness of the fear and gloom that hung over the caravan, Bilqis let her eunuchs help her into the howdah and then ordered the caravan to proceed.

The stars were out in a magnificent array of brilliance with only the wind, light and fresh, to remind them that dawn was on its way.

Usually Bilqis enjoyed this early morning time, but with Il Hamd's predictions of disaster still lurking in the dark corners of her mind, she wasn't able to think of much else. She was determined not to be persuaded to go back, but then she had to admit there must be constant vigilance, "just in case."

The camel drivers sang as usual but instead of the rousing, joyful songs, they now sang songs that were wild and sad, rising and falling in semitones.

The whole day was filled with fearful anticipation of some fatal accident, some evil band of raiders or a desert storm stirred up by the Jinn or the envious gods of this strange country.

Late that night they reached the camp chosen for them near some wells. The tents were already pitched. The evening meal consisting of cracked wheat stewed in broth and young spring lambs roasted on a spit gave the day its final touch of well-being. No Jinn had struck and no strange gods had taken revenge. "The queen has luck like her father" was the whisper that went round the campfires that night.

For any sheik or king there were three requirements. He must be courageous, a leader, and have an unusual quantity of luck. To most of them the third quality was the most important, and they had not expected to find it in a woman.

Bilqis went to sleep relieved that Il Hamd's predictions of disaster had not materialized. They were now well into the strange new country of the desert tribes and no evil had befallen them.

She slept soundly, and before she knew it dawn was breaking over the vast emptiness of sand and scrub. Close by there was the sound of a woman half humming and singing the age-old leben-making songs. She could plainly hear the steady, dull thumping sound of the goatskin hanging from a tripod being swung back and forth in the ancient process of making leben. Then there were whispered orders and the soft padding of bare feet going out into the paling moonlight to gather bits of kindling and dried nettles. There would be warm bread, leben, and honey to eat before they set out on the well-worn track to the famous trading center called Mecca.

Bilqis enjoyed watching the goathair tent swell and lower like a living thing in the morning breeze. The dividing curtains moved with the hypnotic swaying motion of the tent poles. Beyond them in the next section she knew her maidens were all bedded down on straw mats.

She thought of the long way they had already come. Her pleasant valley with the great dam, Ilumquh's temple, and her alabaster palace all seemed far away and almost unreal. There must be something of the roving nomad in her veins, she thought. How unfortunate it would have been to have listened to Il Hamd and turned back. Now they had safely passed over into the far country and no Jinn had struck, no harm had come to them.

She watched the tent's slow undulation that moved almost in time to the leben-maker's song, and before she knew it she had drifted off again into a deep and dreamless sleep.

Several weeks later the caravan pitched camp outside the town of Mecca and immediately the dignitaries who had been anxiously awaiting the queen's arrival preferred their invitations. Mecca had many rich merchants, and they all vied for the privilege of entertaining the queen of Sheba. Some had huge feasts in her honor, others staged feats of daring and dexterity by local entertainers. Two times she went in full royal array to the Great Temple.

There in an oval courtyard had been assembled hundreds of sacred stones and images. Most had strange stories associated with them of battles that had been won and the stone or image captured and brought back as one of the richest trophies of the battle. To have the sacred stone representing the god of one of the neighboring countries or tribes was to have captured its source of power. Even if the god didn't switch his allegiance and back his captors, still it was believed he was powerless to come against them.

Most prized among the stones was a black one that was elevated to the place of prominence in the middle of the courtyard. It was supposed to have power to grant all wishes and make all ventures succeed if only touched.

That night, sitting in the receiving tent in the midst of her people, Bilqis entertained visiting noblemen and rulers from the city. "In my country we have a famous city called Sana which, tradition says is the oldest city in the world. Our wise men tell us it was founded by one of the sons of Noah after the great flood. Tell me," she asked them, "who founded your city? How old is it?"

Some of the gray-bearded counselors looked around the tent until their eyes focused on one man sitting in deep thought at the outer edge of their group. "Come, Ahmed," they urged, "you are our storyteller. Tell the queen how our city was founded."

The frail old man seemed startled at first, then recovering his composure along with some prodding and pushing, he came forward. "Tell me," Bilqis said again, "how was your city founded? Who first came here to this place?"

Small fragments of light from the wicks in hanging alabaster lamps gave his face and form an ethereal, unreal aspect. He was urged to sit on a huge cushion at the queen's feet. For a moment there was silence. No one moved or spoke as they fell under the spell of the sandalwood fragrance that filled the tent. Somewhere outside a wolf's lonesome howl made most of them shudder and instinctively draw closer together.

The old man nervously fingered the folds in his smooth, well-worn robe until he began to speak, and then he seemed to be transformed. His voice was mellow-toned, his eyes at times closed as though he were seeing everything just as it had happened.

"Our tradition," he began, "says that it was a great sheik from Chaldea named Abraham who sent his concubine away with her son because of his jealous wife. The concubine wandered alone across the barren wastes of rock and sand. Her waterskin was soon empty and the dates she had brought with her were all gone. The sun beat down upon her without mercy and the sand blew in sharp, cutting thrusts against her tender skin.

"The child she held by the hand and shielded with her own mantle grew weak and listless. He begged constantly for water and finally dropped from exhaustion. The distraught mother held him in her lap and cried tears of frustration, railing first at her mistress who had treated her so cruelly and then at the husband who had so easily abandoned her with the child.

"The child grew so weak he could no longer move even his lips. His hands became limp and lifeless and the mother knew he was dying. It was then, so the story goes, that she cried out to the God of her master and asked for help.

"To her surprise a well of clear, cool water sprang up at her side and both she and the boy drank their fill and were miraculously revived. The descendants of the woman's son became a great nation, and this city that grew on the spot of the concubine's prayer is their greatest city," the story-teller concluded.

For a long moment, they thought about the strange events of the past that had made this city different from all others. Then Bilqis stirred and the spell of the storyteller was broken. "Is the story true?" Bilqis asked. "Was there really a concubine and her son?"

"The story is true," the old man said. "The well is still here and people are drawing water from it just as they have since it was discovered."

"I'd like some water from that well," Bilqis said. "It must be some of the most wonderful water in the world."

The old man clapped his hands and a young servant moved out from the shadows of the tent. The soft thud of running feet on hard sand could be heard for a moment and then there was silence.

Later, when the visitors were ready to leave, the servant returned with the water in a golden ewer.

"Here, O queen, drink of the very water of life that saved the concubine and her son," the old storyteller said, bowing low and handing her the ewer.

After the visitors had left, the queen called together the three men in charge of the expedition. "We have now seen that neither Jinn nor strange gods can keep us from reaching our goal. Where do we go from here? What kings are yet to be visited?"

"My queen," one of the men said, unrolling a large parchment, "from here we cross back and forth following the path of the wells and oases."

"Undoubtedly your majesty doesn't want to be bothered with the de-tails of the trip," the sharp-nosed younger man said, as he started to reroll the scroll.

"No, no, on the contrary," the queen objected, "I want to know everything."

"My queen," the older man said, "everything is determined by the wells. Our camels can go nine days without water, but the sheep we must have for our food can only travel five. So we follow the wells, and it means we sometimes must go out of our way."

"Then where is our next important stop?" she said almost impatiently.

"There will be several other towns, all small centers of trade, but the next major stop will be at the rock city of Sela, where the Edomites have their kingdom."

"And Hadad is their king?"

"Yes, my queen."

"Tell me all you know about this king. How powerful is he? How has he gained his power?"

Now the sharp-nosed little man reached for the parchment and stepped up to her throne. "See, my queen," he said, "all the trade routes of Arabia come here to Sela." With one hand he held the top of the scroll and with the other finger he traced the thin line from the Hadramaut through Marib, Nagran, Mecca, Medina, Dedan, and Hegra, where the caravans were met coming from Riyadh and the gulf coast. "More than that," he said, "there is another caravan route from the base of the two rivers near the ancient Ur that comes across to Jauf and ends at Sela."

"So this Hadad is very rich and very powerful."

"Of course. From Sela there are only two routes, one going across the desert to Gaza and the other up the King's Highway to Damascus. If Hadad could free himself from Solomon's yoke, he would be very wealthy and strong."

"So, he is planning to join with Shishak of Egypt and Rezon of Zobah, who is now in Damascus."

"So we've heard."

With this Bilqis dismissed the three men, but she sat meditating for a long time. She could see that if Shishak, Rezon, Hadad, and she herself all joined together to come against Solomon, they could easily defeat him. It seemed the wise thing to do. Much would depend on her impression of Hadad. She'd sent messengers announcing her coming and she should be hearing news from them soon.

*　*　*

Hadad was well aware that the queen of Sheba was traveling up the old caravan route on her way to Jerusalem. He had first received a warning from Shishak, who'd advised him to stop her going further than Sela at all costs. Then there had been the gossip of traders that passed through his kingdom and finally her messengers arrived with the formal announcement.

He knew he had to be most careful in making his plans. He must not arouse the suspicion of Solomon. In fact, he must make every effort to keep Solomon from finding out that he had returned from Egypt ready after all these years to take back his kingdom. Years before, Solomon's father, King David, had realized how strategic this capital was and had sent his general Joab down to wipe out the rebellious tribesmen.

Joab had killed most of the men of Edom, and Hadad, a mere babe at the time, had been spirited off to Egypt by some of the palace guards. "Shishak," Hadad speculated, "has been clever enough to play the game both ways. Solomon has the Egyptian princess, and I'm married to the sister of the queen. A queen is greater than a princess, and so I would wager Shishak is betting on my winning this struggle."

He had received messengers from both Shishak and Rezon warning him that he must discourage the queen of Sheba from her proposed visit to Solomon. "Solomon has a reputation for being irresistible to women. The queen could be charmed against her better judgment to join with him against us." Shishak had spelled the matter out quite graphically, leaving no doubt of Hadad's responsibility in the matter.

"I must be about the same age as Solomon," he thought. "It would be a brilliant means of getting even for all the treachery of his father, David, if I myself should waylay the queen. Poison her mind against Solomon. Win her confidence. Even marriage may be necessary to carry out my plans," he gloated.

Quickly he called together his stewards and counselors. He wanted to make the most of this opportunity and it would take fast work and careful planning to stage a reception equal to the magnitude of his ambition.

* * *

In Jerusalem Solomon tried to piece together the information he had received. It was becoming quite clear that Pharaoh Shishak wasn't the friend he had once seemed to be. Everything had changed once the news reached the pharaoh that Israel had started building ships at Ezion-Geber on the Red Sea. Now he was fast becoming a dangerous enemy, and with Tipti being the pharaoh's eyes and ears right in Solomon's bedchamber there was nothing he didn't know.

"How can I get to the bottom of this?" Solomon asked his brother Nathan late one night as they visited the caged animals in the quarters behind the palace.

"It won't be easy. Tipti knows you are suspicious."

"It's even worse than you suspect. Our mother has warned me that Jeroboam, my trusted confidant, friend, and main supporter among the northern tribesmen is being influenced by Tipti."

"I wouldn't have thought she'd go that far. How has she managed it? He's always been so loyal."

"It seems she's been encouraging him. Telling him he has all the qualities of a king."

"That's preposterous. Hard to believe he'd listen to such a thing."

"You remember I sent him to Egypt with her dead cat. Shishak himself sat with him and flattered him outrageously."

For a moment the two stood watching the old lion that had been a mere cub twenty-two years before when Solomon came to power. The lion had been dozing but on hearing footsteps opened one eye rather cautiously. He heard his name called and with a great effort roused himself and walked leisurely to the door of the cage where he rather lethargically began scraping at the lintel with his paw. "See, he wants me to let him out." Solomon was all attention as he talked softly to the lion and quietly lifted the latch. "Come, old friend," he urged.

"One of these days you'll let the wrong animal out," Nathan said nervously.

The great beast nosed the door open and walked out into the courtyard. He rubbed his mane against Solomon's leg and began a great purring rumble down deep in his throat. Solomon tousled his tawny mane, stooped down, and looked him in the eye. "There are some good things about old age," he said turning to Nathan. "When he was a cub we were the best of friends. He followed me everyplace. Then he grew strong, fierce, and unfriendly, but now he's back being my friend."

"He's lost his teeth," Nathan said laughing. "He hasn't changed his disposition."

"He could still cuff me across the courtyard with one swipe of his paw," Solomon said defensively.

"Well, what do you think has changed him then?"

Solomon stood up and let go of the lion. They watched him pad softly around in the moonlight and then nose open the door to his cage, go in, and lie down. "He's lost interest in everything. Nothing excites him anymore. There's no challenge worth the effort and no place he really wants to go. He's bored and unhappy with the way things are. His old courage is gone."

"Are you talking about yourself or the lion?" Nathan asked cautiously.

"Both, I'm probably talking about both." With a resounding thud Solomon let the bolt fall into place. "I've seen courage revive even a severely injured person, but when courage dies, what hope is there?"

Nathan didn't answer but stood looking at his brother in the moonlight as though seeing him for the first time. Something was wrong, very wrong. Gradually words began to form and came haltingly. "Our hope, Israel's hope, is in our God as it has always been." The words weren't said as a criticism but rather as a comfort—a reminder.

Solomon turned his head so Nathan couldn't see his eyes. "The God of Israel hasn't been speaking lately. I don't feel His presence. He's suddenly left me alone to manage hostile enemies, vengeful wives, and a fool for a son. It's His fault if things go wrong."

"You know what our father would have said, don't you?"

Solomon turned to him with the pained look in his eyes that was beginning to be his normal expression. "No. What would he say?"

"Why, I'm sure he'd say again as he said so often, 'God is our helper in time of trouble.' However, we both know, a man may ruin his chances by his own foolishness, then blame it on the Lord."

Solomon suddenly relaxed and almost smiled. "He also used to remind us that when a person is gloomy, everything seems to go wrong; but when he's cheerful, everything seems right."

"Perhaps even now help is on its way."

"What's on its way here is more trouble. Badget tells me, and one of her messengers announced, that the queen of Sheba has already left and is on her way here for a visit. I can't help but suspect there is some trick involved."

"There may be a blessing."

"I doubt it, but I did need your encouragement."

"That's what brothers are for," Nathan reminded him, "to help in time of need." With a renewed feeling of closeness the two walked out to the waiting counselors and scribes. There was no time to discuss further the queen's visit. Nathan turned the possibilities over in his mind. It was strange. The trip was long and hard, no one went to that much trouble without some very good reason. Impulsively he had told his brother it could be a blessing on its way and he hoped with all his heart that it was true.

12

*W*ord spread quickly in Jerusalem. Almost at once everyone was talking about the visit of the queen of Sheba. To each person it meant something different. To the merchants it meant more sales, to the weavers and dyers who supplied the court with their gowns and robes there would be long hours at the looms and the dye vats, to the goldsmiths a challenge to create the ultimate in gifts and ornamentation. All Jerusalem was stimulated into a regular hive of activity.

No group or coterie was more energized than Solomon's harem of wives, and among that group no one was more interested than his Egyptian princess, Tipti.

Tipti had given up all thought for the time being of moving to Gezer. Instead she had called Jeroboam, Solomon's chief builder, and had ordered him to have her palace totally redecorated. There were two reasons for doing this: one was that she wanted to have the most elaborate quarters as befitted her rank, and the other was that she wanted to have an excuse to see more of Jeroboam.

Jeroboam was handsome, perceptive, and always flattering. He caught on quickly to the dress and manners of a courtier. He had learned to prefer nothing but the best. Though he was a building supervisor, he dressed like one of the princes. His hair and beard were shaped and perfumed, his short tunic impeccably white due to the care given it by his widowed mother. She first wove it of the finest linen and then had it regularly whitened by the fullers down in the valley. His outer garment was seamless and decorated with long fringes while his sandals were carefully tooled by Jerusalem's most renowned leather craftsman.

With all this he wasn't a man dawdling his time away in parties and celebrations. He had worked hard and had the strong, muscular build that went with his trade.

Tipti had watched him with interest and slowly began to develop a plan that would bring her the status she needed and the power. She had not been able to have a child, and so she had been constantly reminded that one day Rehoboam, the son of her loathed rival Naamah, would inherit the throne from his father. Lately she had developed almost a hatred for the thin, scholarly, self-righteous prince.

Rehoboam had none of the charm of his father. He was blunt and always critical of anyone who was not a part of his own entourage or that of Naamah. The two of them together were formidable, and Tipti had been well aware of the many barbs thrown her way by this archenemy and her son.

Tipti was a clever woman. She decided not to appeal to Solomon but to take matters into her own hands, form her own defense and battle strategy. From the moment she first noticed Jeroboam, he became a vital factor in her plans.

She had seen him from the roof of the old palace soon after she had come to Jerusalem. She had gone to the roof often with her maidens for fresh air and to view the progress of Solomon's extensive building program. Bored and listless, she had noticed that one of the builders walked with such majesty and spoke with such authority that it was hard to believe he was not one of the princes.

She had sent one of her men who spoke Hebrew to inquire about him and found that he was from the north. He had no real family ties, only a very devoted widowed mother. This suited her plans exactly, and the next time she saw Solomon, she announced that she had found the Israelite to build her palace.

It was at a time when Solomon could deny her nothing, and so he had ordered the young Jeroboam to temporarily leave the building of the Millo platforms and instead take charge of building the palace for the princess.

Solomon had actually been pleased that she had chosen one of his own workmen to build her palace. He had been worried at first that she would insist on bringing large numbers of workmen from Egypt. Building in Egypt was so different. There were no large quantities of pliable rock there and the weather was mild and pleasant with almost no rain. The palaces in Egypt consisted more of pillared walks and pleasant garden grottoes. Of course, this wasn't possible in the crowded little city of Jerusalem.

Jeroboam had been flattered and inspired by the attention of the princess. He was quick to learn and observe everything, from the way her servants conducted the schedule of her day to the many imported treasures and artifacts from Egypt. He couldn't imagine why she had chosen him. He soon realized it wasn't for a romantic dalliance. Neither was it because he was able to manage his workmen so efficiently. There was more to it. He sensed much more.

When her cat had been killed and he had been chosen to take it to Egypt, a whole new world had opened to him. There he saw life lived for pleasure and time spent in endless frivolity. Everyone seemed effortlessly beautiful; even the air was perfumed with mysterious, intoxicating scents. For the first time in his life he had experienced the pure pleasure of having servants wait on him and the heady authority of being someone the pharaoh was entertaining.

Since he had returned his whole relationship to Tipti had deepened. She was always teaching him niceties. She let him taste the rich food she took for granted and insisted on his spending some time with her each day just to talk.

In turn he shared with her the news of Jerusalem and, what was more important, the customs and practices of these people that were so foreign to her. Jeroboam's loyalty had gradually shifted until finally, without even being aware of it, he had made the Egyptian princess his first concern, the object of his whole attention. She for her part rewarded him by announcing that she was adopting him as her son. She also made it clear that as her son he would have equal claim to the throne with Rehoboam.

Jeroboam was an intelligent young man. He understood just what the princess wanted from him and he was immensely flattered. Looking back he could see that from the moment she had arrived in her ebony palanquin, curtained in gold drapery and painted with peacock feathers, she had totally replaced the true queen, Naamah, and all the other wives and concubines in Solomon's heart.

Naamah's anger had been terrible to see. It was rumored that she had sworn destruction on the princess and her cat god, and there had been charms and incantations against the Egyptian made regularly at her shrine to Moloch in the Valley of Hinnon.

Despite all this, only the sacred cat had suffered while Tipti had not been visibly hurt or moved unless, as some whispered, she had been cursed with childlessness. It was obvious that though she ruled Solomon's heart temporarily, with his death her influence would end and Naamah with her hated son would be in charge.

So, Jeroboam had become Tipti's solution. Like the Egyptian princess in the past who had drawn Moses out of the water and had adopted him, she, Tipti, had chosen a son, a son she felt was far superior to Naamah's son Rehoboam.

* * *

Passover had come and gone, the Omer had been counted for fifty days and the Feast of Weeks had been celebrated with the wheat harvest. It had been a good harvest. Now it was early summer and the beginning of the dry season and the ripening of fruits. It was the perfect time to build and restore granaries and cisterns, strengthen walls, and repaint or white-wash the mud and dung walls.

Tipti had brought artists from Egypt to restore her frescoes and had appointed Jeroboam as the one person to whom they were all to be responsible. It seemed that she was with him constantly. Before the workers arrived in the morning, she gave him instructions and after they left at night she detained him. "We need to go over the work and see if it meets our approval," she said.

On this day it was the frescoes they examined. "You see," she said, "in Egypt there is sunshine all the time and everyone is happy." The fresco they were examining was of wild geese in a marsh on the delta. Jeroboam thought it was much more appropriate than the picture that had been there before. The central figure had been Bastet, in the form of a lion-headed man holding an ankh, though the jackal-headed Anubis with the scales of fate and the recorder of destiny the ibis-headed Thoth, were quite prominent also.

They moved from the frescoes out into the courtyard, where Jeroboam noticed that the doors of the cat shrine were closed and work-men had been rearranging the whole area to look like an Egyptian garden. Vines had been trained to crawl up over the bare stone surfaces, small trees seemed to spring out of openings in the pavement, but most amazing were the water lilies that now floated on her pond. "See, my brother sent these from his own garden," she said proudly pointing to them.

Jeroboam was always impressed with the magic she seemed to produce in everything she touched. His eyes glowed with admiration. "You must miss Egypt very much," he said.

In all the years Tipti had been in Jerusalem no one had ever understood her yearning for home, and she was immediately touched beyond measure. "I wish it were possible for you to go study in Egypt. That's where someone with your talent belongs. But since that isn't possible, I have other plans for you." She smiled and patted the cushion beside her.

"Plans?" Jeroboam said sitting down rather diffidently, as he wasn't used to the familiarity with which she treated him now.

"Yes, yes," she said with a smug smile, "I pulled you out of that disgusting work at the Millo so you could be here, where we can more easily make our plans."

"Yes, of course," Jeroboam said, "and I'm grateful to you. I've worked my men hard building the Millo and they haven't been too pleased."

"That's another reason I've wanted you here. People must associate only pleasant things with you if my plans are to succeed."

Again Jeroboam looked puzzled and Tipti looked around to see if anyone was listening. Then in a very low voice she began to explain.

"As I've told you, there are going to be big changes here very shortly. The countries that have been bypassed by Solomon's fleet are furious."

Jeroboam's eyes grew large and bright with excitement. "The queen of Sheba is on her way here. Is that part of the plan?"

"Undoubtedly. My brother and Hadad, Rezon, and the queen of Sheba all plan to come against Israel at one time. They'll depose Solomon and his foolish son and I'll have you ready to ascend the throne. It is all so simple."

"It sounds simple but . . ." Jeroboam was hesitant. Everything was moving so fast he found it hard to comprehend just what she had in mind.

"It is simple. By the time all of them are ready to march against Solomon, we'll have our plans completed." She pushed back the coarse black hair of her wig and looked at him with a long calculating gaze. "Secrecy is important. No one must know."

"Is it certain that the queen of Sheba is joining with the others?"

"Of course. She has to. Why else would she be making this long trip?" Tipti's words were sharp and her eyes were hard as emeralds.

"I've heard from the traders that she's coming to prove Solomon with hard questions."

Tipti toyed with the fringe on one of the cushions. "Don't believe such foolishness," she said. "Supposedly she's coming in peace, but once here, you'll see, she is one of Solomon's worst enemies."

As always in Jerusalem, though the sky was still light, dusk descended on the narrow streets and lanes within the city. The pillared portico that edged Tipti's pool was shadowed. A slight breeze blew across the lily pond just as the silver trumpets within the great temple area announced the time for evening prayer. Tipti motioned for her small serving girl to light the oil lamps and was about to order a cool drink when Jeroboam rose and knelt beside her.

"My most revered queen, could you spare me for two days?"

Tipti was stunned. "Spare you? Why?"

"I need to go to the holy place at Shiloh. There's a wise man of God there. I need to ask him if the God of Israel will be with me in this plan of yours."

Tipti was at first affronted and indignant that Jeroboam would dare to submit her plan to one of Israel's uncouth, ragged, holy men. She sat up very straight, her delicate face flushed with anger and then just as quickly her whole demeanor changed. "That's just what you should do," she said. "I'm sure that if the God of Israel has any wisdom at all, he'll also see the reasonableness of our plan."

Jeroboam left Tipti's small palace glowing with pride and happiness that this austere queen had chosen him to confide in. More than that, she seemed determined to adopt him as her son. He could hardly believe his good fortune. As to her plan to make him the next king, he preferred to consult Ahijah, the holy man of Shiloh, to determine if the plan would succeed.

✳ ✳ ✳

The next morning Jeroboam rose early and made his way through the narrow village streets of Shiloh until he came to a small shrine. This shrine was all that remained of the tabernacle of Yahweh that once stood here. The shrine was dark and smelled of dry blood and cheap incense. There was something depressing and gloomy about the gray stones and the door that stood gaping open. It was like a corpse, a dull, dead thing.

Jeroboam turned from its empty interior and made his way through the thistles and thorn bushes around to a gnarled and hoary old tree. This tree had once stood in the outer court of the tabernacle when Samuel and Eli were alive. It was the only thing that even hinted at the glory of what had once stood on this spot.

Jeroboam moved to a better vantage point under a great, spreading fig tree. The sun was just coming up and the birds were beginning to stir somewhere up in the top branches of the tree. From one of the round openings high in the shrine's wall came the plaintive call of a turtle dove. There was an air of peace that hung heavy over the deserted shrine. "Lonely but peaceful," Jeroboam decided.

Suddenly, a quavering figure of an old man materialized from the gnarled roots of the tree. His beard was long and smokegray in color, matching his worn and threadbare robe. His hair was white and stuck out in small tufts around his bald head. His bearing and dress were so colorless that it was almost startling to see that his eyes under their heavy eyebrows were piercing and intense.

He reached behind the tree and brought out his long walking stick before he said anything. "Jeroboam," his voice was cracked and shaky. "You're Jeroboam ben Nebat. I've been expecting you."

"My mother told you I was coming?"

"I didn't have to be told. I knew you were coming." The old man came over to Jeroboam and looked at him intently. His eyes seemed to drill right into Jeroboam's soul. They penetrated all his defenses, and Jeroboam drew back in sudden aversion.

He was completely unnerved by this ancient priest, who seemed to have become as weathered and tattered as the shrine he guarded. He wondered what answers an old man like this could possibly have.

"I've been told," Jeroboam began, "by persons of influence, that I will become king of Israel after Solomon." He said the words hurriedly as though they almost burned his tongue.

"And . . ." the old man said, striking his stick impatiently on the outcropping of rock.

"And I want you to inquire of the Lord to see if it is His will."

The old man became very agitated, backed off, and began muttering something Jeroboam couldn't quite hear.

"What is it, old man? What are you saying?"

"I don't need to ask the will of Yahweh. It is plain, the prediction must be false. Though you know there is no love for the young prince, still the tribe of Judah and Benjamin will never turn against the house of David. At best you would have only the ten northern tribes."

Jeroboam reached out to him eagerly and then drew back without touching him. There was something of dust and ashes about him. Something almost unreal. "My father," he said, "I would be willing to take the ten tribes and rule from Shechem."

The old man's laugh was high and cracked. There was no real mirth in it as he said, "You forget Jerusalem. They would have Jerusalem and the temple and that is like having the heart. Without the heart, you would have nothing, my son."

"Let them worship in Jerusalem if they like. I can rule from Tirzah or Shechem if necessary. We can build shrines and temples of our own."

Again the old man became very upset. "No, no, my son," he said, "you don't understand. If the people go to Jerusalem to worship, they will look to Jerusalem for their king. We can't compete with Jerusalem."

"We can build other shrines."

"Look, my son, at this dead thing," the old priest said tapping the stone wall of the shrine with his stick. "Never forget this. It is in Jerusalem our God has put his name."

The old man had become so upset and agitated that Jeroboam backed off. He whispered his thanks, blessed the old man, and kissed the ragged hem of his garment in respect. Then without looking in at the dark, yawning emptiness evident through the open door of the shrine, he hurried away and up the street toward his mother's small house.

Late the next day he was back in Jerusalem. His fine clothes were limp with perspiration, his short beard and eyebrows were almost white with dust from the road, flies clung tenaciously to his arms and legs. He headed directly to the public bath. He wanted to wash off not only the grime of the road but the terrible disappointment of having the priest of Shiloh negate his ambitious plans.

More than anything he dreaded telling Tipti the old man's pronouncement. She would, of course, try to find some alternative. She was not one to give up easily. More than that, she wouldn't understand that the old man was right. Jerusalem was where the God of Israel had placed His name. Everyone had seen His shekinah glory flood the temple on that first day of dedication. He himself remembered how awestruck they had all been.

He remembered the priests carrying the Ark to its new home in the temple. There hadn't been a dry eye in the tightly packed crowd. Tears came to his eyes again as he remembered how the sun glinted on the worn gold of the box. It had been a deeply moving experience, so moving that no one seemed to be aware of the Ark's smallness or the primitive workmanship. All they saw was the great symbol of their faith that had blossomed in the wilderness with Moses and the two tablets of the law.

Despite the glory of the new temple, with its golden doors flashing in the sun, its pillars with their twined chains and hanging pomegranates carved into the flared capitals, the huge tank held by twelve oxen, the altar piled with sacrificial offerings, all of this was as nothing beside the small gold box that still contained the two tablets of the law given to Moses on Mount Horeb.

Jeroboam sat in the darkened bath letting the slave dip tepid water over him. He was aware of the steamy moisture coming from the heated rocks, the musty odor of water on old, worn stone, and the pots of glowing coals with small bursts of fragrance as fresh herbs were thrown on them. He was totally aware of his surroundings and yet his mind was busy replaying the events of that day the temple had been completed.

No one had known what to expect. They certainly hadn't anticipated such a dramatic demonstration. It had been so overwhelming that the great mass of people had fallen on their faces partly in worship and awe and partly because the sight was too wonderful to behold. As he remembered, it had happened not just once but twice during the dedication. He himself believed at the time that, like Moses, he was seeing the glory of God and would surely die.

When the priests had disappeared with the Ark into the temple, no one breathed. Some even thought it possible that the priests who carried the Ark and placed it in the Holy of Holies beneath the wings of the cherubim would die. The moments they waited to see if they would return had seemed an eternity. The singers, Asaph, Heman, and Jeduthun with all their sons and brothers, stood motionless in their glistening white robes to the east of the altar. One hundred twenty priests with trumpets, flutes, lyres, and harps stood waiting immovable, suspended in terrible anticipation of what might happen.

Then the moment came when the priests appeared at the door of the temple. They had not been killed. The Ark was in its place at last. They raised their hands in adoration, the chorus burst into a song of lilting praise while cymbals crashed, trumpets blared, lyres and harps joined in. All exploded with the joy of their message, "He is so good! His loving kindness lasts forever."

One moment the chorus, players, and multitude had been singing with hands raised and tears of joy running down their faces and the next moment they were frozen in astonishment. Jeroboam sitting on the hard stone seat in the bathhouse instinctively covered his eyes even at the memory.

It wasn't just a fable invented by the priests. They all had seen it. They had seen it and everyone of them knew what it meant. They would never be the same again. In fact, they would never come to the temple mount without remembering just what had happened. They would tell their children and their children would tell others but words were too inadequate to describe the joy. The glory, the shekinah glory had come down and filled the temple.

It was light, bursts of light radiating from the door of the temple so brilliant it blinded them so that they hid their faces and fell to the ground. The God of Abraham, Isaac, and Jacob, the God of their beloved King David had come down and they had all seen His glory as it filled the temple.

It had happened once again after Solomon had offered his prayer of dedication and the priests had prepared the altar for the great sacrifice. Actual fire had burst forth upon the sacrifice and at the same time the shekinah glory had flooded out of the temple so that they all fell to their faces again and worshiped.

Jeroboam reached for his clothes. He had determined he would not go to see Tipti as he had planned. Just remembering all that had taken place at the temple's dedication had sobered him. Tipti would never understand that the Lord God Jehovah was not like her cat god that could be manipulated and used. He was real and powerful and they had all seen that it was Jerusalem He had chosen for His dwelling place.

He knew Tipti would be very disappointed. She had built all her hopes around him and the possibility of his becoming king. At the thought of trying to explain all of this to her, he found his stomach knotting and his mouth dry with dread. Tomorrow at the latest he must tell her the result of his trip to Shiloh.

13

*T*he next day when Jeroboam arrived for work at Tipti's palace, he was relieved to find she wasn't there. She'd gone down to her quarters at Gezer and was expected back sometime late in the afternoon. Jeroboam was now so familiar with her schedule that he knew just why she had gone. It sobered him considerably, making him even more reluctant to tell her the bad news from Shiloh.

She went to this old pagan city her brother, the pharaoh, had given as her dowry because there she could secretly receive messengers from Egypt. It was always the same: she either sent a message or received one every fortnight. Most of the time it was by runners, but if there was some urgency, she had whole cages of trained pigeons she could send.

In this way she advised her brother of Solomon's activities and in return received the pharaoh's instructions and advice. Now that there was a major plot forming against Solomon, it was doubly important for them to exchange information.

On this afternoon she was disturbed by the message from her brother. It seemed that the queen of Sheba had given no real commitment to the Egyptian ambassador. In fact, she had talked more of an investigative visit to Solomon than an invasion. "Everything depends on Hadad in Edom," the message read. "When the queen visits him, he must convince her to join the rest of us in marching against Israel. If this fails I will need to depend on you to convince her with cunning appeals."

Tipti brushed back the twined black hair of her wig and read the report again. Then she ordered all of her maidservants from the room. She needed to be alone to think. She walked out onto her balcony and looked eastward toward the road that wound up to Jerusalem. The foothills were covered with olive and fig trees, and low stone walls bordered the terraces. It was a pleasant sight, but she noticed none of this. Her mind was racing ahead to ponder her ambitions for Jeroboam in the light of this new information.

She felt sure the queen of Sheba would join in the coalition once she understood the advantages. Surely Hadad, the charming, persuasive Hadad, would make her change her mind. However, if none of these measures worked, she would have to make other plans to bring Jeroboam to the throne. It would take much longer; perhaps even waiting until after the death of Solomon. If she succeeded, the wait would have been worth it. With Jeroboam on the throne of Israel, Israel would virtually be an extension of Egypt. At least a strong ally.

Tipti frowned. Right now all of her plans for Jeroboam depended on the advice of some ancient old priest at a deserted shrine in a small Ephraimite village called Shiloh. This was something she hadn't counted on. Jeroboam had never seemed very religious. She must find a way to rid him of this weakness.

She had never understood Solomon's devotion to his unseen God. She only knew that it had taken every bit of her ingenuity to pry him loose from its rigid rules. It was through the king's curiosity she had won a foothold, but with Jeroboam there was no curiosity, only ambition. She pondered how best to proceed. This religion had some mysterious hold on him. She didn't like it. "I must find a way to break down, root out, get rid of this strange fixation he has. Imagine telling me he was going to get advice from one of those old priests."

She shuddered at the thought then wondered if Jeroboam was still in Shiloh or had already returned. With a determined step and toss of her head she went through the beaded curtain that closed off the balcony from the small private garden. "Run," she ordered the old man who was tending the tuberoses, "tell my maidens I'm ready to go. We must leave for Jerusalem at once."

＊ ＊ ＊

Back in her own palace in Jerusalem, Tipti asked for Jeroboam and found to her alarm that he had gone to the temple for evening prayer. Solomon had not called for her, but the report was that he had been seen more with his son Rehoboam of late. All of this was unsettling. It was unthinkable that Naamah's magic could be working so well. Undoubtedly her own cat god Bastet was still angry that she hadn't managed to have the priest that killed her cat beheaded. She'd have to make some sacrifice that would please her cat god and make him forget the terrible affront to his dignity.

In the meantime, she paced nervously back and forth beside her lily pond while her serving maids peeped anxiously through the gauze curtains. When the queen was in such an angry mood, none of them wanted to risk her displeasure. She could be so charming when things went well, but when angry she was entirely capable of having them whipped or even sent back to Egypt for execution.

Looking around and seeing that the courtyard was empty, Tipti picked up the gold-handled mallet and hit a resounding blow on the large oval brass gong. Instantly her serving men and women came running and stood with ashen faces just inside the west portico. "I'll be entertaining this evening here beside the lily pool." Her words were clipped and her eyes flashed as though giving a command.

As her servants hurried away in all directions to carry out her wishes, she motioned for her chief steward. "Go quickly to the southern gate of the temple and find Jeroboam. Tell him I wish to see him immediately about important matters."

* * *

Jeroboam was surprised that Tipti had known where to find him. He was even more surprised to find that she had prepared a feast fit for Solomon, but he himself was to be the only guest. Though he knew that to sit and eat with one of the queens alone like this was considered a terrible affront to the king and could be punished by death, he was flattered. He quickly dismissed all such thoughts from his mind as he sat down on the cushion beside her.

He knew Tipti was curious to know the result of his trip, but he found himself reluctant to tell her the discouraging news. Finally it was Tipti who brought up the subject. "My son," she had taken to calling him this lately, "I have had some disturbing news from Egypt. It seems that the queen of Sheba is not yet committed to join the coalition." She paused, waiting to see what effect this would have on Jeroboam.

Jeroboam shifted uneasily under her gaze. "I wish I could bring you some good news, but mine is also discouraging."

"The priest was not in favor of our plan?" Tipti's voice was honey sweet, but her eyes flashed dangerously.

"He was most discouraging."

"And what reason did he give?" Her voice was still sweet, but her mouth was rigid and stiff.

"He pointed out that both the tribes of Judah and Benjamin would go with David's tribe even if they didn't like Rehoboam."

"And ..."

"They would hold Jerusalem and the temple. People would still come to worship and trade on the feast days in Jerusalem and I would have nothing to offer them that was as grand."

Tipti threw back her head and laughed a hard, brittle laugh. "Is that the only problem? We can easily remedy that."

"I don't understand." Jeroboam was astounded. He had expected her to be as discouraged as he was.

"My son," she said lightly touching his arm with the tips of her jeweled fingers. "The God who dwells in Solomon's temple isn't very attractive to most people. In Egypt, given a choice, no one would choose to worship such a god."

"But ..."

"No, no, don't say anything until I explain. This God your people worship does nothing for the farmer who wants rain or the young man who wants sex and love or the wife who wants a charm against her husband's new love. Your God fills none of the needs of ordinary people. Now if you brought up from Egypt the golden calf once worshiped by your people ..."

Jeroboam was horrified at the suggestion. "That was the great sin of my people. The golden calf was evil."

"That's what you were told by your priests. In Egypt the Apis or Mnevis bull is even more powerful than Bastet or Mihos. In his temples they have dancing girls and lovely festivals where a magic potion made from a grain called ergot releases the worshiper from all his inhibitions, and only enjoyment is important."

"But in Israel all of this is a great sin and wouldn't be accepted."

Tipti held some large dried dates on a golden plate. Now she picked up one with her own jeweled fingers and laughing held it up to Jeroboam's mouth. "Is all pleasure then a sin here in Israel?"

Blushing at such familiarity he bit into the date and almost choked. "We take pleasure within limits. It's forbidden to use the plant ergot or worship idols," he stammered.

Tipti licked the stickiness of the dates from her fingers. "Why should it not be possible to give your people the advantage of worshiping both the God of Israel and the Apis bull? And as for the ergot, it grows with the rye quite naturally. It gives such lovely dreams and visions. One becomes like a god. Had you thought of that?"

"How could I convince the people?"

"You say your God created everything, but you worship him in a very narrow fashion. How much better it would be if you let the Apis bull represent also your God Jehovah. Then plant the ergot so your priests will have visions and . . ."

Jeroboam was horrified at the suggestion. He didn't know what was really wrong with it. He just knew the worship of the golden calf in the wilderness had been one of the greatest sins Israel ever committed. The ergot was dangerous too. Some pagan priests had died after taking too much.

Tipti saw the look of horror on his face and quickly brought up her most convincing argument. "My lord Solomon has permitted a shrine for the bull on Olivet along with shrines to other foreign gods. He has even secretly taken the ergot and found it to bring most pleasant dreams. He sees no harm in it at all."

Just as she had thought, Jeroboam was impressed.

"You think then that I need not worry about the loss of Jerusalem."

"Of course not. Let the tribes of Judah and Benjamin keep their harsh God and gaudy temple if it comes to that. You can give the people something easier to understand and enjoy."

"What about the coalition? If the queen of Sheba doesn't join, what will happen then?"

"Then our plans will have to wait. But hopefully this won't happen. It's to her advantage to join with Egypt and Egypt's friends against Solomon."

Jeroboam sat thinking of all she had said and trying to piece together the various aspects of her plan. Tipti seemed to be preoccupied with sipping from her goblet of choice wine, but all the time she was watching him to determine his reaction to what she had said. She noted that while at first he had been resistant to many of her suggestions, now he seemed thoughtful and accepting. "It's just a matter of time," she thought, "and he'll agree with me completely."

Both Tipti and Jeroboam had been so engrossed in their conversation that neither had noticed that one of the serving women who seemed most anxious to be helpful was also listening to everything that was said. This woman, though dark haired and dressed exactly like the other Egyptian handmaidens, was actually a Hebrew and a gift from Solomon's mother, Bathsheba. She had not heard everything, but she had heard enough to gather that a plot was afoot to place Jeroboam on the throne either by deposing Solomon or waiting to edge out Rehoboam, the heir. She began to devise a plan whereby she could see Bathsheba and warn her of the alliance between Tipti and Jeroboam and the plans they were making.

* * *

When Bathsheba heard of Jeroboam's visit to the Egyptian princess, she was upset. But when she learned that he had been served dinner alone as though he were Solomon himself, she was furious. She dropped the balls of wool she was carding and struggled to her feet. "Solomon must know this at once. The punishment is death for such an affront to the crown."

"My queen." The young maid was on her knees clutching the hem of Bathsheba's robe. "There is more. I've only told you the circumstance not the news."

Bathsheba turned and looked at the girl in alarm. "News, what news could you possibly have that is worse than what you've already told me?"

"My queen, the Egyptian has plans to put Jeroboam on the throne of Israel as her son and heir."

At this disturbing revelation Bathsheba drew the young maid aside and plied her with questions until she knew all that had taken place in Tipti's palace. "I must go to the king at once," she said as she nodded dismissal to the maid and summoned her crown and royal robes to be brought.

* * *

Solomon was in the Hall of Judgment sitting on his golden throne with the lion armrests when he heard that his mother was on her way to see him. As her palanquin arrived at the entrance to the great hall, he sent six of his pages to escort her up to the throne.

He watched with keen curiosity as one of the young men pulled aside the curtains and helped Bathsheba to alight. He was surprised to see how very frail she was. With some effort she climbed the six marble steps. Though she stood straight, her head high, and had the same proud demeanor he had always admired, she was still leaning more heavily than usual on her gold-handled cane.

His throne was built low and wide and made comfortable with tasseled cushions. Most of the time he sat in the oriental fashion with his legs crossed. Now he made room for his mother beside him, ordering more cushions and a footrest to make sure she would be comfortable. Then knowing she had some important message, he ordered his pages, trumpeters, and counselors to move away from the throne.

"So, what disaster has brought you out in this hurry?" he asked with a twinkle in his eye.

Bathsheba fretted at the gauze mantle, smoothed her long sleeves, and looked around to see if it was safe to talk. "My son," she said anxiously, "you must not take this lightly."

Solomon smiled, he was tempted to laugh. His mother always wanted to make sure even before she said anything that there would be the proper reception. "You know that I always take your words seriously," he said.

"You remember I told you of the serving girl I had placed in the Egyptian's service."

He was amused. She never deigned to call Tipti by her name. She was always "the Egyptian."

"Yes, of course," he said, "I remember. Has she brought some interesting tidbits for us to mull over?"

"Not tidbits, my son. Treason and treachery is more the name for it."

Solomon was suddenly serious. "Treason! Who is involved in this treason as you call it?"

"It will be hard for you to believe, but it is none other than your man Jeroboam. Tipti has dared to entertain him alone for dinner."

Solomon's countenance clouded and his jeweled right hand, gripped his scepter so hard the veins stood out on his hand, but his voice was steady and controlled. "I should have him flogged and publicly beheaded."

Bathsheba turned pale. "It's what he well deserves. But your wife Tipti is the real culprit. How could a humble workman like Jeroboam refuse the queen? No, no, it's plain to me that Tipti is the one to be flogged and sent home in disgrace."

"What was the occasion for this dinner?" Solomon asked with an apparent calm demeanor. Only his eyes, hard and penetrating, told a different story. "Did the maiden also know that?"

"Yes, yes. She told me everything, and it is a sorry tale full of treasonous plots and ambitious designs. It seems that the Egyptian has plans for this upstart, Jeroboam, to usurp your throne after your defeat by the coalition."

Solomon didn't answer right away, but his agitation was evident by the way he pushed back his crown and pulled at his short beard. He seemed to be struggling to take in all the aspects of this startling news. When he finally spoke, his words were clipped and had a bitter edge to them. "So the plans are that complete. I must say I'm surprised. I wouldn't have thought either Tipti or Jeroboam could be so treacherous."

"There seems to be one problem. They must have the queen of Sheba's backing if the plan is to succeed."

"They aren't sure of her?"

"They don't seem to be. She evidently hasn't committed herself yet."

"Aha, then there is a good chance their plans can be foiled."

"You can have Tipti exposed, sent back to Egypt, and Jeroboam executed."

"Mother!" Solomon said feigning shock. "Tipti's valuable. Now she's probably even more valuable than ever."

"I don't understand. She has an Egyptian knife pointed at your throat."

"I'm amazed that you don't see how it works."

"I see all too well how it works."

"No, no, mother. You don't understand. Now that I know for sure that Tipti repeats everything to her brother in Egypt, all we have to do is give her false information to report. That is the better revenge. To outwit the enemy is far sweeter than to have him flogged."

Solomon's whole demeanor had changed, but Bathsheba wasn't convinced. "That won't be nearly as easy as you seem to think. For instance, what information can you give Tipti that will make the pharaoh give up his plans? It's too difficult. Tipti knows everything."

"Well," Solomon said, stroking his short beard impatiently. "Let me think. Surely there's some bit of information that would be difficult for Tipti or her spies to check and yet would be totally discouraging to the pharaoh."

"It is impossible. Tipti has ways of discovering everything. Just think of one thing that would be impossible for her to ferret out."

Solomon liked a challenge of wits. "The one thing that no one can find out," he said almost to himself, "is what I am thinking. Am I right?"

"Of course," Bathsheba agreed.

"It is also true, I'm told, that I am known for my ability to have women fall in love with me."

"Unfortunately, that is also true, but what has that to do with the problem?"

Solomon laughed a mirthless, harsh laugh as he explained.

"What do you think would happen if Tipti was told and the pharaoh informed that the queen of Sheba had fallen in love with Solomon and that Solomon for a change had fallen in love with her?"

"They wouldn't believe a word of it. They would know it wouldn't last. None of your relationships with women have lasted. You're always tiring of them."

Solomon didn't answer for a moment, and when he did he was no longer joking. "There was a woman once that never bored me."

"Shulamit?"

"Yes, Shulamit. But since she died nothing has been the same."

"God doesn't make mistakes, my son."

Solomon looked over at her and his eyes were dark with pain, his mouth tense. "Actually I've often wondered how God could have made such a botch of things. To give the son to Naamah and only daughters to Shulamit. I've never understood."

Bathsheba was shocked. Though she had often thought about the strange turn of events that had given Naamah, the Ammonite queen, the son that would rule Israel, she hadn't imagined that Solomon had also pondered over the strangeness of it all. She felt a twinge of guilt as she remembered that she had been the one that had urged his marriage to Naamah. "I did wrong to force the marriage," she said. "I was so ambitious. I wanted you to be king at any cost."

Solomon turned away. He knew that what she said was true, and yet it did seem that God could have intervened.

Bathsheba sighed and began to reach for her cane. "So, you think the pharaoh will be utterly discouraged if he hears you are in love with the queen?"

"He would know that if the queen should fall in love with me, his coalition would be demolished, and without one battle being fought. Just gossip would accomplish everything. Tipti's displacement and the pharaoh's plans foiled."

Bathsheba shook her head dubiously. "That's what you have always done. It never ceases to amaze me. You are always marrying your worst enemies."

"This will be a little more difficult."

"Really!"

"Yes. I've good evidence that the queen has a lovely face and is quite accomplished, but she has one flaw."

Bathsheba was leaning forward eagerly. She couldn't believe what she was hearing. "A flaw?" she questioned.

"Yes. Badget the trader has seen with his own eyes that she has the feet of a donkey."

Bathsheba gasped in shock. One hand flew to her throat and the other grasped the armrest of the throne. "It can't be true."

For a moment Solomon was almost enjoying himself. He loved to astonish his mother. "He swears it is true and I intend to examine her feet before I make any proposals."

"I should say you must. But how can you do such a thing?"

"I don't know, but given months to think I shall come up with something. In the meantime I'll begin to give Tipti information that will make it seem utterly plausible that the queen and I are in love with each other."

Bathsheba turned with anxious eyes and grabbed his arm. "And the treachery of Jeroboam. What will you do to him for daring to dine with your queen?"

"In time. Everything will be settled in time. I have found there is a time for everything under the sun."

"Be careful. It's dangerous to toy with a queen's heart." With that she motioned to her bearers and her pages. The curtains of the palanquin were pulled back and Solomon helped her to rise. She went down the steps with the same regal dignity with which she arrived. She refused the hands that reached out to help her and by herself entered the palanquin.

Solomon stood watching until the ebony box and its carriers had disappeared. His thoughts were mixed. His outrage at Tipti was cooling as he thought of the intrigue and complexity of their new relationship. He almost preferred this to her love. The challenge was at least invigorating. It was like the game of jackals and hounds. The queen of Sheba would be his piece to play against her jackal, Jeroboam.

He was sorry for his outburst of bitterness toward God for giving Naamah his firstborn son. He had hidden his resentment all these years and had not imagined it would burst out at such a moment. He was doubly angry at himself as he realized his mother was blaming herself for all that had happened.

* * *

Down in the old city just outside the palace gate at the house of Badget the trader, an interesting game of wits was also being played by his two wives. Terra, the new wife, was happily pregnant with Badget's first child while Yasmit mulled over various plans to regain her lost position of importance.

Yasmit was astounded at the attention this plain, unassuming little woman seemed to have attained just by being pregnant. It rankled and galled her that Terra with no real effort on her part should have gained Badget's complete devotion. Everything that she had learned and practiced in the art of attracting a man's attention seemed of no effect against this new menace.

To make it all more difficult, she found it impossible to hate Terra. The woman was like a ray of sunshine. She didn't even notice when she was slighted. She seemed to be just naturally happy and content.

It wouldn't be easy to discredit Terra or get rid of her, Yasmit decided. She would have to think of some other way to regain her lost position.

Gradually a plan began to form in her mind and the more she thought about it the more she was pleased with it. It would have to involve the old apothecary who had his shop at the very edge of the marketplace. She knew she could trust him not to divulge her secret.

The next day she ordered her mule saddled while Badget was out and then very carefully made her way down the back lanes of the city until she came to the shop. The old man was sitting way at the back on a raised wooden platform covered with a richly woven tapestry. The shutters of his floor-length windows were flung back so he could take in the colorful activity in the marketplace that spread out below his window. He was drinking his regular barley gruel while his two assistants sat on the floor at some distance working with mortars and pestles to fill an order for the king.

When Yasmit arrived, one of the assistants tied her mule to the doorpost and led her back to where the old man was sitting. They knew each other well and he quickly ordered a cushion and honeyed drink for her. "Now what can I do for the wife of my good friend Badget?" he asked.

* * *

That evening as Terra and Yasmit sat together waiting for Badget to come home, Yasmit said, "I have some exciting news to tell our husband when he comes home. It is quite unexpected. He'll be surprised. In fact I can hardly believe it myself."

Terra had just started to dip a piece of bread into the rich brown sauce in the black earthen bowl that sat between the two of them. "It's good news then."

"The very best of news. If you promise not to tell our husband, I'll let you be the first to know." Terra's eyes shone. "How very kind you are to me. Of course I'll keep your secret."

"At my age it rarely happens, and after all this time, but . . ."

Terra dropped the piece of bread and leaned over so she could whisper and not be heard by the maids. "Can it be that you are expecting a child too?"

Yasmit nodded and smiled. "How did you ever guess?" she said almost blushing.

Terra impulsively hugged her. "How wonderful. You must tell our husband at once. He'll be so pleased. Two children to look forward to. We'll plan everything together."

Yasmit again nodded and smiled as she readjusted her mantle under the gold coins that framed her face. She didn't want to discuss it, and she was more than surprised at the response she had gotten from Terra. The girl had not an ounce of jealousy in her, it seemed. She was genuinely pleased. It made Yasmit feel somehow craven and mean. It had taken all the joy out of her triumph.

* * *

That evening as Solomon waited in the chamber of the eastern gate for his son Rehoboam to join him for evening prayers, he thought again of Tipti's careful plans to replace him on the throne. He was no longer so sure he could thwart them. He was reminded of the way he had been chosen to rule and then his amazing encounter with the God of Abraham, Isaac, and Jacob. It had been so real and he had been promised so much if he was willing to obey God's rules.

Somehow he'd done everything wrong, made all the mistakes possible. Worst of all, his son Rehoboam was weak and unfit. It made him sick to think of it. Of all his failures this was the biggest. "The father of a fool has no joy," he muttered to himself.

In despair he found himself praying, "O God of my fathers, is it possible that you can still bring some good thing out of this chaos? With all my wisdom I've failed in the most important areas of my life."

At the last moment a messenger arrived saying that his son was entertaining some friends and couldn't come. Solomon, with a determined set to his jaw and considerable anxiety over the choices this son was habitually making, moved off toward the temple surrounded by his counselors and tribesmen.

14

*B*athsheba was not the only one with spies in the house of the Egyptian princess. It was well known that Naamah, as the ruling queen, was obsessed with the need to know even the most intimate details of life in her rival's palace. It was a fact that several of the servants had risen to dizzy heights of power within the confines of the harem just by giving her some choice bit of news about the Egyptian.

Now on this, the ninth day in the month of Elul, during the olive harvest, Naamah, concerned about the reports from her spies, set out for the grotto of the ugly god Moloch. She was convinced that Moloch could frustrate any plans the Egyptian queen might have.

The grotto had been constructed with Solomon's reluctant blessing in the Valley of Hinnon not far from the city's Dung Gate. Here since time immemorial the refuse of the city was burned and there was a continuous pall of malodorous smoke hanging over the area. After much discussion, and considerable objection from Naamah, the grotto had been placed here so the burning flesh of small children would not bother the inhabitants of Jerusalem.

On this particular day Naamah rode one of the white mules but kept her face covered and wore garments of dull gray, like a peasant woman, so no one would recognize her. Slung from the pommel of her mule's saddle was a large woven basket that she protected from the glaring sun with a piece of finely tooled leather.

When she reached the steps that led down into the cave she surprised the maidservant that rode with her by insisting on carrying the basket herself and presenting it to the chief priest. "My lord," she said, "I've brought the jewels you requested. Now may the god grant me success when I go to confront the Egyptian."

The priest had the look of an ordinary man with heavy eyebrows that flared out partially obscuring his small, deepset eyes. His garments, in contrast to his appearance, were richly embroidered, almost garish. He reached for the basket, but Naamah shook her head. "Not yet. I myself must present them to the god."

The priest turned and led the way down the steps into the dark interior, where the only light came from a fire in the belly of the huge idol. The fearful creature sat cross-legged, with metal arms outstretched over leaping flames always greedily waiting to receive the next victim.

The priest bowed, then prostrated himself before the idol. When he finally rose, he proceeded to throw incense from a leather pouch that hung from his waist by a braided cord.

Naamah also prostrated herself before the ugly form. For a few moments there was only the crackling sound of the flames and a hissing noise as more incense was thrown on the fire by the priest.

Slowly Naamah raised herself, and lifting her head so she could look up into the glass-fixed stare of the idol, she chanted, "O Moloch, you are far greater than the cat god Bastet of Egypt. You must not let the cat and her devotee the Egyptian succeed in their evil plans. It is my son, Rehoboam, who must rule Israel."

She sat back on her heels, a plump, ordinary-looking woman whose face was turning crimson with the heat. Her gray hair hung in damp spirals from under her mantle and there was just the barest hint of a small, gold crown on her brow. Sweat poured down her face, running freely in the deep creases, but she was oblivious to all this. Her whole attention was focused on the image.

"See," she said as she rummaged in the basket, "I've brought you jewels given for the temple of Israel's God. I stole them for you. We'll make a crown for you and you'll honor my son and make him the next king of Israel."

At this the old priest hurried forward and put out his clawlike hands. "Yes, yes, Moloch needs a crown. A crown of gold and jewels more glorious than the king's own crown. We'll have it made."

Naamah looked at him questioningly before she put the jewels in his hand. "Old one, there is a plot afoot; a plot designed by the Egyptian to overthrow Solomon and put the upstart Jeroboam on his throne. My son would be ignored. Promise me this will not happen."

The priest had drawn back at her sharp words and daggerlike stare.

His hands were still held out, but his eyes had taken on a frightened, haunted look. "Give Moloch the jewels for his crown and everything will be yours."

"Everything?"

"I swear, everything."

Naamah breathed a sigh of satisfaction. "Tell the god, when he's in a mood to listen, I want the Egyptian out of my way. Back in Egypt or better still dead of poison or a broken heart."

The priest's eyes glinted with greed as she dropped the large, finely cut jewels in his hand. "Take care that no one steals them," she said as she removed the lid of the basket and felt around for more. She handed them to the priest, but when she turned to put the lid back on the basket, the head of a huge snake appeared above the rim and filled the opening. It was obviously temporarily crazed by the light and heat of the fire. "Zizi has guarded the jewels well," she said with a coarse laugh. "None of the women would dare open any of my baskets."

With a swift movement she nudged the snake back in the basket and fitted on the lid, then rose and turned to leave. "Remind the god that I have given jewels worth a kingdom for use in his crown."

As she lumbered heavily up the steps, she was tempted to look back. She yearned to know that the god had at last forgiven her for not sacrificing her firstborn to him. All these twenty-four years since Rehoboam had been born she had been thinking of new and better ways to buy him off, settle the debt.

It was true that Solomon had built this shrine at her insistence. At the time she had hoped Moloch would accept this in exchange for the life of her son. But Moloch was greedy. He was always wanting more. Never satisfied.

The God of Israel never asked for human sacrifice. A payment of shekels in exchange for the life of a firstborn son was the only requirement. How easy it was to worship the God of Solomon. In spite of this, she would never give up Moloch for the God of Israel. The God of Israel couldn't be seen or bribed, and what good was a deity that couldn't be bribed?

At the top of the steps she paused to catch her breath and wipe the dripping sweat from her face with the end of her mantle. She hung the basket back on the pommel and let her maid help her onto the mule. Then with a sharp command she ordered the mule forward out of the sacred grove and up the rock-dusty trail toward the Fountain Gate.

Back in the court of the women she found her son Rehoboam impatiently waiting for her. "I heard you wanted to see me," he said rather sharply.

"Is that so strange?" She undid the basket and lifted the great snake out. "There, there, Zizi, you've been terribly uncomfortable. I understand."

Rehoboam drew back. "It's always the snakes. It's peculiar. No one else . . ."

Naamah's eyes flashed dangerously as the snake wound itself around her shoulders. "Your father has all sorts of animals running through the palace. Are you critical of him too or is it just me?"

"He says he's studying their ways, but snakes . . ."

"Zizi has just protected a fortune in jewels. They sat right here in this basket within reach of everyone and no one dared touch them."

"A fortune in jewels! I could use a fortune right now. I need a new house for one of my wives."

Naamah smirked. "Your wives are all spoiled and selfish. I don't approve of anyone of them."

While she had been talking, Naamah had walked through the courtyard of the harem to her own place of authority. At the far end of the court a dais with a canopy had been built and fine tapestry carpets spread over the stones and out some distance in each direction. There was a cushioned throne that had been designed much like the king's throne except there were no carved lions and the gold and ivory inlay had been used more sparingly.

Naamah settled herself on the low-cushioned seat and patted the space beside her for Rehoboam. "We must talk," she said.

Rehoboam found there wasn't much his mother didn't know. She already knew of the coalition plotting to come against Israel and that the queen of Sheba was still uncommitted. She knew that Solomon was building another fortified city at Tadmor for trade beyond Damascus. She even knew that the king was often depressed these days and instead of calling for women from the harem, he was spending time with his brother Nathan. "I have heard," she said, "that he goes around muttering, 'Vanity, vanity, all is vanity.' What does he mean by that?"

145

Rehoboam shrugged and toyed with a large emerald ring he wore on his right hand. "It's strange. All these years he's emphasized having wisdom. He says that wisdom is the main thing necessary to rule well. There's only one problem: it seems to me he's gotten so much wisdom and knows so much that nothing's really interesting anymore."

"And what will you do when you're king?"

A smile flickered briefly around the sensual mouth of the prince. His eyes took on a speculative look. "I'll seek wisdom, but not his kind. It'll be my own wisdom. There'll be no more old counselors, only my own young friends, and I'll not ask the advice of any of the gods."

Naamah was shocked. "One must always appease the gods, my dear. They control everything and everyone."

Rehoboam fingered the fringe that hung from his waist. "I've been watching the gods worshiped around here. I don't like cats, and sacrificing babies seems meaningless, so there's only the God of Israel left."

"And what will you do with him?" Naamah spat out the words with venom.

"Appear at the ceremonies, take part in the prayers, offer the sacrifices, keep the feasts; but as to anything more than that, I'll leave the gods alone if they leave me alone." He stood up ready to go, then bent and raised his mother's hand to his forehead in a show of respect.

Naamah was smiling now. Her son did look kingly like her own father. He was a little soft from lounging in his harem with too much rich food and honey beer, but once he became king all that would end. "Remember the Egyptian princess is a snake waiting to strike, and watch Jeroboam."

With that word of warning ringing in his ears, Rehoboam turned and walked through the clusters of women that made up his father's harem. "One thing for sure," he muttered, "I'll have even more women in my harem than my father has."

* * *

If either Naamah or Rehoboam had known where Jeroboam was at that moment they would have been very uneasy. Jeroboam had ridden out of Jerusalem on a short errand to the north of the city. It was a beautiful day at the beginning of the olive harvest. Young men with sticks were beating the branches and old women and children huddled beneath the trees gathering the olives as they fell. Still others were carrying large woven baskets on their heads filled with the green nuggets. They were taking them to the various presses where the oil would be squeezed out and put into jars.

Jeroboam loved this time of year. The skies were clear, the sun bright, and as the harvest was good, everyone was happy. It was dry and dusty so that he had to ride with his headpiece over his nose and mouth and for that reason it took him a few minutes to realize someone was calling his name. He pulled on the reins and the donkey came to a stop under a carob tree. He shielded his eyes from the sun and looked around.

Once again he heard his name being called and turning in the direction from which the sound came, he saw an old man standing in a freshly plowed field. It was impossible to make out any details, but Jeroboam knew it had to be Ahijah.

He tied his donkey to the tree and made his way across the field to where the prophet was standing. It was indeed Ahijah. He looked different. He no longer wore his old tattered garments but instead had a new robe that must have been acquired especially for this trip to Jerusalem.

"Do you have business in the city?" Jeroboam asked.

"Business of a sort. I've come to see you."

"How strange that I should meet you here."

"Not strange at all. I was told that I would find you here."

Jeroboam frowned. He didn't like to think that everyone knew just when and where he was coming or going. "No one knew I was riding out today. How did you know?"

"Don't bother yourself about such things. My knowledge is not gotten from people." The old priest never lowered his eyes but stood looking at Jeroboam with a most penetrating gaze.

"I had almost forgotten you were a priest. Forgive me, my father."

"Not just a priest but one of the few prophets left. I've been given a message for you. I told you wrong when you visited Shiloh. What I told you then was by my own wits, but the message I bring you now is from the Lord, God of Israel."

Jeroboam found himself shaking and suddenly cold. He couldn't imagine what the message could be, but it frightened him. "Is it good or bad? Tell me so I can prepare myself."

Ahijah didn't answer but instead unwrapped the sash that held his robe in place and folded it carefully on the ground. Then he removed his new cloak and to Jeroboam's utter surprise began to rip and tear it into pieces. Each time he tore a section from the robe he handed it to Jeroboam, but all the time he refused to say anything.

"Your garment is new," Jeroboam tried to protest. "You need it for the Feast of Tabernacles." His protestations were ignored and the old man went about his task as though it were a matter of the greatest importance.

"Count them," Ahijah said finally as he stepped back still holding the last piece of the ruined cloak in his hand.

With a puzzled look on his face Jeroboam began to count the pieces in his hand. There were eight in all.

"Two more, you need two more," the old priest said as he proceeded to tear two more pieces from the cloak.

"What's this? What does it mean?" Jeroboam was genuinely mystified.

Ahijah still said nothing. He stooped and picked up his girdle and wrapped it around his linen shirt, then stuffed the last piece of his cloak in his belt.

"Here are the pieces," Jeroboam said, holding out the shredded remains of the old man's cloak.

"No, no, my son. Those are yours. The Lord God of Israel has spoken and said, 'I'm going to tear the kingdom out of Solomon's hand. Ten tribes will be given to you, Jeroboam.'"

"And the piece you have in your belt?"

"The Lord God has decreed that the tribe of Judah and the city of Jerusalem where He has put his name will remain for David's sake with Solomon and his seed."

Jeroboam had broken out into a sweat. "Why, why should He punish the king?"

"The Lord said, 'He's forsaken me and worshiped Ashtoreth of the Sidonians, Chemosh of the Moabites, and Moloch of the Ammonites. He's not walked in my ways nor kept my laws as his father, David, did.'"

"And what have I to do with this?"

"Ten tribes will be taken from Solomon's son and given to you. If you walk in the ways of the Lord God of Israel, and keep His statutes and commands as his servant David did, then will he build you a dynasty as enduring as the one promised to David."

Jeroboam was stunned. He fingered the torn pieces of cloth and tried to comprehend all that was being told him. There were so many questions, so much he wanted to know, but already Ahijah had picked up his walking crook and was preparing to leave. "Wait!" Jeroboam cried. "You must tell me more. What of Rehoboam and Jerusalem?"

"He will have a tribe, the tribe of Judah. The Lord Himself said in his own words, 'So that David, my servant, will always have a lamp burning before me in Jerusalem where I have chosen to put my name.'"

"How long will this be?"

Ahijah had again turned, ready to go, but now he stopped and looked back at Jeroboam. He fingered the oblong piece torn from the cloak that protruded from his girdle. "He said he would humble David's descendants, but not forever." With that the old man turned and started walking across the furrows toward the road.

Jeroboam stood for a moment, pondering what he had said, and then ran after him. "What does he mean, 'but not forever?!'"

Ahijah seemed not to hear him and kept walking with his face toward Shiloh. Jeroboam shrugged and fingered the torn pieces of cloth as he watched the old man disappear around a rocky projection. "How strange. He tore up a perfectly good cloak." Jeroboam muttered as, clutching them in his fist, he headed back to his donkey. His errand was forgotten. He wanted only to hurry back to tell Tipti the good news.

✳ ✳ ✳

Despite Solomon's periods of depression, his interest in the gods of his many wives never seemed to slacken. At first it had been out of curiosity that he spent time talking with their priests. Then he had found some of the ceremonies and the potions taken mysteriously stimulating. When his brother Nathan had warned him against such practices, he had explained, "If we understand their gods and know their secrets, then we can control them and use their power for ourselves."

He saw no conflict with his own beliefs, since he went regularly to the temple for morning and evening prayer. He boasted that he had as yet found nothing in the pagan religions that could not be explained by some trick of magic or a natural phenomenon twisted to appear new and different. In fact, he enjoyed the reputation he had gained for being able to control both the good and evil forces abroad in the world.

Quite often now Nathan and Nathan's son, Mattatha, went with him to the temple for the morning sacrifice. On the occasions when Rehoboam was with them, Solomon was acutely aware of the vast difference between the two young men. At such times his depression became almost unbearable as he saw that his son had none of the leadership qualities or the spiritual strength that Mattatha had in abundance.

On this morning Solomon joined Nathan, Mattatha, and Rehoboam at the great arched doorway of the palace, where the standard-bearers, swordsmen, and thirty of Israel's Mighty Men stood waiting to escort him to the temple. At sight of the king, the signal was given, and trumpeters on the wall raised their silver instruments for the high, stirring salute to the house of Judah.

The king's entourage moved like shadows up the marble steps to the large courtyard called Solomon's Porch. Here and there bits of light flashed out from lanterns carried by serving men, and small squares of polished marble became visible and then were again lost in the darkness.

Solomon loved this time of day and enjoyed the gradual lifting of the mist as light came from behind Olivet to transform the dark, shrouded marble edifice into a flashing jewel of tiered splendor. Slowly the great golden doors of the eastern gate, those doors that took twenty priests to open, reflected the first light. The marble pillars around the Court of the Women emerged out of the darkness and the fifteen steps up through the great golden Nicanor Gate were highlighted.

Later, after the sacrifice and after the incense, the priests would stand on these steps and sing. The hauntingly beautiful half tones of their chant would rise and fall until suddenly, high and clear, a bell-like voice would rise on the luminous air of the morning straight up to the gates of heaven.

Now as the king arrived to take his place on the porch of the temple the crisp, bright blast of the trumpets sounded once more, letting the people know they were free to flock into the large, open Court of the Women.

As Solomon watched them come, he felt a sudden surge of joy such as he had not felt in weeks. They were his people, his sheep coming into the fold. A splendid, marble and gold, gem-encrusted fold. Their garments and headpieces of every color were like jewels spread out across the Court of the Women.

Some of the priests had been awake and on duty for the past hour, washing both hands and feet at the laver, tending the fire, and checking the sheep that were to be sacrificed. Still others were at this very moment in the Hall of Polished Stones drawing lots to determine their position for the day.

It was still dark enough that the eternal fire glowed on the altar, warm and golden. Solomon wished the altar could have been made of finer stuff than the rude, unpolished stones, but that was how it had to be. That was one of the instructions that had been very clear and impossible to change.

Slowly the light had increased until with a sudden flourish the sun rose over Olivet. It glinted and danced on the golden doors, highlighted the pillars of the porch with their capitals of a hundred flowers set in a delicately carved network, while the symbol of Israel, a great golden vine with huge clusters of grapes above the doors was almost blinding in its brilliance.

Solomon saw all this with delight. "Surely," he thought, "this temple I have built will last as long as the pyramids in Egypt. What could destroy so fine a work of art? Certainly not an army. It is God's holy precinct, His dwelling place, the place where He chose to put His name."

He squared his shoulders as a feeling of pride enveloped him. The God of Israel wasn't like other gods that could be taken captive by an enemy. No, that was one thing Israel didn't have to worry about. Their God would never be humiliated in that way. It was equally certain that He'd never let this lovely house built with such care and precision be destroyed.

He had hardly noticed that the priest had taken coals from the altar until he heard a dull resonance as the Magrephah was struck. Soundlessly the priest passed close beside him and went inside the Holy Place to put the coals on the altar of incense.

This summoned the Levites to move to their places on the steps for the morning hymn. All was now ready. The sacrifice had been laid on the altar and the salt sprinkled on it. The priest in the Holy Place waited for the signal to commence the burning of the incense. At last the signal was given and with one accord the people fell on their faces before the Lord like waves of ripe grain falling before the scythe. Solomon and his whole company had turned toward the great doors of the Holy Place and with the rest of the people had fallen to their faces before the Lord.

It was then a strange thing happened. Solomon heard clearly the voice of the Lord. He heard it as though it came from a great distance some-where above the pillars and the flashing brilliance of the golden vine above the temple door. "Solomon," the voice said quite clearly. It was the same voice he had heard twice before. The voice that had commissioned him and warned him. He felt heat at the back of his neck and his hands on the cool paving stones of marble began to sweat.

"Solomon, you have not kept my covenant or my statutes which I commanded thee. For this I will surely rend the kingdom from thee and give it to thy servant."

With a cry of anguish Solomon fell prostrate along the floor and hid his face in his hands. "I am to be like Saul?" he cried in a torment.

Now almost gently the voice continued, "For David thy father's sake I will not do it now, but I will rend it out of thy son's hand."

"The whole kingdom lost?" Solomon pled.

"Not all the kingdom. I will give one tribe to thy son for David my servant's sake and for Jerusalem's sake which I have chosen."

There was the rustle and surge of the huge assembly getting to its feet. A cough here and there. No one else seemed to have heard the voice or Solomon's answers. Solomon let Nathan and Rehoboam help him to his feet. He felt weak, smitten with a terrible wound someplace deep inside where no balm could reach. He tried to hold his head high and control the trembling and the weakness in his knees as he struggled to concentrate on the familiar chant of the Levites at the Nicanor Gate.

Automatically he walked down the steps and out the southern gate toward the Hall of Judgment. His head reeled with the message he had heard. He tried to calm himself with the reassuring words that none of this would happen in his time.

Settled on his throne in the Hall of Judgment, he found himself unable to concentrate on the cases brought before him. Instead he pon-dered the strangeness of it all. His father, David, had sinned grievously taking another man's wife and having the man killed. He, Solomon, had always been careful never to commit such an outrage, but now he was being judged, put out, disowned in a way his father never had been.

He knew he'd taken foreign wives and this had been forbidden. But then without the wives and the treaties they brought with them, he would have been involved in as many wars as David had been. David had not been able to build the temple because his hands were covered with blood. "I built the temple because I was a man of peace."

Quickly his mind ran on to that other sin. He had been forced to let his wives build temples to their gods. First Naamah. She had insisted on the temple to appease the ugly Moloch. It had seemed at the time the life of Rehoboam was in mortal danger. Then the Egyptian had pouted and pled until he let her have her way. It seemed so harmless at the time. Others had followed until the Olivet especially was dotted with forbidden grottoes, sacred gardens, and heathen shrines.

He pushed his crown back on his head and ran his fingers through his short, well-trimmed beard. He waved away the counselors and petition seekers. He wanted to think. He wanted to be alone, and that was almost impossible.

There was something else in the message that his mind now settled on that sent a cold chill down his spine and made him wince with sudden alarm. "'My servant!' The voice said that the kingdom would be taken from my son and given to my servant." His eyes went round the room looking at each counselor, each fighting man, each tribesman. Somewhere within this body of men before him the culprit who would steal the crown must be even now standing undetected. He must find him, search him out, and then, perhaps, get rid of him.

His shoulders sagged beneath the terrible revelation. He'd asked in a moment of clarity for some reprieve, some good to come out of the bungle he'd made of his life and his calling. Now the answer seemed certain, final, hard as a rock. The kingdom would be lost and with it all hope of some redeeming goodness. God had spoken. Only Jerusalem, God's little plot of earth, the place He'd put His name, was to be left to his son Rehoboam.

He buried his head in his hands. "Is everything then lost?" he prayed. "Is there no hope for the future of Israel?" There was no answer, and he knew that the God of Abraham, Isaac, and Jacob had given the verdict, and apart from some miracle, the kingdom was doomed.

✳ ✳ ✳

Jeroboam had not gone to the morning sacrifice, but he had come to the great Hall of Judgment looking for one of Solomon's chief counselors. He stood at the back of the hall half hidden by one of the great pillars. He found himself pondering for the hundredth time all that Ahijah had told him. He found it almost incomprehensible that he, a building supervisor, the son of Nebat, should be elevated to king of ten tribes. He found it even more astonishing that he had been adopted, almost like the revered patriarch Moses, by the Egyptian princess.

He sensed he was walking on dangerous ground. If the king should hear that he had dined alone with his Egyptian queen, it could mean death. He shuddered. He had been so overwhelmed with the honor and the persuasiveness of Tipti that he hadn't taken time to think much of the consequences if he should be caught.

Now he looked at the splendor around him. The hall of pillars was like a forest of stone. The huge stone blocks that made up the walls were carefully chiseled, and along both walls were arrayed golden incense burners and candelabra.

More majestic and regal than any of his works was the king himself. Jeroboam had almost worshiped him at one time. The way he held his head, the confidence that was evident in his walk, his slow, amused smile, and most of all the noble forehead and intelligent eyes marked him as a king among kings.

He saw the foreign dignitaries that had come with petitions and many others that had come with some puzzlement for Solomon to unravel. Their faces were a study in awe and admiration. They always went away marveling at the simplicity and yet the accuracy of his pronouncements. Even in Egypt his fame as a man of great wisdom had flourished.

He saw the two scribes that sat on either side of the throne to catch each word and record it. One scribe might not get the exact word and so there were two, and now on each side of the marble steps there were others writing, recording as though his words were gold.

As usual there was an animal nearby. Today it was a small monkey that had arrived with the most recent shipment of goods from Africa. When Solomon became tired of the petitions and the endless reports or questions, he would summon the little monkey to the arm of his throne and talk to him. "Solomon can understand the animals," people were saying. Jeroboam didn't doubt it.

"I can practice being like him, but I will know inside that I am not like him and never will be. He was born to be a king, and I was born to be a building supervisor and no more. Gold runs in his very guts, luxury is his heritage, and the affairs of state come naturally to him."

He ran his hand down the solid marble pillars and looked again at the throne, noting every detail. The throne itself was a marvel of artistry, it was all of delicately carved ivory inlaid with gold. The marble steps and great carved lions guarding it were more than impressive. Then there were the banners unfurled behind the throne, the trumpeters, pages, elders, priests, and counselors, all blending together to make this the most outstanding court most travelers would ever see.

All this splendor, pomp, and elaborate apparel would never be part of his share. It was represented by the one torn piece of the cloak that Ahijah carried away with him in his belt. However, he had the ten pieces—ten tribes would be his. His to rule and to make great. His to build into a far greater kingdom than that of David.

He turned and pushed his way toward the door. The last thing he wanted to do right now was talk with the king or, for that matter, have the king talk to him. He was still bothered by doubts. The whole idea of his being king seemed at times alien and strange. If it had just been Tipti's idea, he would have discarded it as a jealous effort of one wife to get even with another. Tipti had never been able to accept the fact that Naamah's son, Rehoboam, was going to inherit the throne. However, it wasn't just Tipti's idea. Now the revered priest of Shiloh, Ahijah, had sworn, and had affirmed by tearing his cloak into ten pieces, that he, Jeroboam, would rule after Solomon.

He paused for a moment in the deep shadow of one of the great pillars and looked back at the king on his throne. He rubbed his hands together and smiled a slow speculative smile. He had been chosen just as David and Solomon had been chosen. At times he found himself impatient, impatient to get started. He didn't want to wait. In fact, he wondered if it was really necessary to wait.

"And what have you to smile about?" The words were spoken softly as though the person didn't want anyone else to hear. Jeroboam spun around and found himself face to face with Rehoboam. He noticed that the prince had evidently stopped on his way to join his father.

"Good things, many good things are coming my way," Jeroboam answered.

"How do you know? How are you so sure?"

"That's easy, both the stars and the priests have said it."

"Watch out that you don't take such things too seriously."

"What do you mean?"

"It has reached the king's ears that you dined with his queen. He was not pleased. You exalt yourself beyond measure. Don't forget you are just a building supervisor who knows how to build houses, terraces, and temples. You are that and no more."

With a threatening look and a toss of his head, Rehoboam moved out into the lighted aisle while Jeroboam, feeling badly shaken, ran down the steps and headed for the palace of the Egyptian queen. He had to see her. He had to warn her not to say anything about the dinner they had enjoyed together or about the prophecy of Ahijah. Men had been killed or banished for far less.

15

*N*aamah had neither slept nor eaten until word came that the Egyptian queen would receive her. Then in a flurry of activity she summoned her serving girls, called for her most elegant robes, had her thin, graying hair crimped, curled, and finally braided and wound around under her crown. She leaned into the brass mirror and ordered kohl to edge her eyes and then color for her cheeks. In sudden disgust she decided it made her look old and haggard. It all had to come off. She would go as she was, only wearing her most elaborate crown.

Though she hated the Egyptian queen, still she found herself constantly in awe of her, and Naamah was not used to being in awe of anyone. She was not only in awe of her but curious. She wondered how the Egyptian managed always to look so young and vital and how she made her palace something that was marveled at by all the most prominent people. She had never been inside the Egyptian's palace, she had only heard of the wonders to be found there; furniture of finely, carved ebony, alabaster lamps, and a pool made fragrant with scent drawn from thousands of tuberoses.

On feast days or new moon celebrations she had been very much aware of the Egyptian queen and her constant array of eunuchs, pages, maidens, and counselors. On these occasions Naamah as well as the other queens and concubines were always envious of her clothes. They were of sheer gossamer material that had never been seen before in Jerusalem. Her ornate wigs and crowns were impressive too, but it was her jewelry that they coveted most. Wide collars encrusted with jewels, ankle bracelets, toe rings, and girdles that matched or were even more ornate than the collars.

For years Naamah had made a point of telling Solomon how disgraceful, how vulgar and tasteless his Egyptian queen was. She pointed out that her off-the-shoulder dress was indelicate, her haughty manner rude, and her lack of consideration for Israel's religious customs impossible. "How very insensitive the Egyptian queen is," she often said, "to flaunt her cat god and his shrine right at the very door of the new temple."

It infuriated her that Solomon did nothing. He just listened to all she told him and did nothing. Consequently with the news that Tipti was plotting to put Jeroboam on the throne of Israel, she had decided to handle the matter herself. She knew that if she told Solomon, he would do as he had done in the past: listen and do nothing. She wanted action.

At the last minute she ordered her royal palanquin with the curtains embroidered with twin lions in gold thread. She would go in splendor befitting the queen of Israel.

Her indignation carried her with great confidence to the door of Tipti's palace. There she dismounted and with an arrogant flourish followed the footmen through the entryway.

Just inside the door to the atrium she stopped and gasped as she looked around in amazement. Tipti was nowhere to be seen but her maidens were sitting very prettily on cushions at one end of a lily pool. They were laughing and talking but held instruments as though ready to play at their queen's command.

Naamah noticed with growing envy the quiet charm and leisurely atmosphere. Tall, statuesque girls with nothing on but jeweled girdles and turquoise and gold necklaces stood with ostrich feathered fans near what seemed to be the queen's chair. Black Nubian eunuchs with jeweled slippers and scarlet and gold trousers waited with trays of food. Two peacocks with furled tails paraded before the shrine of the cat god.

Naamah suddenly wished she hadn't come. The opulence and splendor were unnerving. Her own clothes, the best she had, looked suddenly garish. Even her crown was overdone. No wonder Solomon had liked coming here to this tranquil retreat. It was evident that this woman had never found it necessary to resort to love potions and threats to win a bit of his time. She couldn't imagine this proud Egyptian queen making her way to the apothecary's shop for mandrakes to stimulate love or potions to ease her own sleeplessness.

"Come." The invitation was from a very young girl with a black, stylized wig, gold neck collar, and jeweled girdle. Naamah didn't respond. She was too shocked at the girl's state of undress. Instead she kept her eyes on the fine jeweled sandals the girl wore.

"Come," the girl repeated, "the queen will see you in her formal receiving room."

The receiving room was not large, but it gave one the impression of almost uncluttered opulence. A soft light came through alabaster openings in the wall and highlighted the polished marble floor and the decorated pillars set into the walls. The marble floor was mysteriously laid in various colors of marble making it appear carpeted. The odor of jasmine hung heavy on the air and seemed to come from two tall golden incense burners. A small table of carved ebony held pieces to one of the strange games played by Egyptians, and, finally, at the far end of the room were three chairs of carved ebony decorated in gold. The center chair was obviously a throne.

As Naamah came farther into the room, she was even more impressed with the utter barrenness. It was so different from the cushioned, tasseled, and carpeted disorder of her own apartments. It was like the austere simplicity she had found so distasteful in most of the furnishings of Solomon's new palace.

"You may be seated," the young girl said motioning to one of the chairs.

Naamah had never before experienced sitting upright in a chair, and she found it very uncomfortable. She didn't know what to do with her feet. Finally, with some effort, she folded her legs under her as though she were sitting at home on one of the cushioned divans. This was still terribly uncomfortable. The chair was hard and the seat too narrow. Once again Naamah felt a surge of anger that she, the queen, should be placed in this unpleasant situation.

She was jolted from her frustration by the distant cacophony of trumpets, the roll of drums, and shouted commands that echoed down the long hall through which she had just come. With no more fanfare, a host of laughing maidens came and took their places both behind and on each side of the throne. Two Nubians came to stand guard while several scribes and young slaves bearing large feathery fans advanced to the throne.

At last, framed in the doorway, was the Egyptian herself. Everyone fell on their faces with their hands outstretched along the floor, and Naamah felt renewed anger that there had been no such demonstration when she, the true queen, entered. She also found herself resenting the dazzling beauty of this woman.

She reached into the hidden pocket in her sleeve, touched the magical rock she had gotten just that morning from the priest of Moloch, and secretly cursed the Egyptian. "May she turn ugly as a warted toad, may her nails fall off and her teeth rot," she muttered pressing the stone between her thumb and middle finger.

Tipti with head held high swept into the room, ignoring everyone, including Naamah. As Naamah had feared, she sat down on her throne with her feet on the floor and her legs going straight down from the seat of the chair in the most uncomfortable manner. Naamah, seeing that this was indeed the proper way to sit on such a thing, stiffened and unfolded her legs so they also hung over the edge of the chair.

Tipti had her maidens arrange the fans, readjust the footrest, and then, finally, when everything was to her liking, looked at Naamah. Her small cherry mouth managed a forced smile, but her eyes were hard as olive pits.

"So you've come to visit me at last," she said.

Naamah hesitated only a moment, then she decided to plunge in and state her business and leave as soon as possible. "I've come to warn you," she said, "not to visit."

"Warn me?" the queen laughed. "What could you possibly have to warn me about?"

"Jeroboam. You must stop this foolish planning to make Jeroboam king. He's no king. He has no claim to the throne."

Tipti had taken in Naamah at a glance. The ill-fitting, dull clothes, the laughable way Naamah had tried to sit in the chair with her legs tucked under her, and yet her haughty—almost frightening—demeanor.

"I have no son and so I've decided to do as another Egyptian princess did long ago. I'll pick my own son."

"And so you've chosen Jeroboam."

"Exactly. Since this is my right, I've no need for advice from anyone." She sent a scathing glance at Naamah.

"Well, it's a waste of time for you to make such plans. Your Jeroboam has no credentials. To have credentials he must have the blessing of a prophet. He must be chosen by the God of Israel just as David was chosen."

Tipti smirked and looked down as she idly fingered the tassel on one of the cushions, "Oh, but he does have credentials. The same credentials that have always given Israel her kings."

"What credentials? He has none. He's the son of a humble man. A worker and that's all." Naamah was sitting up very straight; her face was flushed and her eyes bulged.

"Why, I would have thought someone would have told you."

"Told me what?" Naamah's eyes became mere slits as she studied her adversary.

"Told you that it has been predicted, by a priest from Shiloh, that Jeroboam will rule ten of the tribes and your son, Rehoboam, will be left with only one."

Naamah clutched her throat, rolled her eyes to the ceiling in disbelief, and then began to laugh hysterically. She grasped the arm of the chair and struggled to her feet. "What priest dared to tell you that?" she demanded with eyes flashing dangerously.

Tipti ignored her show of anger and smiled sweetly. "Why, the venerated old priest named Ahijah. He even made a big show of it by taking his own robe and tearing it into eleven pieces. He gave Jeroboam ten and kept the one that represents Rehoboam's share. He said the ten pieces of his cloak were for the ten tribes Jeroboam would rule."

"I don't believe it. Let me see the pieces. There aren't any." Her tone of voice was now sure and confident, and Tipti ordered one of her maidens to go fetch the stack of pieces representing the ten tribes.

No one spoke, but Tipti ducked her head and looked out from under her long lashes at Naamah and laughed. Naamah, feeling uncomfortable but sure of victory, tossed her head in the air and turned so the Egyptian couldn't see her face. All the time she was rubbing the evil stone and thinking dark thoughts that would poison Tipti if the charm really worked.

The young girl returned with a reed basket and handed it to the Egyptian.

"See," said Tipti pulling the pieces from the basket. "See, these are the ten tribes Jeroboam will rule. It has been prophesied."

"You lie." Naamah shouted as she tried to grab the pieces from Tipti. "You lie, no priest would tear his own robe."

Tipti laughed a harsh, bitter laugh. "He did. He prophesied that Jeroboam would rule ten tribes."

"Never, never, never." Naamah shouted as she tried to tear the pieces from the Egyptian's hands. "He'll never rule even one tribe. He's not of the house of David. It's impossible!"

161

Tipti held the pieces high over her head and called for the guards to take Naamah to the door.

With one lunge Naamah missed the pieces but grasped the elegant black wig of the princess and pulled. The wig came off in her hand and the Egyptian stood with her head bare and shaved as befitted a princess of Egypt. "You ugly little snake," Tipti cried as she charged after the quickly disappearing queen. "I'll have you flogged for this, this insult to Egypt!"

Naamah turned at the door. "A queen, a queen of Israel you will have flogged?" Her laughter, high and bitter, rang after her down the hall as she retreated to her waiting palanquin.

Tipti turned just in time to see her maidens stifling a laugh. "Anyone who laughs will be punished," she said. "Now go and bring me a new wig." She pointed to one of the older maidens who went hurrying from the room. Tipti walked with all the dignity of a pharaoh back to her throne and sat down as though nothing had happened. "I'll see that the queen from Rabbath Amman learns a lesson," she said loudly enough for those nearby to hear her.

On reaching the harem, Naamah went straight through her rooms to the small, intimate courtyard. She was furious. She had not thought the Egyptian would dare be so bold as to mention Jeroboam. To think that she had also claimed this upstart had credentials from the priest at Shiloh was the final indignity. She paced the floor wringing her hands and muttering beneath her breath curses and threats. "I'll ruin that woman," she said. "I'll make the name of Jeroboam so distasteful the king will have him killed and will banish her."

Of course she would have to tell Solomon. This time he would listen. This was no game of jackals and hounds. It was deadly serious. She stopped and let the ecstasy of sure revenge sweep over her. Here at last within her grasp was the weapon that would finally unseat the Egyptian in Solomon's heart. Moloch had given her the victory she had bought from him with the jewels.

It wouldn't be easy to get to see Solomon. He no longer would answer her summons no matter how urgent, and his guards had orders not to let her near him. It would take cunning, bribes, and a clever plan, but she must see him. She herself must deal the blow that would forever tear the Egyptian from his heart.

She paced the floor deciding first on one strategy and then another but each time finding them inadequate.

She clapped her hands for the maid. She was ready to retire. Now she could rest knowing that everything was almost in place to bring about the defeat of Tipti.

The maiden came, and at the same moment another idea, both vengeful and malicious, dawned upon Naamah. While she waited to see Solomon, this evil trick would be most amusing. Impulsively she snatched up one of the baskets harboring her most dangerous snake and handed it to the girl. "Here," she said, "take this to my chief eunuch and tell him to be sure it is delivered into the hands of the Egyptian queen with my compliments."

As she settled down for the night she had to stifle a laugh. She hadn't laughed in years, but she laughed now. Everything was going her way at last. Hopefully by morning the news would come that the Egyptian was dead.

16

When Yasmit found the potion from the apothecary's shop was of no effect, she devised another plan. It would cost a few pieces of her better jewelry, but it would be worth it. She was desperate. She had to do something, and this was her last chance.

She waited until Badget was off on another trip before trying to implement her scheme. She planned everything carefully. Terra must notice no change in the usual schedule and none of the servants must get suspicious.

When the morning finally came she rose early, lifted the loose tile in the floor of the storeroom, and reached down for a sandalwood box containing her most precious jewels. She pulled out necklaces and earrings, bracelets and hairpieces. Each item suddenly seemed too precious to waste on such a venture. One after another she put them back in the box, keeping out one silver necklace and a gold ring she had never worn.

She tied the jewelry in a small scarf and then slipped it into a deep pocket in her wide sleeve. She closed the lid of the box and put it back in its hiding place. She made her appearance in the courtyard just as Terra was coming out of her room.

She noticed with envy that Terra was already beginning to show evidence of the child she expected. She wanted to hate Terra, cut her down, make her life miserable, make her feel as bad as she herself felt, but Terra was too sweet, too trusting.

Terra came to her smiling, and gently led her to the shade of a grape arbor. "You are probably feeling nauseous," she said. "I'll have them bring you some nice fresh bread and barley gruel."

"Nauseous?" Yasmit asked.

"I'm just getting to where I feel a bit better now," Terra said. "It's always that way at the first." Yasmit began to understand that Terra was talking about her supposed pregnancy. It dawned on her that she would have to learn all the symptoms if she was serious about carrying this deception to its conclusion.

"I have felt faint," she said accepting the bread and earthen pot of gruel.

As soon as possible she excused herself saying she had to go again to the apothecary for more herbs. No one noticed that unlike her usual trips to the various shops she took no servant with her but went alone and seemed to be in a great hurry. Yasmit knew well the neighborhood she was heading for. She was familiar with every twist of the lane, each door that led into the cramped courtyards, and most of all the smell. It was not only the smell of grime, dirt, and unwashed children but the bitter smell of souring milk and aging cheese.

She had grown up in abject poverty and she hated the necessity of setting foot in this old section of the city. It was in the southwest corner not far from the Dung Gate and was called the section of the cheese makers. The odor proclaimed the occupation long before one reached the crumbling walls and moldering courtyards.

Yasmit's younger sister lived here as the second wife of the son of one of the cheese makers. She had eight children and was now pregnant with the ninth. She had wept when she realized that it would mean one more mouth to feed, one more child to crowd into the room she and her husband shared with the rest of their children. Yasmit had already broached a solution, but her sister had assured her that her husband wouldn't agree.

Now Yasmit was desperate and ready to implement any plan or strategy. The facts were evident, she needed a child and her sister had too many. The answer was simple. She would go with her sister to visit a distant relative and when they returned, the child would be hers. With enough gold all this could be accomplished without too much objection from the rest of her sister's family.

She let the wooden knocker down with a dull thud and then pulled the latch and let herself into the courtyard. Almost at once she was surrounded by a swarm of children. Several chewed on rounds of bread, but others looked hungry. They were all barefooted and wore scanty, moth-eaten tunics. The smaller ones wore no clothes at all and were covered with flies. Their hair was stiff with dirt.

Yasmit pulled the end of her mantle up over her nose. "Where's your mother?" she demanded sharply of one little boy as she pulled her skirt out of his grubby hand.

Several of the older children disappeared and returned with Yasmit's younger sister. Yasmit was shocked. It had been some time since she had last seen her sister, and she looked old and tired. She wore no kohl around her eyes or henna on her hands and feet and her hair fell loose under her mantle. There was no jewelry, and it was obvious to Yasmit that though the cheese business was good, it couldn't support adequately the needs of two wives and all these children, let alone the other brothers and their wives. She was at first appalled and then encouraged. Surely her sister would give up this child she carried for the jewelry she had brought.

There were at least five rooms around the courtyard. Yasmit knew that each of the brothers had a room for their wives and children and there was one room for the parents. The men slept on the roof in good weather and in bad, moved into the small storeroom which was also on the roof.

Yasmit followed her sister into her dismal room. She noticed the sleeping mats were neatly piled along the wall, and in the various niches there seemed to be a few articles of clothing. "You know why I have come," she said as she rejected her sister's offer of a mat to sit on and bread fresh from the outdoor oven.

"Yes, I know. I've been expecting you. Those potions from the apothecary seldom seem to work."

Yasmit ignored her remark and got right to the point. "Will your husband let you give up the child?"

"I must tell you truthfully. He doesn't want to agree, but he said that if you offered enough, I was to take it."

"And you, what about you, how do you feel?"

"You're my sister. Since I was a little girl I've always given you whatever you wanted."

"Then you'll agree."

"Just satisfy my husband and the child is yours."

Yasmit was ecstatic. "You must tell me everything. All the signs. I will have to appear to be pregnant."

"First, you have to remember not to take to your bed with the monthly flow."

"That's easy. I was past that a year ago. What else."

"At times you must appear nauseated, have strange yearnings for certain foods, and feel weak and exhausted."

"All of that is easy."

"But how will you appear to be getting larger?"

For a moment Yasmit looked puzzled. She looked down as her hands flew to her stomach and she compared her size to that of her sister. "Don't worry, I will manage. Perhaps my garment maker can be of some help."

"Don't trust her. You can't trust anyone."

"You're right. I'll think of something." She was about to turn toward the door when her sister reminded her.

"Nothing can be agreed on without my husband's consent." She held out her hand and Yasmit reached into the pocket of her sleeve and pulled out the bit of cloth holding the jewelry and untied it. She put the necklace into her sister's hand.

It was not enough. She added the ring. "Will this convince him?" she asked.

"He's very greedy. He thinks all the time of when his sons grow up and support him so he doesn't have to work. He thinks this will be another son and is very reluctant to give him up."

Yasmit hesitated. Her sister was gentle and sweet but the husband was a different matter. He was known to be a sharp bargainer. Quickly Yasmit took off three of her gold bracelets and then added her golden earrings. "Tell him I have given you even my own personal jewelry and that is all I have."

She could see that her sister was pleased. She waited while she stuffed the small treasure in one of the empty clay honey jars on a shelf and then went out into the courtyard. The odor of cheese and urine mixed with that of poverty and filth was almost stifling. She hurried to the gate, said a quick goodbye, and then breathed a sigh of relief as she heard the big wooden door close behind her.

She paused only a moment. "I must not lose Badget," she thought. "Without him I'd be right back here crowded into a corner of that ugly room. I must make this succeed." With that decided she hurried up the crooked, narrow streets to her own front door.

It would be easy to fool Badget, and Terra was too sweet to even imagine such plotting. As she figured it now, she and Terra would both have a child at the same time. What good fortune it would be if Terra's turned out to be a girl and hers was a boy. Then she would not only be the first wife in name but in fact. Everything would be like it used to be before he married Terra.

* * *

In the palace Naamah was growing impatient. She had tried every way she knew to gain an audience with the king. She knew he wanted nothing to do with her. He wouldn't accept her messengers nor would he send any sort of answer. Finally, in desperation, she devised a plan. If it worked she would be able at least to tell him of Jeroboam's plot and Tipti's treachery.

There was no time to waste. That same evening Naamah sought out the chief eunuch and demanded to see the record of the women called by the king within the past month. Glancing at the scroll, she saw that Solomon was calling certain ones quite regularly. "Who is the one he calls most often?" she asked.

"A princess from Sidon. She plays the kinnor and sings," the eunuch said.

Naamah thanked him and then pressed into his hand a pure gold necklace with Egyptian workmanship. "The next time he calls her, I wish to take her place."

"But . . ." the eunuch stammered in fright.

"Don't worry. I have news for the king he must hear. He'll have forgotten all about the girl when he hears what I have to tell him."

The eunuch looked again at the necklace lying in his hand. Even if he were dismissed, he could live a lifetime in quiet luxury with what this would bring. His hand closed on it, and Naamah, satisfied that he would do his part, went back to her apartments to wait for the summons.

It came sooner than she had expected, and there was no time to think of changing her clothes or fussing over her hair. She would have to go just as she was. She felt a slight twinge of anxiety at tricking the king, but when he heard the news, surely she would be forgiven.

She called for her ointment of jasmine. She had heard it was a favorite with the the young woman from Sidon. She had her maidens rummage in her chest of clothes until they found her wedding mantle all embroidered with gold and small pearls. She squeezed her feet into the jeweled sandals she had worn as a bride and last of all she called for a harp to be carried by her maid. At first glance, with only the alabaster lamps for light, she hoped the king would mistake her for the maiden from Sidon.

Just as she was ready to leave, one of her maidens came running to tell her the favorite from Sidon had fainted and then went into hysterics upon hearing that someone else was taking her place. Naamah stiffened. "Just be sure she gets no message to the king until I've seen him first."

With that she took the scepter from the eunuch and followed him up the stairs to the king's pavilion on the roof.

As the curtains parted she saw Solomon sitting with Rehoboam, Nathan, and a few of the tribesmen. She waited in the shadows until they were dismissed and then she took the harp from her maid and stepped inside letting the curtained covering of the door drop down behind her. She saw him smile, but it was a sad, remote smile compared to the joyful smile she remembered. For the first time since she had devised the plan she was fearful.

Straightening her shoulders and stiffening her resolve, she came forward and knelt with her face hidden in the deep folds of her mantle. She held the scepter out to him and felt him take it in one hand and then reach for her hand. "Come, my lovely Sidonian," he said. "I have forgotten your name but not your music or your other charms."

Naamah let him help her to stand and then she threw back her mantle. She saw him draw back with horror and aversion. He let her hand drop and was about to call the guards when she stopped him. "My lord," she said, "the Sidonian will come, but first I must tell you there is treachery afoot in the palace and neither you nor our son Rehoboam is safe."

Solomon was hesitant and cautious. "Treachery! What treachery can be worse than the treachery you are mixing most of the time?"

"My lord, don't make light of this. I love my son and will not see him bested."

"Yes, yes, it is true you do love your son."

"Now listen carefully. There's a plot to put Jeroboam on the throne either with the success of the coalition against you or after your death. You know this. You also know the plot originated with the Egyptian."

"Yes, yes," Solomon said waving his hand in impatience. "All of that has been told me. Is there anything new? That's all I care to hear."

Naamah knew she had to hurry or he'd not hear her through. "My lord, I've been to visit the Egyptian."

Solomon spun around and looked at her with utter disbelief registering in his eyes. "You what?"

"Visited the Egyptian and ..."

"Why should you do that?"

"Wait, I'll tell you. I went to explain to her how futile it was to back Jeroboam since he hadn't been anointed by a priest or chosen by Israel's God."

"And ..."

"She told me he had been both chosen and anointed. The priest at Shiloh, Ahijah, came clear to Jerusalem to announce to Jeroboam himself that he would be king over ten tribes."

Solomon's whole demeanor changed. He sank down among the cushions of his throne, his head in his hands. Suddenly her words broke through his despair. "Ten tribes," he said. "There are twelve. What of the other two?"

"One is the priestly tribe and the other is Judah. Judah and Jerusalem are all this liar says will be left for Rehoboam. Of course, you must kill the plotters immediately. Even your God can't save a man with a sword thrust through his heart."

"Are you sure the priest actually said Jeroboam would be king?"

"Quite sure. As the Egyptian told the story, this priest actually tore his garment into eleven pieces and gave ten of them to Jeroboam. I saw the pieces. I counted them. There were ten."

Solomon's face had turned deadly pale. He was remembering the encounter he had experienced in the temple. He had been searching ever since for the man that God would choose over him and his son. "So it is the upstart Jeroboam," he muttered.

"And the Egyptian. They are together in this," Naamah added.

"Ah, the Egyptian. That woman I've sold my soul and all Jerusalem to have." His laugh was bitter and cynical.

"Get rid of her. Have her exposed and beheaded."

"You have obviously forgotten she is a queen, a sister of the pharaoh."

"Then send her home in disgrace." As Naamah spat out her resentment Solomon was deep in thought. He didn't even notice that she had backed from his presence and slipped out through the curtains. She had accomplished what she had come for and now it was up to him to act.

Solomon mulled over every aspect of the situation. He dissected each word spoken to him in the temple and every revelation of Jeroboam's duplicity. Actually it was within his right to have the man killed for dining with his queen. He wondered now how often it had happened and how much could be explained by Tipti's wanting a son to compete with Naamah.

He thought of calling Jeroboam in and talking to him. What would they have to say to each other? Things had gone too far. Even the priest at Shiloh had spoken, and Solomon didn't doubt it was God's word that he spoke. It had the same ring to it as the message he had heard in the temple.

He finally determined that he could not deal harshly with Tipti. He must instead try to win her back. No doubt she was resenting all the other women that were taking up his time and crowding her out. He could ease things over with her, but Jeroboam had to go.

He would put out an order to have Jeroboam killed. Surely both Tipti and Jeroboam himself could expect nothing less. It would be punishment enough for Tipti to have her favorite removed. As to his being God's man, chosen to rule Israel, well, it was God's business somehow to protect him and it was Solomon's business to have him removed.

With that settled in his mind he called in Beniah, captain of his house guards, and ordered him to do away with Jeroboam as soon as possible. "The man has been plotting to join our enemies and take over the kingdom."

No sooner had Beniah left than Solomon began to think of what was likely to happen next. He always did this. It was a pattern he had developed years ago. Most people acted and then were surprised by the result, but Solomon went through each possibility in his mind until he was very seldom surprised. "A truly wise man avoids conflict whenever possible," he thought.

He could see that if Jeroboam were killed, Tipti would never forgive him. He would always be the enemy. There would be no reconciliation possible. At the same time he could see that he must deal harshly and strongly in this situation. Finally he determined that to keep Tipti from hating him he would have to warn her of what he intended to do. Of course this would make it possible for Jeroboam to be warned and escape, but there was nothing else to be done as far as he could see.

It was his custom to talk everything over with his counselors and fellow tribesmen. In this matter they probably wouldn't agree with his final decision, but he would at least have the benefit of their best thinking. He raised his hands and clapped three times. The guard appeared in the doorway. "Send for Nathan and the tribesmen," Solomon ordered. "I must consult with them."

When they arrived both Mattatha and Rehoboam were with Nathan and some of the older tribesmen. They scattered around the room and waited to hear what the king had to say. He told them everything he knew about the Jeroboam revolt but neglected to tell them he had gotten the news from Naamah. He also told them his solution, and they were in agreement with everything but objected to his warning Tipti. "She'll tell Jeroboam and he may escape," Rehoboam said.

"That is the chance we take, but at least the Egyptians will feel we have been fair. They were warned." Solomon held to his point and though most of them couldn't agree with him, they understood that he could do nothing else. "This is a delicate matter," he said. "Who shall I send with the message?"

It was finally agreed that one of the serving men should go, making it known that he was coming at Solomon's request.

That settled and seeing it was late, they were about to disband when the thud of hooves was heard on the pavement below. A series of questions by the guards and then muffled answers carried on the clear night air.

Within minutes three men appeared in the doorway. It was evident they had ridden hard and were greatly disturbed. As they came closer, Solomon recognized them as the men in charge of gathering tribute from the Edomites. He was more than annoyed that they had come at this time of day. He couldn't imagine any news worthy of such an intrusion. "Speak, speak," he ordered impatiently.

The men fell to their knees and only the leader spoke. "My lord, the Edomites have captured the queen of Sheba. They are holding her in their stronghold."

This was indeed news worth listening to, and Solomon was immediately interested. "For what purpose? Are you sure she's been captured? Maybe that is part of her plan to join the coalition against me."

"I don't think she is joining the coalition," the leader said.

"How do you know? What makes you think this?"

The three men looked at each other and finally the tallest spoke. "As far as we have heard, Hadad is demanding that she marry him, and she is objecting."

"Marry him!" Solomon was surprised and shocked. "Why is he doing that?"

"My lord, she's a beautiful woman," one of them ventured.

"Her support is needed for the coalition, I'll wager. She could be as ugly as a witch and he'd make love to her just to get her to join them." Solomon was now pacing nervously. "She's inside the Siq is she?" he asked.

"Most of the caravan waited outside while she went in for one of their fairs and celebrations, and now he won't let her back out."

"And how did you come by this news?"

"Your men stationed at the entrance to the Siq reported to us and we came directly to you."

"So this bit of southern baggage with the feet of a donkey may need my help."

"She must be desperate. The wedding is to be within a few days."

"Are you sure she is opposed to the marriage?"

"It seems so from what we've heard. She's a virgin, my lord."

Solomon laughed a jolly, amused laugh. "I've no doubt the woman's a virgin. Anyone with the feet of a donkey could hardly be anything else. However, we just may need to rescue her."

"Hadad is calling in the tribesmen from the desert."

"Ah, then we must be prepared to act quickly. He's always planning some revolt. Alert your men in case they are needed. We need more information before we rush in and stir up Hadad's hornet's nest."

As soon as they were gone Solomon again grew thoughtful. "It's hard to know what to make of such news. This may very well be a carefully contrived plan to lead my men into a trap. The Edomites are good at that. We won't move until we know exactly what is happening."

* * *

Tipti was lounging near her pool watching the brilliant fish glide and float through the water. They had been a recent gift from her brother the pharaoh and she found it entertaining to sit and watch their slow, graceful movements. Though she seemed relaxed, her mind was actively at work plotting the next step in her plan to bring Jeroboam to the throne.

She heard the sound of running and then a loud knocking on her door. Then her gateman was asking questions. She hoped he would send the man away, as she wasn't in the mood to deal with news of any kind. She leaned over and looked in the pool. One of her earrings was missing. She clapped her hands for her maid and was surprised when no one came right away.

"Sureeyah, where is Sureeyah?" she called in a slightly irritated tone.

The other maidens by the lily pool held their breath. Tipti didn't have much patience with a maid's dalliance when she was needed. They were just looking from one to the other in nervous anticipation of the queen's outburst of anger when Sureeyah rushed into the room and hurried to the queen and fell at her feet.

"My queen. I have bad news. I must see you alone."

Tipti never liked bad news. She didn't really believe there was bad news for a queen. She should be able to manage things so nothing could happen that wasn't to her liking. Now she looked at Sureeyah and plucked a big, ripe grape from a golden dish before she made up her mind to hear what she had to say.

"Where is this news from?" she asked as she leisurely flicked a fly from the grapes on the tray.

"My queen, the messenger was from the king and the news is of Jeroboam." At this the queen sat up very straight and her eyes became narrow and calculating. She nodded to those sitting near her and they quickly got up and moved away.

"What news of Jeroboam do you have?" she demanded.

"Solomon has declared Jeroboam a traitor and has sent Beniah to execute him."

"Execute him!" Tipti jumped to her feet and paced back and forth. She knew that if Solomon had already given the order it would only take Beniah a short time to find the young man, and there was no doubt that he would put a swift end to him. Tipti also quickly surmised that Solomon was giving her an equal chance to rescue him. Now it was her wits against Beniah. She knew where Jeroboam was, and she knew she would have to go to him and persuade him to flee. He wouldn't even have time to go home to say goodbye to his mother. In fact, he must not go home, as that would be the first place Beniah would go to look for him.

"Get my mule and have it ready to go. Alert my men I want them with me." The queen knew she would have to go in disguise. She'd even have to ride the despised mule. She quickly changed clothes with Sureeyah and was soon on her mule riding out the valley gate.

She found Jeroboam just where she had known he would be, in his small olive grove supervising the pickers. She hurriedly told him all that she knew and then she cautioned him, "You must not go home. No doubt Beniah is there all ready. You'll have to flee from here just as you are."

"Where am I to go?" Jeroboam asked.

"Why, to my brother in Egypt. You can march with him when he comes against Solomon."

"And what if he doesn't march against the king?"

"Then you'll wait. Make plans, and when the king dies, you'll be ready to challenge Rehoboam."

"And the pharaoh, your brother, will he accept me?"

"Here, take this and he'll understand everything." Tipti lifted a golden chain with her own cartouche hanging from it and placed it around Jeroboam's neck. The strange drawings on it spelled out her name. Not Tipti but the formal Egyptian name by which her brother always called her.

Jeroboam held it in his hand for a few moments and seemed to study its meaning. Then he tucked it inside his robe lest it be a temptation to robbers. He seemed to be stunned by the sudden turn of events. He had pictured everything so differently. "Then we'll see what comes of a priest's predictions," he said finally.

Tipti reached into one of the saddlebags and drew out some nondescript pieces of cloth. "Here are the ten tribes promised you by that priest from Shiloh. Keep them. It's a fair prediction that will give you much comfort while you wait in Egypt. Now, you must go. Forget the olive harvest. You have bigger things to tend to. Beniah must not catch you or all our dreams will come to an end."

Jeroboam stooped and kissed the hem of her garment, then looked at her as though wanting to remember this moment during all the time he would be in exile. Finally, glancing around at his grove of trees, he shrugged and started off on a shepherd's path that would take him to Bet Shemesh, Gath, and then the River of Egypt, where he would be safely out of Solomon's hands.

* * *

It was late that night, as Solomon sat with his brother Nathan, that he finally received Beniah's report. "Jeroboam has fled to Egypt."

Those words were like Beniah—short and to the point—and yet to Solomon they fell like a hammer of doom. "So," he said to Nathan, "Jeroboam is the man. If Beniah had killed him I would have known to look for someone else."

Nathan had heard of Solomon's fateful encounter in the temple and he had found little comfort to give him. It was painful to watch the depression that came down over him like a dark shadow. "All my work, everything I've done means nothing. A fool will inherit my throne, my palace, my temple. An ambitious builder will be given most of my kingdom. The riches I have amassed will do nothing for my people but attract thieves and robbers like the pharaoh. How could things have gone so wrong?"

"You mustn't imagine that the bad erases the good. The beauty you have brought to all of us can never be destroyed. The glory you have given Israel will be talked about for generations."

"But Nathan, I started with so much promise and will end so infamously. Where did I go wrong? I know the foreign wives I married and their temples have been like spittle in God's face. But with them I've kept peace. It's not easy to be wise and be king."

They sat in silence so profound that neither of them noticed Solomon's pet hedgehog that edged out from behind one of the cushions and began to tiptoe across the carpet toward the tray of sweets. Nathan saw him first and was startled. "What's that animal doing in here?" he asked.

"I'm seeing if I can make friends with him," Solomon said. "He's quite a clever fellow. Causes no disturbance and will eat insects and spiders."

"Have you tamed him?" Nathan asked.

"I haven't learned his ways yet. But sometimes if I sit very still he watches me out of his beady little eyes as though trying to decide whether he'll let me stay or get rid of me."

Nathan laughed. "How you have time for all these animals I don't understand. What interests you about them?"

Solomon held out his hand and the small barbed animal edged forward and then back as though trying to decide whether it was safe to trust this giant being that was trying to enter his small world. "Have you no curiosity, Nathan? God made all these little creatures. They're all constructed differently—and no matter how we try we can't make anything like them. I can build with stone and wood, gold and silver, but can't make even a flea."

Nathan was impressed. "Just as a man loves to have his work admired, I'm sure it must please our God to have His small masterpieces noticed."

Just as quickly as he had been diverted by the little hedgehog so now he became morose again. "I wonder how far Jeroboam has gotten. Do you imagine he is sleeping right this moment on some rock and seeing visions like our ancester Jacob?"

"Solomon, you mustn't let this thing poison your life. It's draining you of all the good things that are still yours."

"I see no good things. I see only failure and I don't know why I've failed. I tried so hard."

"You may as well go on and say it. You're angry at God. You're almost afraid to think it, but you can't see that He's been fair. Am I right?"

Solomon didn't answer, but Nathan could tell by the quick way he turned away and concentrated on the billowing cloth of the ceiling that he had hit the root of the problem. "You can't even bring yourself to say it, but you're thinking that you've never committed adultery like our father, you've never had a man killed to gratify your own selfish lust like our father. You've obeyed most of the law scrupulously and asked forgiveness and made the proper sacrifices when you did wrong. Most of all you did the one thing God commissioned you to do—you built a temple for His name. And such a temple you have built. He need never be embarrassed by some idol's having a grander dwelling."

"Yes, I have tried so hard, and yet He holds against me my foreign wives and the small temples they've built. I've never put another god before Him. He's always been first."

"And I'm right that you've been puzzled by these things."

Solomon didn't answer but seemed to be watching as the little hedge-

177

hog burrowed again under the nearby cushion and disappeared.

"Look," Nathan said, "perhaps it's a bit like you and the hedgehog. You hold out your hand and are delighted when the little creature trusts you enough to come toward you. If he would actually trust you enough to come eat from your hand, you'd be ecstatic. Am I right?"

"I don't see ..."

"Maybe God is like you with the hedgehog. He treasures most of all our responding to Him."

Solomon was very quiet. The lamps flickered and the incense grew almost oppressive. Finally he turned as though dismissing all such serious thoughts and lightly said, "You mean I've been so busy doing things for Him I don't even know who He is anymore."

"Something like that," Nathan said.

The spell was broken and Solomon stood up. "Right at this moment the queen of Sheba could be deciding our fate. If she joins Hadad and Shishak, it would be a very strong, unbeatable combination."

"That 'if' makes all the difference."

"The way things are going, I have no illusions. This could be the end of everything."

"On the other hand it could be the beginning of a new start, a new opportunity."

Solomon reached out and hugged his brother. "I need large doses of your optimism," he said. "These days I'm inclined to see the dark side, the hopelessness of everything."

The two left together, and when they parted at the base of the marble steps, Nathan noticed that his brother walked with his head held high and a hint of the old debonair spirit that made him such a magnetic personality.

*B*iqis paced the cold stone floor of Hadad's winter quarters. She realized she was in serious trouble. It was increasingly obvious that she should have known better than to have been enticed into the Edomites' stronghold. She hadn't seen any danger until it was too late. She had made a mistake in thinking that by leaving most of her men outside, Hadad wouldn't dare pressure her in any way. However, there was no way she could have known the nature of the secret entryway into this rockbound kingdom.

She went over and over again in her mind every aspect of the situation from the very beginning. Haded was such a dashing, attractive ruler. He was every bit a desert prince, and yet he had all the polish of Egypt. He had been raised there and even his speech had an Egyptian flavor to it.

He also had adopted some of the charming ways of the Egyptians. She had first been impressed by the riders he had sent on a full day's journey into the desert to escort her to his palace. When they had come to the Siq, a long, narrow cleft between high rock cliffs that led into his fortress, it had seemed perfectly natural to ride in as the prince suggested. This cleft was just wide enough for donkeys or camels to go through single file and it was easily defended by a few men.

Once in the Siq she was made uneasy by the hawks and ravens that dove and swooped overhead emitting their incessant screams that echoed and bounded off the walls of the passageway like voices of doom. She experienced further alarm when she realized how long the Siq was and how much time it took to go from one end to the other. Then finally, when she came out into the valley itself and discovered that it too was surrounded by high cliffs of red rock, she was convinced she had made a serious mistake.

She tried to reassure herself that everything was all right since she had left most of her army and wares outside, taking with her only her own personal bodyguards, serving maids, and retainers as well as her cousin,

Rydan. She had thought it best to separate Il Hamd and Rydan lest they plot against her while she was gone.

How could she have guessed that Hadad cared nothing for her treasures, and was instead obsessed with forcing her to join the confederation against Solomon. Still worse, on seeing her he had quickly revised his plans to include marrying her and keeping her right here in this fortress as his ally.

By the time she understood Hadad's plans and the nature of the rockbound city he ruled, it was too late. There was no way out and no way her men could rescue her.

"You needn't try to escape," Hadad said. "I've everything carefully planned. I've already sent word to your caravan that you have changed your mind about going to Jerusalem. Instead, you are staying right here and marrying me."

"But . . ." she tried to object.

Hadad leaned back among the cushions of his divan and smiled a slow, calculating smile. "You saw the Siq. No one can enter without my permission, and once someone is inside, they can't leave against my will. If you are thinking of escaping, it is no use. My men are everywhere."

"You pay tribute to Solomon, and he'll see that I'm rescued," she countered indignantly.

"Of course, if he knew, I suppose he could rescue you. But you'll be married before word reaches him."

"I've heard that Solomon knows everything. Even the evil Jinn, ghouls, and demons are supposed to obey him. Aren't you afraid of him?"

Hadad's face clouded over. "He's my worst enemy and for years I've sworn to get even. Now with the coalition, Shishak of Egypt, Rezon of Syria, and you with your army from Sheba, we can utterly defeat him. I'll not let anything stand in my way."

"So you think that by marrying me you'll have the support of Sheba?"

"At least you won't be able to join him."

"What makes you think I'd join him?"

At this Hadad appeared nervous. "It's well-known that women can't resist him. You'd be no different from the rest."

"So you think to win me over by holding me captive in this disgraceful manner and marrying me against my will. Well you are wrong. Even if

Solomon doesn't rescue me, certainly Ilumquh, the god of my people, will deliver me," she said tossing her head with a bravado she didn't feel.

Hadad laughed. "If he should try to rescue you, he would find the god of my people is greater and stronger."

Bilqis was immediately alarmed. "And who is the god of your people?" she asked.

"Dusares," he answered.

Bilqis's eyes grew thoughtful. "Du means 'Lord;' but what does sares mean?"

Hadad glanced at her in astonishment. His women were not interested in such things. He didn't like it that a woman should ask about the name of a god. She had no need to know such things. He remembered just in time, however, that he wanted to impress this queen, and so he answered, "Shara or Seir is what these mountains are called. He is Dusares, lord of all these mountains."

"Our god is Ilumquh. He is the shining being that rises at dusk and gives us light in the darkness, brings seeds to life, and gives us a way of numbering our days."

Hadad smirked. "I have studied the gods of Egypt. Ra is greatest of them all. Without his shining we would be in darkness all the time." He said this in such a smug way that Bilqis felt he was dismissing Ilumquh as unimportant.

"If Ra is so great and powerful, why is he not the god of the Edomites?"

Hadad again shifted uneasily. "This isn't a matter for one as beautiful as you. Don't concern yourself. Leave it for the priests and tribal leaders."

Now Bilqis felt insulted. "You speak to me as though I were only a woman," she said trying to control her voice. "I'm not a woman, I assure you; I'm a queen."

For a moment Hadad was taken aback. He looked at her closely and then broke out into a hearty laugh. "Of course you are a queen, and it is fitting for you to ask such things. Now I remember. You are supposed to be traveling to the all-wise king in Jerusalem to ask him questions that will tell you what is truth."

Though he seemed to be saying the right things, Bilqis felt that underneath he was still amused that a woman should ask about one of the gods.

"Truth is important," she said. "How can we worship until we know who is the true god?"

Hadad was amazed. He had never thought very deeply about such matters. "Why, it's quite simple. In Egypt I worshiped Ra and now that I am here I worship Dusares."

"Can I see this god of yours?"

Again Hadad shifted uneasily. "He is in the form of a white stone, very sacred. The priests guard him night and day. They may not let a stranger see him."

Bilqis was now quite interested. "He is a white stone? Your god is a white stone? You can touch him and could even crush him if you wanted. Ilumquh is totally unreachable. He's above the tallest trees and the highest building. He rules in every place. Each night I see him no matter how far from home I might be. He is much greater than your white stone."

Now Hadad was angry. "Have you ever touched Ilumquh? No, of course not. Well I have touched Dusares. No matter what god or gods ride by in the sky, Dusares rules here in Seir."

Bilqis felt a chill of fear. It was true that not only was she hemmed in by these mountains but Hadad's god seemed to be in complete control.

In desperation she began to devise a plan of escape. Her only hope was somehow to get a message to Solomon in Jerusalem. Hadad was his vassal and still answerable to him.

She went over in her mind each person in her company and found that only Rydan could manage such a feat. He would not only have to escape from this stronghold but he would then have to find his way up to Jerusalem. She wondered also if she could trust him. It was entirely possible that he would join Il Hamd and together they would seize her throne and ride back to rule Sheba. The time was short and she would have to act quickly.

Once she had determined Rydan was her only hope, she had to figure out a way to see him alone long enough to devise a plan. Hadad or his servants were with her constantly, and it wasn't until the night of an elaborate banquet held out under the stars that she was finally able to talk to her cousin.

Rydan seemed surprised when she singled him out to sit beside her. She noticed that he was nervous and could hardly eat. He answered her questions with deference and was overly courteous. He no longer seemed to be the strong-willed, insolent young man she had so disliked in the past.

The opportunity to speak privately to him came unexpectedly when Hadad was called away on business. "My cousin," she said, "you know that we are all being held prisoner here. Hadad is now insisting on marrying me and forcing me not only to join him in the conspiracy against Solomon but to stay right here as his wife." She could see by Rydan's expression that he was horrified. "I must find someone who can escape and get word to Solomon. Can I trust you to do this?"

"There's a camp of Solomon's men just outside the Siq," he whispered. "They're stationed there to keep the Edomites from doing anything rash. Each day a small battery of mercenaries rides through the Siq to check on them. If I can get to them, maybe there is some hope."

"There isn't much time. Within three days Hadad has told me there will be a great sacrifice and immediately after that the wedding."

The next morning as Solomon's guard marched through the Siq into the city some of them noticed an old woman dressed in rags begging for alms. She held out her hand and kept her face covered as though she was embarrassed to be engaged in such a humble occupation. Several of the guards were incensed to find her sitting so close to their station, and they accosted her, insisting she leave and find someplace else to beg.

Strangely enough, no one seemed to notice that when the soldiers left and rode out through the Siq, the woman had also disappeared.

That night when Hadad again prepared a feast and entertainment, Bilqis noticed that Rydan was missing. She breathed a sigh of relief knowing that he must have found a way to leave the fortress, but she doubted that he could get help in time.

* * *

The sacrifice to Dusares was planned to assure the success of Hadad's plans to defeat Solomon. He insisted that Bilqis be present. "Tomorrow," he said, "you will come with the men of Edom to the high place, and there you will witness the power of Dusares. It has never been permitted before for a woman to witness this ceremony, but then, never before has a queen been my guest."

Bilqis knew instinctively that he was taking her with him so there would be no chance of her escape and to impress upon her his dedication and commitment to the coalition and their plans. "This sacrifice," Bilqis asked, "what will it do for you?"

"You'll see. After the sacrifice, the wedding, the victory over Solomon, everything will happen as I want it."

"Can the god of a white stone do all of this?"

"I sacrifice to Ra of the Egyptians also. Ra and Dusares are stronger than the God of Israel."

"And me. How do you think your god can force me to marry you?"

Hadad laughed. "That's the easiest. You are here in Dusares' territory. Your god has no power to protect you here."

Bilqis was frightened but still curious. "What sacrifice will give you such power?"

"You'll see. However, I must warn you," he added, "if it were found out that you were a woman, even though you are a queen, it could cost you your life. I'll give you a man's garb, cloak, and head covering. You'll stay near me, in my company. Of course you can't speak or ask questions, and no matter what you see, you mustn't cry out or object." He looked at her as though he were enjoying her discomfort.

That night she slept fitfully as she wondered whether Rydan had succeeded in getting to Jerusalem and if he had been able to deliver the message. There wasn't much time left. Once the sacrifice was carried out, the wedding would soon follow.

She wondered at the mysterious way in which Hadad had talked of the sacrifice. He seemed to be so sure his god would free Edom from Israel's control. The very fact that women weren't allowed made her suspicious. Could it be that she was about to see some dark horror? She would have to summon all her courage not to flinch or cry out no matter what was involved.

* * *

The altar of the Edomites was at the top of one of their high stone cliffs. Bilqis, standing beside Hadad, shivered in the predawn darkness and wondered how they were to scale this sheer cliff. As the priests began to light torches, she saw a narrow passage in between two rocks that led to steps cut in the rock.

The climb was steep and the steps worn. Bilqis had only gone halfway up when she felt exhausted. She saw Hadad and the rest only as dark shadows, and there was no sound but a steady chanting of magical phrases. She wished she had asked more questions. As this involved some vow Hadad was about to make, it could be something very serious. She knew that Hadad would be willing to pay almost any price for freedom from Israel.

They arrived at the top and fanned out in the space behind the altar. Remembering Hadad's warning, she edged away from him and off to one side where she could see everything but wouldn't be easily seen. As the sky brightened she saw that there were dark outlines of two men, bound, standing in the well-defined circle near the raised area that was entirely covered with gold. Four steps led up from the golden platform to a low but broad limestone altar.

She was vaguely aware of chanting and priestly rituals. Somewhere above them she could hear the flapping of giant wings, see exaggerated shadows on the rock face as huge birds circled and swooped and at times gave out the same wild call that had first startled her in the canyon.

Across the valley beyond the dark mountain peaks, the sky grew crimson. One of the captives had been drawn by lot and was then given a drink from a golden ewer. The chanting ceased. There was only the steady, low insistent beat of drums. Every eye rested on the dark form. He was still only an outline against the sky. His features were blurred and indistinct. Someone coughed nervously. It became evident that everything must be ready before the sun rose.

There was an audible sigh of relief as the victim sank into the priest's hands and then was lowered to the altar. Just as the sun rose there was the glinting flash of a knife and the body lay motionless, head hanging over the altar's side and a stream of blood flowing down into a catch basin.

Bilqis had not been able to take her eyes from the awful sight. She found her lip sore from biting into the edge of her cloak. In Marib, back in her father's time, there had been a threat of famine, and a human being had been sacrificed. She had never really thought about it before, but now she wondered about many things. Would this really accomplish what Hadad wanted? Were the gods pleased with such devotion? Could they be bought with such sacrifices?

There was a slight stir as Hadad stepped up to the altar's edge, dipped his finger in the blood, and wiped it on the four edges of the altar. Then in a loud, militant voice he cried, "O mighty Dusares of Seir and Ra of Egypt, by this blood I pledge to free your fortress of Edom from Israelite bondage. I'll bring Solomon down to defeat. See that his eyes are put out, his sons slain, his wives desecrated, his house become an abode for vultures, and his temple ashes." He paused, and then in a lower, more controlled voice he pled, "Grant me success, grant Edom success, and grant Egypt success. May our enemies be as dung."

Bilqis cringed. If Dusares and Ra were really as strong and as powerful as Hadad thought, then there was no hope. She stood transfixed by the horror of it all until suddenly, like a great tidal wave, there was first a rough, gutteral sound and then bursting upon the morning air the militant shout of men waving their arms, stomping their feet, and shouting "Edom, Edom" over and over again.

Quickly the solemnity of the past hour changed to jubilation. Men rushed past Bilqis shouting and laughing in a hurry to get down to the valley, where the festivities were to take place. She edged to the side of the cliff and turned her face to the wall lest they see that she was a woman and almost faint with loathing. When all but the priests had gone, she turned to find her way back down the worn steps. She hugged the rough cliff side and tried not to look at the altar that now was flooded with bright sunlight that glinted and flashed from the golden platform. Though she didn't look at the altar, she couldn't ignore the sight of great ugly vultures that were swooping in and landing, ready to tear apart the sacrifice.

With averted eyes and trembling lips she made her way down the steps to the oleander grove where she had left her retainers and her palanquin. Without a word she stepped in and let them pull the curtains while she leaned back exhausted and terrified. "This Hadad would stop at nothing to accomplish his goal," she thought. "Even if Rydan can get to Solomon and gives him the message, there seems very little hope that anything can be done."

Hadad was waiting for her as she dismounted near the guest rooms.

"The vow has been recorded, the sacrifice made, and tomorrow we will have the wedding." His smile was smug and calculating.

"I'll need more time. Queens can't be married like common women." She tried not to let her anger show.

186

Hadad laughed. "It's the same everywhere. Women are always reluctant to marry, always finding excuses. They have no idea of what's best for them."

Bilqis started to leave but was quickly stopped as Hadad reached out and grasped her arm and swung her around to face him. "You'll find me to be a tireless lover. I'm a passionate man." His eyes glinted with lust and Bilqis shrank from him.

"I'm afraid you'll find me quite cool to your ardor. I am a queen, not a simple village maid." She pulled away from him and joined her maidens as they mounted the steps to the guest house. Behind her she could hear Hadad's laughter. He hadn't taken anything she said seriously. He had no doubt but that his plan would work.

* * *

Bilqis spent a sleepless night. She paced up and down, restlessly looking out at the moon and wondering if there was a moon god named Ilumquh. If there was, did he care that his queen was hopelessly trapped in this small rockbound city? She thought briefly of Il Hamd and realized that he could say nothing to comfort her. She no longer believed he knew any more about the mystery of the gods than she did.

The next morning there was still no news from Rydan and the wedding was to take place at sundown. She stalled for time, but it was useless. Each hour was now bringing her closer to her fearful fate. She stormed and raged and threatened but knew that without some miracle, Hadad would have his way.

Just as she had given up all hope, there was a stirring among the maidens. They looked startled and whispered among themselves. Half of them disappeared and later reappeared looking nervous and frightened. Then to everyone's surprise a young man plunged through the doorway and shouted, "The queen. Our king, Hadad, is calling for the queen."

Bilqis stood up and summoned her maidens, then, with head held high and a defiant look in her eye, she followed the young man out into the open courtyard. She had gone hoping to confront Hadad and demand her release. She had her threats prepared and her bargaining organized. But she was taken aback by the sight that met her.

Hadad wasn't anywhere to be seen. Instead, her own cousin Rydan stood in the midst of the courtyard with what seemed an army of light. Their helmets were of leather trimmed with glistening metal, the breastplates of highly polished brass, and their greaves of brass laced with leather thongs. Their shields were of pure beaten gold that sparkled and glistened in the sun. Over and around them, rippling in the breeze, were brightly colored banners embroidered with lions rearing to attack. It was obvious that these valiant warriors were Solomon's men and they had come to rescue her.

"How did you get through the Siq without being detected?" she asked.

Rydan pointed to the cliffs above them, and for the first time she saw that there were men standing with drawn bows pointed at the king's palace and the open courtyard where the wedding was to have taken place. "Solomon understands these scoundrels and knows how to handle them," Rydan said. "When I got to Jerusalem, the king had already been told of Hadad's treachery and was sending his men to rescue you. This isn't the first time he has had to put Hadad in his place."

*　*　*

By dusk the queen was back in her own camp with the familiar tent over her head and the whole episode of the last few days seeming like a bad dream. She had honored Rydan and elevated him to one of her chief counselors. He would be invaluable, she decided, in dealing with the Hebrews.

"We're to go on to Jericho tomorrow," he told her. "The king has a winter palace there. When it is cold in Jerusalem they say it is warm and pleasant in Jericho. He knows you will need to rest before you make the last part of your trip up to Jerusalem."

"Then you actually saw Solomon?" she asked.

"No, it's very difficult to see him. I saw one of his brothers. A young man named Nathan. He will also be the one to meet you in Jericho."

"And Jerusalem. Did you go to Jerusalem?"

"Yes, my queen, I went to Jerusalem, and it is all they have said and more, much more."

"Tell me, what was it like?"

Rydan struggled for words and finally said, "If I told you, you wouldn't believe me. You'll have to see it to understand. It was like nothing I've ever seen before."

The queen was suddenly tired. She needed to rest if she was to make the long trip to Jericho on the next day. She decided to wait and see for herself.

* * *

Late that night Solomon was in the small quarters of his chief clerk looking over the lists of men that were to send supplies to the palace for the next month. He was holding the parchment and studying the lists when to his surprise it was snatched from his hands rather roughly. At the same time there was the familiar chattering exuberance of his little monkey. The agile creature bounded from the low floor-level writing desk to the window lattice and then to the lintel above the door.

The clerk was obviously frightened of the boisterous little animal, and he cringed in a corner while Solomon, losing all dignity, stood begging and coaxing the little fellow to come down. The monkey turned his head and ignored all pleading. Several pages heard the commotion and came to see what was happening. They also tried and couldn't coax him down.

Finally some of the older counselors crowded into the small room to see what was happening. "He's frightened now. We'll never get him down like this." Solomon was obviously enjoying the challenge. "We must find something the little creature likes more than the parchment. He'll never give it up otherwise."

The men looked at each other and shrugged. "Who would know what a strange creature like that would find more interesting?" one of them asked.

"Why, it's quite simple. He loves a juicy coconut. Run, page, and crack one open for him. You'll see, he'll probably snatch it out of your hand."

When the page brought the coconut and the men saw how quickly the monkey dropped the parchment and sprang down to claim his prize, they whispered among themselves, "See, it's uncanny how he manages the animals."

Solomon sent one of the pages to bring Nathan to him. There were delicate matters to be decided, and he needed his brother's help. He had received word just a short time before the episode in the clerk's quarters that his men had freed the queen of Sheba and she would be heading for

Jericho the next day. He wanted Nathan to go to Jericho and welcome her and then bring her to Jerusalem with all the pomp and splendor she would certainly expect.

When Nathan came to Solomon's bedchamber he found him strangely morose.

"This queen from Sheba," he said, "will be in Jericho within the next few days. I want you to go and make her welcome in my winter palace. Let her rest there for a few days. She probably needs it after the ordeal at Petra."

"She may be beautiful," Nathan said.

"What difference does that make?"

"I've never known you to avoid a beautiful woman."

"But this one . . ."

"I know, I know. You told me about her feet. Of course I don't believe it."

"Then you'll go?"

"You know you can depend on me but I have a better idea."

"A better idea?"

"It's quite important that the queen see Solomon at his best. I think you should go and meet her in Jericho without the crowds and curious members of the court. You need to get away and Jericho is such a pleasant change."

"It won't be pleasant with a queen to entertain. No, I'd rather you go. I'm not my usual self these days."

With that Nathan was dismissed, but he went away feeling it would be much better for Solomon to ride down to the lovely winter palace and meet this queen there. She held their fate in her hands. If she sided with Solomon's enemies, all would be lost. On the other hand . . . Nathan knew there was no use thinking about it once Solomon had made up his mind.

18

*T*o Nathan's surprise, Solomon finally decided to go down himself to his winter palace in Jericho to meet the queen. The brothers had stopped by the treasury after the early morning sacrifice and Nathan had reminded him, "This is going to be a very important visit. You need to go yourself. If it goes well, the queen of Sheba will stand with you against the coalition. With Jeroboam in Egypt just waiting for your overthrow, you'll need all the support you can get."

Solomon knew that what Nathan said was true, but there had been one question bothering him and it had blotted out all other plans and strategies. "If God has rejected me as king," he asked, "is it even worth trying? Won't everything I do fail?"

"The kingdom is not to be lost during your lifetime. It would also be well to remember that some of the greatest blessings have come through those who have failed but didn't give up."

Solomon was unconvinced. "Name some," he said.

"Well, Abraham took Hagar because he didn't quite believe the promise; Jacob stole his brother's birthright; Joseph was such a braggart he got thrown out by his brothers; Moses killed an Egyptian and . . ."

"Enough. That's enough. What does that have to do with my going down to the winter palace in Jericho?"

Solomon was so serious, Nathan had to laugh. "Well, sometimes it's hard for God to bless people when they sit around depressed."

"So you think I might miss some good thing if I don't personally go greet this queen?"

"I don't know. I'm just saying that if you want blessings, you have to be looking for them, expecting them almost."

* * *

Solomon had already ordered vast preparations to be made for the queen's visit. A camping area had been set aside for her caravan on Mount Olivet, a new house had been added to and refurnished for her within the palace gardens, the royal treasury had been searched for appropriate gifts, and several tours of the chariot cities planned. All these preparations had been made by Solomon's able body of servants so that Solomon had done very little real thinking about her visit.

Now Nathan's words struck a chord of hope. He didn't even know what he was hoping for, he just knew that he would go down to Jericho and meet this queen who had traveled so far to see him. "Badget says she is coming to ask questions. She wants to know what truth is. Have you ever heard of a woman thinking about truth?"

Nathan laughed. "Not in all your harem is there one woman asking such a question. This queen must be unusual."

"Probably ugly, balding, and remember the feet."

"She can't be that bad. Hadad was trying to marry her."

Solomon shrugged and smiled. He didn't say any more, but when he returned to his palace, he ordered preparations for the visit to the winter palace in Jericho.

The winter palace was Solomon's favorite retreat. Because the weather was always temperate, the palace was open to the sun and fresh air. There were covered walkways and latticed balconies that opened onto a lush formal garden. There were fountains and pools shaded by palm trees, while every now and then a peacock could be seen with feathers unfurled against the deep green foliage.

As soon as he arrived he found a message waiting for him. The queen had accepted his invitation to be a guest in the winter palace and she would be arriving that evening. However, as she was feeling indisposed she asked that there be no ceremony.

He wondered what she meant by "no ceremony" and finally concluded that he need not order a great feast or plan a celebration. He would simply meet her, welcome her, and put her into the hands of his chief steward and the servants who would carry out her slightest wish.

Later that day, just before sunset, he was on one of his balconies talking to some emissaries from Rabbath Amman when a wild flourish of trumpets announced the queen's caravan. He quickly dismissed the men and went to view the arrival. He noticed that she had left a large part of her entourage outside the city and brought only her own serving maidens, some counselors, and her bodyguard with her.

It was easy to recognize her howdah. Solomon had never seen anything like it. It was covered in gold embroidered cloth set about with precious stones, and the harness and fittings on her camel were all of gold and rubies. Light from the setting sun glinted and sparkled from its dazzling surface until it seemed almost a vision of ethereal radiance.

Solomon was fascinated. He moved out to the balustrade of the balcony so he could see her when she dismounted. "What kind of creature must it be that would come wrapped in such a splendid cocoon?" he thought.

He hurried down the marble stairs and then walked with dignity befitting his kingly position out to the steps leading down to the drive. He was just in time to see the driver jump down and order the camel to kneel.

There was only a pause and then the curtains were parted from inside. Solomon noticed nothing but the woman that looked out at him. He who had seen many princesses and hundreds of beautiful women was for a moment spellbound. One small, jeweled hand still held the embroidered curtain, and the golden ornaments that framed her face made a pleasant tinkling sound as she leaned forward to view the new surroundings. Then she noticed him. Their eyes met and held briefly as her face registered delight. "And you are Solomon's brother, Nathan," she said to cover her embarrassment.

Solomon remembered that with the invitation he had told her his brother would be her host. He was about to explain that he wasn't Nathan when he changed his mind and made a quick decision. Perhaps it would be better for the moment to let her think he wasn't the king. Maybe then they wouldn't drift into the formal aloofness he so despised.

He smiled the relaxed, boyish smile that had over the years endeared him to so many and reached for her hand to help her alight. The servants were surprised. They had never seen the king so forget himself as to help someone down from a mount. For a moment he stood holding her hand and again their eyes met in wonder and fascination. She wasn't more beautiful than dozens of women in his harem, but there was something of openness, excitement, and zest for life that radiated from her, and he was immediately captivated.

He found himself wanting to stay by her side instead of retreating to his quarters as he had planned. He was glad the steward had ordered an impressive repast.

To everyone's surprise he stayed and exhibited uncommon devotion to the queen. He sat beside her, his elbow unconsciously resting on the same armrest, his eyes brightening when he looked at her, and an animation in his voice that hadn't been heard in a long time.

The repast was being held on one of the wide balconies. The air was fresh and pleasant with the fragrance of tuberoses, birds called to each other in the trees and as the sun slowly disappeared, torches were lit along the wall. The moon rose over the tall palm near the gate, and laughter could be heard from one end of the group to the other.

The food was spread out on finely woven, gold-washed reed mats in golden dishes. The officials the queen had brought with her, including Rydan, Tamrin, and Il Hamd, sat on ordinary long cushions that lined each side of the woven centerpiece. Though they couldn't hear what was being said, they were obviously astounded by the animation of their queen in the company of this Hebrew.

When the light meal was over and the guests were ready to retire, both Solomon and the queen seemed reluctant to part. It was only when she noticed her maidens waiting patiently with their small lamps all lit that she brought the conversation to a close. Solomon, for his part, stood watching them go down the long hall and didn't move until the lights had at last vanished into the room.

Back in his own quarters he puzzled over all that had happened. Of course she still thought he was Nathan, and it would be difficult now to tell her any differently. He wondered how the evening would have gone if she had known he was the king. He also wondered if she was always as animated, as vitally alive. He had gotten so carried away that he had to admit he hadn't even looked at her feet. In fact, as well as he could remember, he hadn't noticed much of anything but her wonderfully expressive eyes, her full, curving mouth, and her slightly exposed shoulders.

He felt such a mixture of strange, unfamiliar emotions he had trouble understanding what was happening. He couldn't really analyze what he was feeling. There was a great fascination with everything she said or did, and then there was an overwhelming desire to be intimate with this woman. To possess her in every way. This frightened him.

She was no ordinary woman. She was a queen, and a pagan queen at that. After the reprimand in the temple, he had resolved never to marry another pagan woman. He felt just about as strongly about marrying a queen. One didn't possess queens. They possessed you.

He resolved to quench the fire while it was still possible. He even considered getting up early and riding back to Jerusalem. Then he realized it would be very inhospitable. He remembered for the first time that evening that he desperately needed this woman's backing if he was to combat the coalition.

For a moment he wished that it really had been Nathan that had come down to Jericho. Then just as quickly he realized that if Nathan had come he himself would have been back in his palace in Jerusalem battling his depression and sense of failure.

No, he decided, he wouldn't trade this one evening for anything, but he must remember to be careful. He felt utterly vulnerable. In just these few short hours this woman had brought him out of the most desperate depression and had pitched him into such a turmoil of emotions that he was thoroughly disturbed. Nothing like this had ever happened to him before. His one love, the Shulamite maiden, had been sincere and beautiful but immature compared with this. This emotion was not something an experienced man like himself should be feeling. It was too much for one his age to handle.

He let his serving men help him undress and then pull back the curtains of his bed. His bed was a welcome retreat. He hoped that with the clear light of morning this madness would have dissipated.

He tossed and turned and tried to forget her eyes, her laughter, her delightful way of seeming both shy and yet forceful. Suddenly in the midst of these memories he had a fearful thought. He sat up in the bed and rubbed his eyes, ran his fingers through his hair, and wrestled with this thought that was so new for him. "What," he thought, "will I do if she doesn't feel the same toward me? Surely I can't endure such a thing." This too was a new thought for him. In recent years he had thought more often of whether he liked a woman rather than whether she liked him.

* * *

The next morning he rose early and went out into the formal garden. He needed to clear his mind, needed to remember he was dealing with a queen who held the fate of Israel in her hands. This could be no pleasant dalliance. He breathed deeply of the invigorating air and walked down the path to the grape arbor.

Suddenly his attention was drawn to a line of ants that crossed his path and wound their way to a sandy spot near the trellis. He stooped down and watched. Ants always fascinated him. They worked so hard. They never seemed to rest, and they would tackle the most impossible feats. Now he pulled out a small crust of bread he had saved for his pet crow and, breaking off a small piece, put it in the ants' path.

"I've always found ants to be most interesting." The voice was soft and melodious.

He would have known that voice anywhere. He turned and saw that the queen was standing on the path with one of her maidens shielding her from the morning sun with one of the elaborate plumed fans used by the Egyptians. He stood up and smiled. "If my people worked as hard," he said, "the whole world would be a paradise."

They laughed and then both stooped down to see if the ant would really carry away the little piece of bread. "How small they are," she said. "They should be afraid we'll step on them, but they don't seem to even know we exist."

Solomon let one of the little creatures crawl onto his finger. They both stood up and watched him make his way round and round the finger. "It is only Elohim, our creator God, who could make such a perfect creature this size."

"Elohim? Is that the name of your God?"

"That is the name we give Him when we think of Him as creator."

"I don't understand."

Solomon stood looking at her for a long moment before he spoke. "We have many names for the same God. Each time he shows himself it is in a different way and we add another name. When we see that He fights for us He is El Shaddai, the Almighty, when he provides for us He is Jehovah-Jireh, when He heals us, Jehovah Rapha. There are more."

"I have come with many questions for your brother."

"So I've heard. What do you intend to ask?"

She stood up abruptly and became very serious. Solomon put the ant back down and stood up beside her and they started to walk toward the grape arbor before she spoke. "I want to know so many things," she said. "Where does the rain come from? What makes the wind blow? Why can some things like snakes kill a person? Why are animals and birds afraid of people?"

She stopped to catch her breath and Solomon laughed. "You think he can answer all those questions?"

"Maybe not all, but some, and those aren't the most important questions."

"The most important? What are the most important questions?"

"Why does Solomon have to obey a law? Which is stronger, good or evil? But most important, what is truth and how can we know what is true and real? How, for instance, can we be sure we are worshiping the true God?"

Solomon was astounded. These were questions he had pondered. He had never known another man to ask such questions, and here was a woman, a frail, beautiful woman asking them. "I hope you won't be disappointed."

She laughed. "At least he can tell me if he keeps the four winds under his throne."

"You heard that I . . . that he keeps the four winds . . ." Solomon burst out in a jolly laugh. "I'm sure he can answer that easily. He may ask in turn that you tell him if the queen of Sheba has the feet of a donkey."

"The feet of a donkey! How ridiculous. He has heard that I have the feet of a donkey?"

"Yes. One of the traders said he had seen them with his own eyes."

She laughed and lifted her skirt just enough to show the dainty feet encased in jeweled sandals. "I can't imagine . . ." she started to say and then stopped and thought. "Of course, my throne is made of alabaster and the legs of the throne are carved into the hooves of a bull. When my skirt is wide it could look as though . . ." She laughed again. This time almost boisterously. "I'll wager it's your trader Badget that's made this report."

"You're right."

"Of course you didn't believe him."

"Well, he said . . ." They both laughed so hard the servants in the palace heard and wondered. Solomon hadn't really laughed like this in years. All formal barriers were washed away in this little episode. They no longer saw each other as foreign dignitaries but as delightful individuals.

In the next few days Solomon was bothered by only one thing; he wanted to confess who he was. Yet each time he tried to tell her he found it would have spoiled the mood of the moment. Finally, on the last day before he left to go back to Jerusalem he told her, "When you come to Jerusalem there will be many surprises. I'll do my best to make them all pleasant ones for your sake. Remember, there is a reason for everything."

* * *

When Solomon got back to his palace, he ordered a great procession organized to bring the queen of Sheba from Jericho to Jerusalem. He called the poets to write songs in her honor, and drummers, trumpeters, and dancers to come before her company into Jerusalem. He had his bravest men with their spears and golden shields to stand at attention down the road that led over Olivet and along the Kidron Valley to the Fountain Gate.

It was to be a festive day with no work for anyone, and so the people crowded up onto the walls and lined the road from the far side of Olivet down to the Kidron. They were singing and waving palm branches, each one hoping to catch a glimpse of the queen of Sheba.

No one was disappointed. The queen's caravan was far more impressive than they had imagined. It was even noted with due excitement that the queen herself had been seen parting her curtains to look at the scenery.

* * *

Bilqis had been reluctant to leave the winter palace in Jericho. She had loved the relaxed atmosphere, the perfumed air, the openness of pillars and lattice instead of high stone walls that shut out the sun. Most of all she had loved the time she spent with the young prince. Here was a man she was in danger of losing her heart to and she had actually found it exciting.

For a short time she had been able to forget she was a queen and just enjoy being a woman. He hadn't said anything about marriage or wanting her to do anything or be anything. He just seemed to enjoy being with her. There had been a few moments when she had experienced a decidedly new emotion. The way he had looked at her and then two times when their hands had touched and the times when they hadn't touched but she had felt a drawing, pulling excitement—these were memories she treasured.

The ride to Jerusalem seemed very short. She had looked out only on two occasions. Once when a young poet stopped the caravan so he could recite a lovely poem in her honor and then again when they were just over the hill and the whole caravan had stopped to look at Solomon's city.

It was all that the traders had described and more. A city of gold and marble ascending on tiers to the pinnacle that was crowned by an exquisite temple. There seemed nothing of darkness or hidden ugliness about this temple. It was all constructed of simple, elegant lines with golden doors that flashed and sparkled in the sunlight and arched courts that seemed filled with light.

Her eyes briefly swept over the maze of marble buildings she imagined were the king's palace complex and on down to the lush, green garden that ran along below the city's walls. She wondered what this king would be like. Certainly he could not be more charming than his brother. His brother was too charming. She had found her mind returning again and again to his smile, his brief touch, and the way they had laughed together.

With one last glance at the lovely city called Jerusalem, she closed the curtains and ordered the caravan to move on. As they approached the gates her own trumpeters blew a royal accolade in her honor. The drummers who had come out to meet her from the city began a stirring beat and dancers and singers sang a lively welcome.

Once inside the gate she pulled out her brass mirror with the snakes entwined on the handle. She smiled remembering the prince's saying they had heard she had the feet of a donkey. She wet one finger and smoothed her eyebrows into an arch, bit her lips to make them red, studied her eyes to determine what the prince had seen that made him look at her with such pleasure. She laughed and put the mirror down. "I must be sure the king gets a glimpse of my feet."

Everything had proceeded as planned. Tamrin, her own emissary, informed her that the camels with the gifts had all started to arrive an hour before and the last of the gifts were just at the moment being brought in before the king. Only the white horse and a few other choice surprises would not be given right now.

The queen's camel knelt and the howdah was removed and placed on the shoulders of twenty Nubians with leopardskin skirts, bright turbans, golden nose rings, and ankle bracelets. They set the howdah down at the foot of the throne, pulled the curtains back and the queen stepped out. Immediately the court erupted with shouts of welcome, the blare of trumpets, singers shaking tambourines, drummers drumming, and now and then the clash of cymbals. No one noticed that the queen stood at the foot of the marble steps in shocked disbelief. All they saw was the king descending the steps, taking her by the hand and leading her to sit beside him on his wide throne.

Bilqis was speechless. It was obvious the prince and the king were one and the same. His eyes met hers with the same delight she had seen in them when they were in the winter palace. However, she felt nothing but indignation that he should have let her believe he was just a prince. She felt embarrassed in front of all these people. To be thrown off guard at such a time was something that had never happened to her before.

She smiled and nodded to the crowded room of people but she refused to look at the king. Even when he stood and publicly thanked her for coming so far and bringing such treasures, she refused to meet his gaze and instead smiled her most enchanting smile for his counselors and tribesmen.

On each side of the throne she noticed women, dozens of them, all with children. Two of them sat on each side of the marble steps on slightly elevated platforms with ebony and gold thrones. One was definitely the Egyptian queen and the other must be the queen from Rabbath Amman. "He'd better not think I'll be swayed by his charms like these silly women," she thought. "I must not forget that I'm the queen of Sheba. I almost succumbed to his charm, but now I'm wiser. I'll not be moved by his subtle sorcery."

* * *

Solomon could see that it would be difficult to mend the breach between them. She had obviously been hurt by his thoughtlessness in letting her believe he was Nathan. He tried in every way he knew to get her aside long enough to explain, but she was careful to avoid any moments alone with him. She was pleasant but distant, and he longed for the bright,

200

unfettered exchange they had enjoyed in Jericho.

In spite of this she managed to take advantage of every opportunity to ask the questions that had been uppermost in her mind. After she had probed every aspect of his new shipping venture in the Red Sea, she began to ask questions about the temple and the God of Israel. He was surprised. Traditionally the main concern of women in Israel was to seek cleansing in the Mikvah once a month and to light the sabbath lamps. In the temple area they were allowed no farther than the Court of the Women. He hesitated even to answer her questions about the God of Israel.

Finally he was persuaded to bring her as far as the porch of the temple and let her look through the folding leaf doors into the splendor of the Holy Place. He saw her eyes fasten with amazement on the gigantic grapevine of pure, sparkling gold that was fastened above the doors. "The clusters are as high as a man," she exclaimed in astonishment.

Then she noticed the careful workmanship on the doors. He saw her reach out and touch with one finger the folded wing on one of the golden cherubim. She lightly touched the palm trees and open flowers all carved into the olive wood of the doors and then covered with gold.

Solomon noticed that as she moved to where she could get a glimpse inside at the Holy Place she drew in her breath sharply. She was obviously impressed to see the same patterned cherubim and palm trees carved into the gold-covered cedar wood that she had seen in the doors.

Her eyes passed over the golden incense burner, lingered for a moment on the table holding the shewbread, and then came to rest on the seven-branched candelabra. She noticed that it was as high as a man, with a seven-petaled pomegranate flower as decoration, and that the bowls to hold the wicks were in the shape of almond blossoms. "How beautiful!" she exclaimed. Her eyes were shining and her mouth slightly open in amazement.

"And," she said, "you do have an idol behind the curtain at the back."

"No idol. It's forbidden," he said as he noted her incredulity.

"Then if there's no idol, what do you have in the holiest place?"

"A golden box," he said as he started to lead her away. The finality with which he said it made it quite evident he wasn't ready to discuss it further. At least for the time being the subject was closed.

While he remained reluctant to discuss the strange furniture she had seen in the Holy Place or the golden box in the Holy of Holies, still there were other aspects of the temple he was eager to talk about. He explained how water from a great distance was piped into cisterns beneath the temple, how the priests must wear only linen garments and must never wear them outside the temple area. Finally he told her that only the high priest could enter the Holy of Holies and that only once a year on the Day of Atonement.

Later he heard her remark to her priest that Israel had no image of their God. They had only a golden box that sat in the place usually reserved for an idol.

He had been careful to explain nothing before she asked. He wondered how long it would take her to ask about the acacia box covered with gold in the small, square room of beaten gold, which was so holy it could be visited only once a year by the high priest. He also wondered if they would ever get back to the idyllic relationship they experienced in Jericho.

19

$\mathcal{T}$he solemn Day of Atonement was celebrated on the tenth of the seventh month of Tishri. At the full moon on the fifteenth of the same month, the joyous Feast of Booths was to be celebrated. Bilqis had been fascinated by everything she learned about the feast days. Each new discovery gave her insight into Solomon's faith, even though he himself seemed reluctant to explain even the simplest tenets. She wondered if it was too private to be shared. Just as she couldn't go inside even the Holy Place, let alone the Holy of Holies, so now she wondered if she would ever get answers to her questions.

From the rooftop of her house she had seen large groups of people dressed in festive finery with palm branches, banners, tambourines, and drums wending their way over Olivet from Bethany, the "house of dates." They were also streaming through the city gates, and all of them seemed to be laughing and singing as though some wonderful event were about to take place.

From the window in her house that opened onto the large courtyard, she had seen the construction of gay shelters covered with palm branches and myrtle. She sent one of her maids down to investigate. On her return she told the queen that they were booths with tables spread and cushions prepared for Isreal's most joyous feast of the year. "The harvest for the year is over and now it's time to celebrate," one of the king's pages had told the maid.

As it turned out, Bilqis and all her company were invited. She found herself in the seat of honor. Not sitting by Solomon, but by a prince she found most charming.

"I'm Solomon's brother, Nathan," he said.

Bilqis was surprised. She hadn't really thought there was an actual person named Nathan. "So the king does have a brother named Nathan after all."

Nathan laughed. "Yes, and I'm the one to blame for the unpleasant meeting in Jericho."

"Oh, I wouldn't say it was unpleasant."

"You see, it had been decided that I would go and meet you, then at the last moment I persuaded my brother, the king, to go."

"Perhaps it was partly my fault. I just took for granted the person I met was the Nathan mentioned by the messenger."

"And he didn't tell you he wasn't Nathan."

"I don't understand."

"If you'll excuse me I can explain. The king has told me that the time in Jericho was so wonderful, he didn't want to spoil it. To tell you he was the king could have made everything suddenly very formal."

Bilqis understood and promptly regretted her reaction. She quickly reminded herself, however, that this king with his seven hundred wives and three hundred concubines, was not someone she dared lose her heart to. Of course, as she had discovered, they weren't all living in Jerusalem. Many of them had gone back to their villages to live with their families while others languished uncalled for in the harem.

She didn't intend to be added to his collection. However, that didn't mean she had to continue her hostility. "The two of you must be very close," she said trying to change the subject. "Are you one of his counselors?"

Nathan laughed with the same unaffected charm that characterized his brother. "I've studied with the prophets. I suppose I'm an adviser of sorts."

"Then perhaps you can tell me what is being celebrated. Is it a religious festival or a national festival?"

"It's a little bit of both. It's a harvest festival but it's also a time when we remember how we were slaves in Egypt and our God brought us out and freed us. Our people lived for years in the wilderness in booths just like this."

"So you build the booths to remember." Bilqis looked around and saw the clay lamps giving off a soft glow that made everyone's face mysteriously luminous. Looking up she could see the full moon and the stars through the palm leaves. There was a beauty and serenity that was conducive to conversation and simple entertainment. Bilqis found herself wishing that Solomon were there. With such a man perhaps one could be happy living in an arbor on the edge of the desert.

"I've wondered," she said, trying to stay on a safe subject, "if you can tell me how your city got its name."

"It's a bit involved; are you sure you want to hear it?"

"Of course," she said as she began to feel it was indeed difficult to get even the simplest questions answered.

"Long ago when the father of our people came here to sacrifice his only son and God provided a ram instead, he called this place Jehovah-Jireh. Jehovah provides, or the place where Jehovah provided. Tradition says that Shem the son of Noah, who survived the great flood, called it Shalem or "peace." It was our God who put the two together and it was called JirehShalem or Jerusalem."

Bilqis sat very still and pondered the story. Everything she heard made her want to ask more questions. Finally she asked, "It seems that every people in every nation sacrifice human beings to their god."

Nathan was startled. "I didn't mean to imply that. In fact, ever since our God stopped Abraham from sacrificing his son and provided the ram instead, we have known that he doesn't want us to sacrifice human beings."

"Even if you were losing a battle or had a very bad famine you wouldn't sacrifice someone?"

"No, never. We have had famines and have lost battles, but we have never sacrificed either our own people or the slaves that we've captured."

Now some entertainers appeared and after them would come the feasting. There was just time for her to make one observation. "How strange. Most other people resort to human sacrifice in time of trouble." The flutes trilled and the drums began to beat, the dancers appeared with joyful songs, and everyone waved palm branches and joined in the singing. It was a scene never to be forgotten of a happy, prosperous people who were free to enjoy a whole week of celebration without the usual work schedule.

* * *

In the two months that followed Solomon made every effort to acquaint the queen with the various aspects of his kingdom and reign. He even ordered her throne be placed next to his own so she could observe his dealings with various problems. He also carefully planned a series of excursions for her benefit. Some of the time he rode with her, being the perfect host, but he always maintained a formality that discouraged the repetition of the happy time in Jericho. At other times he sent one of his brothers and again there was careful attention to her slightest wish.

First she visited the quarries and saw how the stones were cut and shaped so when they reached the site they were simply fitted into place. She laughed. "So nothing was built by the Jinn from magic."

"Nothing," she was told. "It was all done by hard work and careful planning."

Next she visited most of the chariot cities and was told, "The king had twelve thousand stalls for horses and twelve thousand chariots that he bought from Egypt. For the chariots he paid six hundred shekels and for each horse one hundred fifty."

She traveled through the rich valley of Jezreel and heard how Solomon had divided his country into twelve sections and appointed stewards over each section. The stewards were responsible for supplying the food for the king on their assigned month.

She talked to the priests and heard how different ones went up in regular succession to serve in the temple. In one village she visited in the home of a priest who was making a harp of the berosh and prized almug wood. He told her the harp would be used in the temple service to praise God for His goodness. She pondered this. She had never heard of people praising any god. She wondered what this God had done for these people. She resolved to ask further about this later.

She visited the sea coast and saw the dye vats where the murex shell-fish produced the rich purple dyes that made the king's best garments. She watched with great interest as craftsmen inlaid mother of pearl in furniture and carved wedding chests made of cedar.

As the time passed she traveled to the source of the Jordan, then to Tadmor, the new chariot city being built in the desert beyond Damascus. Finally, coming down the Jordan, she saw the place at Zarethan where Solomon's most accomplished craftsman, Huram-Abi, molded in the natural clay all the brass objects used in the temple and the king's house.

Solomon had planned all of this so that instead of just asking questions and getting answers, she would see his kingdom and how it prospered. He tried to refrain from joining her and enjoying her company, since he was determined to forget the madness he had experienced in Jericho. Instead he found that he thought about her all the more. Her face, her gestures, her way of smiling all conspired to make him even more anxious to see her again and to experience the lighthearted happiness he had known at their first meeting.

Against his better judgment he planned to meet her for a few days in Jericho. He reasoned that she would soon be returning to her country and then this strange attraction would be ended. However, at the very thought of her leaving he felt such pain that he was ready to throw all caution aside and arrange the meeting earlier than planned.

When Bilqis finally arrived in Jericho and met Solomon at his winter palace, she was speechless with wonder at all she had seen. There was no longer any misunderstanding between them and it seemed that once again they were to enjoy the carefree, relaxed relationship they had shared at their first meeting. "Have all your questions been answered?" Solomon asked as they sat in the cushioned retreat on one of the balconies and ate from a tray of fruit and dried dates.

"Most of them. But you never did tell me what was in the golden box behind the woven curtains and golden doors of the Holy of Holies."

Solomon laughed and reached for another cluster of lush, sweet grapes. "And what do you think is in the chest?"

Bilqis grew pensive. "I've thought about it all the way to Mount Hermon and down the Jordan and I've decided it must be the most important thing you or your people own. It must be something you and your God value very highly."

"Yes. And so what do you think it is?"

"I have thought it might be all the images you've collected in battle with other nations. Think of the power you would have if you could lock all those gods up in a chest and hide them away in your temple."

Solomon frowned. The very idea of pagan images in the temple was a terrible thought. "No, no, you're wrong. Guess again."

"Perhaps you have some of the evil Jinn locked up in the box so they can't harm your people."

Again Solomon was astounded by her thinking. "Never, impossible, the Jinn would pollute God's holy hill."

"Then it must be the heads of your worst enemies."

"No, no, no. It is blasphemous even to think such thoughts. I can see you'll never even come close to imagining what it is."

"You'll have to tell me. It must be the most guarded secret of your happy kingdom."

Solomon blushed. He was ashamed that he had been so reluctant to tell her all she wanted to know of his faith. Actually it was just that she was, after all, a woman and usually women weren't supposed to think about such things. "I suppose there'll be no peace until I tell you," he said. "I hope you aren't disappointed. It's two tablets of stone given to us by Moses who led my people out of slavery in Egypt four hundred eighteen years ago."

"Two stone tablets?"

He could see she was very surprised. "They have writing on them," he said.

"Oh!" Her eyes were wide with wonder.

"They have laws carved into the stone. Rules to be obeyed if a people are to be happy and wise."

"Ah, the laws that your trader Badget said even you must obey. I thought it very strange that even a king must obey laws. In Sheba whatever I say is the law. How awful to have laws that must be obeyed."

Solomon struggled to find a way of explaining. He could see that it would be very difficult for her to grasp what even the youngest child in Israel would take for granted. "The law is our greatest treasure. We love the law."

"Love laws? I don't understand."

"Perhaps you can understand if I explain it this way: if the sun obeyed no laws, we would never know when it would come up, and if the moon did the same, planting and harvesting would be impossible. If the seeds didn't obey the laws of their kind, we would have no crops, and if the birds no longer followed their laws, they wouldn't migrate to warmer places. Everything but man has laws and rules to obey. Most of the time these laws are built into the very nature of things. It's only man that thinks he doesn't need laws."

"And where did you get these laws that are in the golden box?"

"Our God gave them to Moses on Mount Sinai."

"All of them are written on just two tablets?"

"The basic ones are on the tablets. There are others that have been added out of experience. But God gave Moses only ten."

For what seemed like a long time Bilqis looked out at the stars and the rising moon. "How happy your people, your servants, and your wives to live in such a country with such a king."

"Have all your questions been answered now that you've seen my kingdom, talked with my people, and at last learned what is in the golden box in the Holy of Holies?"

"Only one thing I can't resist asking. You have seven hundred wives and three hundred concubines. You are obviously a man who has loved many women. How does it happen you have never tried to take me to bed or asked to marry me?"

Solomon was startled by her frankness. For a moment he was confused. He had more than anything wanted to marry this woman, to make her his in every sense of the word. And now he knew that she had sensed this and was wondering why he had held back.

"If I had asked to marry you, what would your answer have been?" He was now very serious, and he looked down at the golden wine glass he held and waited for her answer.

"I wouldn't marry you. I'm a queen. No one must control me. But I do need an heir, and I've decided I would like a child."

"So you would like a child, and you've discovered it's impossible by the law of things to get one without a man."

"Yes."

He seemed to be pondering the whole state of affairs. By the look on his face he found some aspects of the situation amusing, but when he spoke he was serious. "When I was very young," he said, "I made a vow that I would take no woman without marrying her. Now I have added to that vow. I'll take no woman who's a pagan worshiping a pagan god."

"Then we have come to a hopeless impasse. I can gladly accept your God. Mine was destroyed long ago. But to marry is utterly impossible."

Solomon was deeply moved. "You can accept my God and my people?" he asked.

"Yes, yes. I see that everything I've learned is true. Your God is not something your priests have invented or one conjured up by drugs. He is one your people have actually experienced. You know Him by what He has done and the ways He has shown Himself to you."

He reached out and took her hands and looked at her with such love she was tempted to respond. Just in time she remembered his wives and the control a man could exert if he was the husband. She pulled her hands away. "You must understand, I can never marry anyone. Why do you insist on marriage!"

"Must you always ask questions?" Solomon said. He sounded impatient, but he knew that she was only doing what he himself had done all his life. In fact, he was secretly delighted to find someone who was as curious about the world and life as he was.

"I see no need for marriage. For most women marriage means the father gives his daughter to a man who agrees to take care of her in place of the father. Marriage also means the father is losing a piece of property he has invested much time and expense in raising. The benefits will now go to the husband, and so the father must have a payment of some kind. I have no father. I make my own decision."

Solomon was amazed at her clear thinking. It was hard to refute. "I'll have to think about it," he said. "I have many wives and concubines, but I've exchanged a formal commitment with each of them. I'm responsible for them now."

"Responsible, what do you mean by responsible?"

"They belong to me and I must see that they have food and clothing and a proper place to live."

Bilqis smiled and reached out for his hand. "I have no need of someone being responsible for me. I myself provide everything I need."

Solomon was puzzled. This beautiful, desirable woman was offering herself freely to him but at the expense of one of his fundamental beliefs. He had the feeling that this same kind of thing had happened to him before. It all sounded so right and yet it could be so wrong. In fact, this was the only strongly held principle he had never compromised on. Would this be a compromise? He didn't know. He wished Nathan were here. Nathan was wiser in these things than he was.

He quickly turned the subject to plans for the next day. He wasn't ready to toss over his values without more thought.

* * *

Badget was also in Jericho on this same night. He had left a day early on his trading venture up to Damascus and was staying in the same inn he and Terra had stayed in when he first brought her to Israel. He had left Terra and Yasmit back in Jerusalem, both with small babies. Babies that cried and disrupted the peace of his house in a way he wasn't used to. He had to admit to the innkeeper's wife that after all these years he was a bit surprised to be blessed with two boys, born only days apart.

The innkeeper's wife remembered the incident when Yasmit had appeared unexpectedly at the inn and had caused such a scene. She was interested in hearing more of the details. "Your young wife confided in me that she was expecting a child, but the other wife seemed to be too old."

"Is anything too hard for the Lord? That's what our ancestor Sarah said when she heard that she was going to be a mother. Strange things can happen, and Yasmit definitely had a child."

"You were there when these children were born?"

"Well, yes and no. I was at home when Terra had her baby, but I was gone when Yasmit had hers. She evidently had a bad time of it right from the beginning. Being older, Yasmit had no milk. She finally had to get her sister to come and feed the child. That seems to have worked out."

"You dare to leave them alone together?"

"Why not? Terra's a sweet little thing. Why, she's mothering both babies. Yasmit is depending on her for everything."

"I can imagine," the innkeeper's wife said. "Being a mother must have been quite a shock to the older woman."

"Not a shock; just an inconvenience. She's not used to children." The innkeeper's wife nodded knowingly, and Badget could see that she was speculating on just what was really going on between women who were so very different.

As it turned out they were to know within the hour of both tragedy and hopeless enmity that had broken out between the two women. Badget was just leaving the inn to manage the last minute details before leaving the next morning with his caravan when the news reached him by runner. "One of your children is dead," the messenger said. "I've been sent to bring you home."

"Dead? One of my little sons?" It was incomprehensible. He had left them both healthy and growing the day before. Then thinking of his wives, Terra who had waited so anxiously for this child and would be almost suicidal if it died, and Yasmit who definitely was far too old to expect a second miracle, he became terribly distraught. "Which child died? Whose child?" he asked.

"That's the trouble," the messenger said. "They don't seem to know. They're both claiming the living child. The neighbors have come in and are trying to settle it."

"Who has the child now?" Badget was almost frantic. He could picture the scene.

"Why, your wife Yasmit. She's taken the child and has locked herself into one of the rooms and won't come out."

Badget didn't wait to hear more. In a terrible frenzy he himself ran down and unhitched his donkey, mounted, and was off on the road to Jerusalem before the astonished messenger could say more.

When he approached his gate he saw a crowd gathered outside and curious neighbors were on their roofs looking down into his courtyard. He had to push his way through the crowd to get to his door. He could hear screaming and shouting on the other side. At first no one seemed to hear his frantic pounding on the door. Only when neighbors on the roof called to the servants to open for their master did the door finally open.

The sight that greeted Badget was terrible beyond belief. In the courtyard, on a cold, stone slab lay the dead child. In horror Badget realized the dead child couldn't be buried until it was decided whose child it really was. How was it, he wondered, his two wives didn't know one child from the other? He'd never heard of such a thing.

"Terra, where is Terra?" he shouted. Some instinct told him that Yasmit would fend very well for herself but tender-hearted Terra could be totally crushed. He pushed his way into the crowded house. Remembering how Terra had loved the child, he became even more distraught. If it was her child out there on the cold slab, she would be grief stricken but if it wasn't. . . . The total horror of the situation gripped him.

"Where are my wives?" he shouted in frustration and to his relief people melted back making a way for him to pass. Then he saw it. The door to his own private room with Terra almost unrecognizable with her hair unbound, and barefooted, pounding on the door and begging Yasmit to open it. Hearing his voice, Terra turned, and he saw her eyes terror stricken, her mouth twisted in pain, and tears streaming down her face. "My darling," he said as he gathered her into his arms. "What's happening?"

Terra could hardly speak. "My child. It's my child Yasmit has in there. She says it's hers."

Badget always liked to be in control of any situation, and this was beyond anything he had ever tried to manage. "Don't you women know your own children?" he thundered.

Terra pulled away from him with a cry of real pain, and hiding her face in her hands fled to the cook room outside, off the courtyard. She slammed the door and lacked it from the inside.

Badget was frantic. He could see he'd added to her pain, and he didn't know what to do. He looked around at his servants and neighbors, and they lowered their eyes not wanting to see their friend and master in such circumstances.

As the complexity of the situation began to dawn on him, Badget realized there was no quick solution. It was obvious the dead child must be buried, but it couldn't be buried until this dispute between his wives was settled. "Where's Solomon?" he asked. "It's not going to be easy to figure this out."

"He's in Jericho," several people volunteered.

"Then we're going to Jericho," Badget decided. He ordered the servants to wrap the dead child in a winding of fine linen, then he ordered some of his men to break down the door to his room. There was cursing and swearing as Yasmit, clutching the baby, was brought out and forced to mount the donkey for the trip to Jericho. When that was done, Badget with apologies and soft words, was able to get Terra to come out from the cook room.

As people in Jerusalem heard of the tragedy they dropped their work and rushed out to follow Badget and his company down to Jericho. No one wanted to miss the drama. They couldn't imagine how, if the two wives couldn't seem to tell the children apart, and Badget, the father, couldn't decide, Solomon could possibly sort it out.

* * *

When Solomon heard that it was his friend Badget at the gate of his winter palace and that tragedy had struck the trader's family, he ordered his guards to bring them into the courtyard. The scene was a strange one. Badget was obviously beside himself with frustration and grief and the two wives told the rest of the story. One of them held the child. She looked slightly familiar. Solomon struggled to place her. He felt he should know

213

her from some time in the past. The other wife was shy and grief stricken.

"These two women each had a child and one died." Solomon was assessing the facts. "Where is the dead child?" the servant came forward and unwrapped the dead child and placed it on the floor before Solomon.

Solomon remembered that the queen of Sheba knew Badget, and his small, plump wife was from the queen's own country. He quickly sent a messenger to invite her to participate in the judgment.

When she came she was told the details and Solomon asked what her decision would be if this were in her country. She quickly came to a decision. "First," she said, "if this were in my country I would side with the small woman because she is is a native of my own country. However, since I am not in my own country I would be tempted to side with the older woman because she is the man's first wife and should have more consideration. Also she is too old to have another child while the other woman can have many more children." She turned to Solomon. "Now, tell me how you will solve this impossible riddle. Undoubtedly you will go about it in an entirely different way and for different reasons.

Solomon smiled. He was genuinely surprised at the way she went about solving the problem. "You're right. In this case I wouldn't go by any set rules or customs, but I must try to determine what is the truth of the matter, who the real mother is."

"But that seems too difficult. Even if the women themselves know, it won't help because neither one will admit she is lying."

"I have been studying the women. It's obvious to me that between them they know who the real mother is. One of them is lying. All I have to do is find out which one is telling the truth."

Bilqis was amazed. "That's impossible. How can you find out such a thing?"

"I can only try." He turned to the two women and asked them to tell what happened. Yasmit stepped forward holding the child. "Your majesty, we both have children born within days of each other. We were together in the same room with our children sleeping. When we awoke her child was found to be dead, but she insisted it was my child that had died."

Then Solomon signaled for Terra to speak. It was obvious that she was frightened, but when she spoke it was with assurance. "Your majesty," she said bowing to the ground and kissing the hem of his robe, then standing she said, "we both were in the same room sleeping with our children. Her child had been sickly, and in the night it died. She evidently discovered this and took my child and placed her dead child in my arms. When I awoke I found the child I held was dead, and it wasn't my child. She was holding my child and claiming it was hers." Terra began to cry and wipe the tears with her mantle.

"So the problem is simple. We may never determine which of you is the true mother, but we can see that justice is done. Bring me a sword."

A hush went over the people that had crowded in the gate to see what the king would do. Yasmit looked defiant and Terra was obviously frightened. One of the guardsmen had stepped forward and offered the king his sword. "Take the child," Solomon said, "divide it in half and give half to the one and half to the other."

Yasmit glanced around the room with a cunning, speculative look. She obviously thought Solomon must be bluffing, and yet she quickly calculated that either way she would win. She cared nothing for the child. With a quick glance at Terra she raised her arms and handed the child to the guard. "That's fair," she said, "let the child be neither yours nor mine, but divide it."

Terra swayed and almost fainted. A cry of anguish burst from her lips as she reached for the child. "No, no," she cried. "Don't harm him. Give her the child if you must, but don't harm him." She fell at the king's feet weeping bitterly.

Gently Solomon reached down and lifted her up then turned to the guard. "Put up your sword," he ordered. "Give this woman the child. It obviously belongs to her."

Terra took the child and held it gently. She cuddled and crooned to it oblivious to anything that was happening around her. Yasmit, however, was angry. She didn't dare dispute the king's decision, but her eyes flashed dangerously and Badget could tell there would be no peace in his house.

He made a quick decision. Stepping forward he begged the king's pardon and asked to speak. "Let it be known before the king and these witnesses," he said, "that I'm divorcing this woman. She's dealt treacherously in my house and brought disgrace upon it. I'll settle upon her the amount due her from her former husband's property, but she'll no longer be a wife to me."

Yasmit screamed and rushed forward but had to be restrained by the king's guards. "Where am I to go? You can't cast me out into the streets."

Badget had spotted Yasmit's sister in the crowd and now he motioned for her to come forward. "You'll go with your sister and I'll settle a fair amount on you so you'll never be a burden to her."

At that Yasmit broke down. She rushed forward and clung to Badget, begging for mercy, but he was determined to be free of her.

With a nod from the king the guards again came forward and led Yasmit outside the gate. Her sister came and carefully wrapped the dead baby in the winding cloth and carried it out while Badget, breathing a sigh of relief, hurried after Terra.

Within minutes the guard had closed the gates and the courtyard returned to normal. For a short time there was the sound of voices mixed with the braying of donkeys and the shouting of guards and then there was quiet. Solomon and the queen retired to their favorite place to talk on the latticed veranda.

For a while neither one spoke. They were busy rethinking all that had just happened. Finally Bilqis spoke. "I came all this way looking for truth. I have seen that you and all your people have no patience with the manipulations and games of expediency most of us play. You want the truth even if it isn't convenient. It was interesting to see how you go about finding the truth."

Solomon looked at Bilqis and noted the seriousness of her expression. He felt a renewed surge of love for this charming queen. How happy he would be to spend the rest of his life with her. He was terribly tempted to accept her on her terms. What did it matter now that he had been rejected by his father's God? Why should he hold out on principle when she was all he wanted?

Finally the only thing that held him back was the realization that she was a determined woman and a queen. There was no way he could persuade her to stay here in Israel; nor was there any way that he could drop everything and go with her back to Sheba. There was nothing but heartbreak for him if he pursued this relationship. He decided that no matter how difficult it was going to be, he would spend less time with her and would guard his heart from loving her.

20

*D*espite his resolutions, Solomon found he could not tear himself away from the lovely queen, and she, in turn, talked less enthusiastically about going home. A week had passed, and though there had been a steady stream of messengers, pages, and tribesmen urging Solomon to return to Jerusalem, he still lingered in Jericho.

These had been strangely rewarding days in which Solomon tried to answer all the queen's questions. Her questions never ceased to amaze him. She wanted to know about good and evil, sickness and health, life and death, but most of all she was curious about Israel's God. "Is He just the God of Israel," she asked, "or can He also be the God of the people of South Arabia?" They were sitting under one of the palm trees beside the blue-tiled fountain enjoying the sound of the water and the antics of Solomon's playful monkey.

For a moment Solomon was taken aback. He had never thought of his God as being a God for other people. Finally he told her, "He is the creator God. He created the whole world so He is certainly the God of all He created."

"Is He the strongest God?" she asked.

"He is the only God. All other gods are false. I've studied and learned the mysteries of many religions, and I've found their gods are either demons that work some magic or are the creation of false priests."

As Solomon was answering her questions, an amazing thing began to happen. He found himself reviewing all the aspects of his own faith and discovered to his surprise that it was stronger than he'd thought. He wasn't just telling her that this was the truth; he was believing it wholeheartedly. He was seeing it for the first time as one outside the faith would see it, and he found it withstood any test.

Though he was becoming used to her questions, at times she still surprised him. Her next question had that effect, and he hardly knew how to answer it.

"To become a citizen of my country," she said, "a person has to be very wealthy. It's quite costly. What must one do to accept your God as his God?"

He saw how her eyes shone with excitement and with what concentration she waited for his answer. "Enter into the covenant," Solomon said at last, rather matter-of-factly, hoping that would satisfy her curiosity. He didn't want to have to explain the whole idea of covenant. When he saw that she was going to ask more questions, he added, "Israel has made a covenant with Him. He is our God and we are His people."

"Covenant! What is covenant?"

"It's an agreement. We agree to accept His laws. He becomes our God and we become His people. It means we belong."

And so it went for several days until one day she announced that she was ready to enter into covenant with Israel's God. Solomon told her all that she must do, and then he said, "Is it so much easier to enter a covenant with my God than it is to enter a covenant with me?"

"What do you mean?" she asked.

"The marriage I spoke of that seemed to frighten you so was just another way of making a covenant together. A belonging."

"I don't understand."

"It's very simple. Even though you must go back to your country and I must stay here, we would know that we belonged to each other."

She thought about it for a few minutes. "And if I belong to you will that mean you will control me?"

Solomon could see that this bothered her. She was a beautiful, sensuous woman and yet she was first of all a queen responsible for a whole country and its people just as he was king. The times when he had reached out for her hand or had in any way tried to show the love that he felt for her, he found her drawing back with a frightened look and a reserve that kept him at a distance. "I don't want to control you," he said finally. "I only want to love you."

"I don't know about love," she said. "I don't know what it means."

"You've never loved anyone?"

"Never," she said looking at him with her characteristic openness.

218

"Don't you want to be loved?"

She broke into a light laugh, as though she were amused. "I really don't see that I need it. I've found it rather bothersome to have people wanting to love me. It has only meant they wanted somehow to control me or get my throne."

Solomon was frustrated. He had never seen such a woman. Those that he'd known were all cloyingly eager to please him. They wanted his love and his attention. "Why did you come so far? What were you looking for? What have you wanted from me?" he said finally in exasperation.

"I wanted to find truth. I wanted to know things."

"What did you think I could tell you?"

"If you were truly the wisest man in the world, I knew you could answer my questions; tell me what was true and important."

For a long time Solomon didn't answer. He knew her questions were important, but he could see that even with her questions answered she would still feel the emptiness that had brought her to him. It was obvious she knew nothing of the emotions. She had shut them out, covered them up with intellect. She felt nothing, perhaps was incapable of feeling anything.

"I've tried to answer your questions," he said finally. "Have I answered them all?"

Her eyes sparkled and her face became animated. "Yes, yes, you've answered all my questions. I've learned what truth is and I've seen your wisdom."

"But I've not yet told you what is most important, and you said you came seeking to know what was true and important. Are you interested?"

"Oh yes," she said. "To know what the wisest man in the world thinks is important would be worth the whole journey."

"Well," he said, "I'm going tomorrow to Jerusalem. There are matters I must tend to, but when I come back I promise that I'll tell you what the most important thing in the world is."

It was late, the moon had gone down, and the crickets out in the garden were at last silent. Solomon stood up and waited for her before he said goodnight, then they followed the servants to their rooms.

The queen dropped off to sleep immediately, but Solomon was awake most of the night reviewing all that had happened since her arrival. He recalled the anxiety he had felt when he first heard of her coming. He almost laughed as he remembered Badget's tale of her donkey feet. He would always be amazed that she had actually traveled so far seeking truth. Then finally he had been forced to admit to himself that he loved this woman deeply. He was also aware, however, that there was little hope of her returning his love. She was as remote as the evening star and perfectly happy to stay that way.

In Jerusalem Solomon was immediately plunged into urgent business. But he realized with surprise that during his stay in Jericho some of the problems that had rested heaviest on his mind had temporarily vanished. Jeroboam, he found, was indeed in Egypt, and Tipti had for the time being moved to her palace in Gezer. Naamah was content. She was convinced that with Jeroboam gone her son, Rehoboam, would have no trouble taking over the kingdom when the time came.

As to the coalition that had been formed against him and was such an ominous threat, it had now collapsed. The leaders had been informed that their plans had all fallen through. The queen had accepted the God of Israel as her God. Her high priest and some of her tribesmen were studying with Nathan. An agreement of cooperation was already being drawn up between the two countries, Israel and Sheba.

Solomon was pleased and relieved with all that had been accomplished, but he was frustrated beyond belief by the queen's refusal to marry him. He knew that there was little time left. She would be making plans very soon for her return trip. He could accept that with difficulty, but to think that their relationship had never blossomed into anything more than lessons in wisdom was, in his estimation, intolerable.

Late that night Solomon was still up talking to Nathan and some of the tribesmen about their progress in drawing up an agreement with the dignitaries from Sheba. Nathan had explained all that he had learned of their beliefs and the temple built to the moon god. He reported that both their superstitions and their wisdom regarding the stars had been recorded. They in turn had been open and receptive to all that he was teaching them about the God of Israel and the law.

Solomon had listened with rapt attention. He was becoming more convinced that somewhere within the queen's past was an unpleasant incident that had made her fearful of love. Perhaps it was somehow linked to the rejection of her own religion and the search for the truth. "Every man has a key and undoubtedly it is also true of every woman," he said. "One has only to find the key, and any problem can be solved."

"And the key, what is this key?" Nathan asked.

"Every person has something they either fear or want. When you discover either of these you can unlock the heart and there are no more problems."

"And so what are you going to do?"

"I don't know yet."

Nathan left and Solomon sat thinking; he was reluctant to retire until he had come to some resolution. Slowly an idea began to form. It was an exciting idea. Impulsively he motioned to one of the pages. "Go to the house of Badget the trader," he ordered, "and if he is still at home bring him here immediately." It was obvious the page had been bored and was eager to be sent on some errand. He bowed, backed from the room, and hurried out into the night.

There was the familiar challenge from the guards, muffled voices, then the sound of feet hitting hard on the marble steps. Still more faint on the night air was the challenge from guards stationed in the courtyard, and then the palace gate. Solomon loved these sounds, sounds that were lost during the day.

A wind had sprung up, making the silken hangings billow slightly and the goathair ceiling rise and fall. The oil lamps sputtered and flickered, the incense burners gave off intermittent twists of perfumed smoke. The wind would in a few months bring the early rains signaling that the monsoons would be blowing to the southeast, and Solomon knew the queen must soon be leaving. It all served again to remind him of the shortness of the time that was left. Quickly he dismissed the thought as too painful.

He deliberately shifted his thoughts to the trader, with the hope that he could shed some light on the situation. "That wily trader owes me a great deal for bringing peace to his house," Solomon muttered.

Badget came in such a hurry that he was still adjusting his outer robe and had forgotten his ornate girdle. At first he listened carefully to the king's questions all the time nodding and smiling. Then he became impatient. He could hardly wait to tell all he knew of the situation in Sheba. Finally, before Solomon had asked all his questions, Badget began to tell him in detail of the queen's refusal of one suitor after another. How even her cousin had been rejected. Then how at last there had been news that she was going to the temple to meet with the god Ilumquh. The god was to be her only husband.

"And why," Solomon asked, "was it so necessary that she have a husband?"

"The people were demanding an heir to the throne. They cared very little whether she had a husband or not, but they insisted she must have an heir."

"And so?"

"We heard of special diets, rituals, and purifications the queen was having to endure if she was to meet the god."

"And this god she was to meet—who was he?" Badget laughed. "He's the moon god. His presence on earth takes the form of an alabaster bull that lives in a special pavilion beside the larger temple. It was odd. I told people myself that neither an alabaster bull nor the moon itself could give the queen the son she wanted."

"They believed she would have a son by this god?"

"They believed it. With my own eyes I saw the queen enter the small temple."

"She actually went to meet this god?"

"She actually went. The people were terrified. They thought the bull god might tear her to pieces."

"Was she frightened?"

"She didn't seem to be, but then who knows, she may have been terrified and just didn't show it. She's well known for her bravery. Then again the priests may have given her a potion they call ergot. It makes ordinary people dream of gods and demons. It can also make them lose their wits. With my own eyes I've seen some of them."

"What came of all this? Did the queen have a son?"

"Oh no, my lord. It seemed to me she wasn't in the temple long before she reappeared, looking upset. She didn't speak to anyone but gave orders to be taken right back to the palace. She didn't even appear in the temple where the people were waiting for her."

"Did she say anything to her people?"

"No, it was all very strange. It was after that she suddenly decided on this trip. Said she was coming to ask you questions. She wanted to find the truth."

Solomon thanked Badget and dismissed the tribesmen, leaving only the harpist and some guards. He didn't want to be bothered. He wanted to think. Badget had told him enough. He could well imagine the rest. He had often heard of the dark, shady practices of pagan priests.

It was painful to think of this woman he loved so deeply, who was so brave and trusting, being put through such an ordeal. Now he understood everything. Her consuming interest in Israel's God, and her reluctance to respond to the love he knew she felt for him. The coalition meant little to her, the fact that he was bypassing her country's trade route for a water route was important but wouldn't have driven her to take off on such a perilous and arduous journey.

He had the key. Now all that was left was to find out how best to use all that he knew. It was obvious why she feared any kind of commitment, and it was also obvious that above all else she wanted a child. "Without an heir to her throne she'll always have the priests and her people troubling her to marry."

He summoned his guards and went to his bedchamber, where he went over every detail of the situation, summoned up all he knew of moon worship and its rites, decided on a course of action, and then dismissed the whole thing. Finally, as he had done so often, he went to sleep and in the morning knew just what he should do.

First he ordered a bed constructed exactly like his own with posts and curtains enclosing the sleeping area so there would be some privacy from servants and the tribesmen that were always present. This was to be put in his own bedchamber directly across from his own bed. Then he called in his counselors and his brothers. "There are some details I want to add to the treaty being drawn up between our kingdom and that of Sheba," he said.

They spent the whole day going back and forth, wording and rewording the treaty until it exactly met Solomon's requirements. There were all of the usual declarations and provisions for a friendly colation. There were also a few surprises. It was suggested that the queen take full advantage of the new sea route by building up the small town of Axum on the African coast of the Red Sea. That way she could benefit by both the land trade and the sea. She could market the same goods from her own country and at the same time build a new market of goods gathered from Africa.

The biggest surprise was a carefully worded portion that promised that with the acceptance of this agreement, Sheba would be given an heir to the throne.

The next day he ordered preparations be made for a great feast. "If the queen accepts the agreement," he said, "I'll send word and announcements can be read in every town and village that a large celebration will be held in Jerusalem."

When Solomon reached Jericho a few days later, he found that the queen had already received the treaty and had been studying it with her counselors. She was puzzled by the suggestion that she make the small town of Axum, on the Ethiopian coast, a center for sea trade. "What should I do with this small town? It's a long way from my capital in Marib."

Solomon smiled. That was just what he wanted her to ask. "If you sign the agreement, we'll be partners and I'll help you to benefit by the new sea route."

"I don't understand."

Solomon called for some parchment and some charcoal. Then he began to draw a crude map of the Red Sea and the coast of Africa. "See, if you are here instead of over here at Marib, you can collect all the ivory, precious stones, animal skins, and spices from this whole country and send them on ships to my port. In turn I can easily ship you the supplies you might need as the ships set out for the distant ports."

She bit her lower lip and frowned as she studied the parchment carefully. "I'll have to think about it. We've always ruled most of the coast of Ethiopia but we've never built any real towns or ports there. I must also think of my trade with countries to the south and east of Sheba."

"That's the whole point. If you stay in Marib, my ships will cut off much of your trade, but if you move you can be right in the center of everything."

She cocked her head to one side and looked at him from under long curled lashes. "And," she said, "what of this section that promises me an heir to the throne?"

Solomon smiled. He'd wondered just how she'd bring up the subject. "Why," he said, "if you sign the agreement, not only will our countries be married but we'll be married. I'd hoped this would be agreeable to you."

"This marriage. What does it mean?"

"It's very simple. I've already ordered a wedding bed for you and have had it placed in my own chambers."

She stiffened slightly. "And so you too will try to control me."

Again Solomon smiled a relaxed, confident smile. "Of course I have no such thing in mind. We'll decide on things together; make an agreement."

"What kind of an agreement?"

"We could agree, for instance, that only if you take something that belongs to me can I claim you."

Now the queen smiled. "Only if I take something that belongs to you. That should be easy. Why would I take something that belongs to you. I have everything I want."

"Exactly," said Solomon. "There's really very little chance that I can claim you. However, if you forget and take something that is mine, then you will belong to me. Isn't that fair enough?"

"It's fair," she said smiling as she rolled the scroll back into its goatskin holder.

So the agreement was signed and that afternoon the queen and her maidens moved her to the apartment of Solomon, where she found that he had indeed designed a marvelous bed. The posts were covered with gold leaf and the curtains that pulled around it were of fine linen with embroidered peacocks and leopards that resembled his own curtains of stalking lions. He had ordered the curtains made when he first heard of her coming. He had thought at the time that they would be a fitting gift for her to take back to Sheba. Now they served the purpose of giving her the privacy she would need in this large bedchamber where tribesmen, servants, and emissaries came and went at all hours of the day and night.

From the moment the treaties were signed the feasting and celebration began. It was the same sort of feast and celebration that always took place at any royal wedding. Each day started with some new adventure, and every night there was a lavish feast. Solomon and the queen were constantly together, but at night, when they retreated to his bed chamber, she was always cautious to remind him that she had taken nothing that was his and so the agreement that had been signed seemed to come no closer to bringing them together than before.

Solomon saw quite clearly that while she desperately wanted an heir to the throne, still she could not bring herself to yield, to give up, to surrender herself. Even if it meant she must go back to her country without her desired heir, she seemed to feel the need to remain aloof. He could tell that she loved him. Her eyes sparkled with animation when she looked at him, and sometimes she almost reached out to touch his hand when they were talking. She had taken to spending longer and longer with her beauticians and hairdressers and had emerged looking devastatingly beautiful.

With his typical penchant to solve problems, Solomon finally made up his mind. He must act and it must be done in such a way that she wouldn't feel trapped or resentful. "It is the habit of the people of Arabia to solemnize a serious agreement with the mutual eating of salt. Tonight we'll have salt in everything, and the queen and I will perform a special salt-eating ritual joining our two countries in peace and prosperity," he ordered those preparing the feast.

Then later, in the bedchamber, knowing she would be thirsty, he ordered a flask of fresh spring water and a silver goblet placed by her bed.

That night after the feasting and festivities had come to an end they all retired to their beds. Solomon said goodnight to the queen but was resolved not to go to sleep until his plan was implemented. He didn't have long to wait. He heard her rise, draw the curtain aside, pick up the flask, pour water into the goblet, and drink not once but twice and then again as though the spices had taken full effect.

In the shaft of moonlight he saw her quite clearly. From the small bare feet on the marble floor to the hair that was now loose and flowing down her back she was a vision both lovely and desirable beyond anything he had ever seen. He must be careful not to frighten her.

Noiselessly he got out of bed and moved behind her. "You realize you have lost the wager," he said softly. She dropped the goblet and deftly he caught it and placed it on the low stool.

She whirled and stood leaning against the pillar of the bed and looked at him with large, frightened eyes that reminded him of one of his high-strung Egyptian horses. "What will you do?" she asked. "It was just water and I was thirsty."

"Yes, it was a rather despicable trick. It was not only the salt but to make sure, I told the servants to add hot spices to your food. I wanted to make sure you'd get thirsty enough to drink my water."

"Your water?"

"Yes, do you agree? This water isn't from Marib, it's from Jerusalem. It's my water."

She stood looking at him with questioning, fearful eyes. Once again he realized that somehow she'd been terribly frightened in the past. Perhaps as a queen she had so schooled herself to be aloof that it was difficult to give even a bit of herself to anyone else. She reminded him of some little animals brought in from the wild that need to be tamed.

She glanced at the goblet. "And so now . . . ?"

"Now I ask only that you play a game. A game you will find very pleasant. Haven't you enjoyed most of the things I've planned for you?"

He could see that she was softening, relenting, but her voice was hesitant. "Yes, but is this a game I can win?" she asked.

In the darkness he smiled and moved closer to her, taking her hand. It was small, warm, and very feminine. "You'll win all the pieces and walk off with the grand prize."

She pulled her hand away and held her hair back as though to see him better. "I'll win all the pieces?" she asked. "I can't imagine such a game played against the all-wise Solomon."

He could see that she was interested. She obviously liked the idea of winning. "And what do I have to do to play this game?" she asked.

"Each night when the moon comes up you'll become a woman," he said. "Perhaps even a simple village woman. For a short time you'll forget you're a queen."

"And who'll you be?"

"Why, I'll be a handsome village lad that has fallen madly in love with you." He could see she was caught up in the magic of the idea, though there was still a skittishness about her.

"I suppose you would be in charge?"

He was a bit taken aback by her abruptness. "Of course. That would be the first rule of the game because you don't even know how to play."

She tilted her head to one side and looked skeptical. "I've never played a game where I wasn't in charge and sure to win."

"Oh you'll win, even when I'm in charge, and you can be in charge as soon as you learn to play." That pleased her. A small smile played around her mouth. "What must one learn to be in charge?"

He took both her hands in his so he could look at her. "You'd have to learn to tell me how much you love me, how handsome I am, and how you want to be close to me and to make me happy."

"And that is what you would do when you were in charge?"

"Of course, that is the whole nature of the game."

"Could I stop the game if I didn't like it?"

"I would say that should be possible, but then you'd have to give me the same privilege when you're in charge." She pulled her hands away and stepped back so she could see him in the moonlight. She seemed to be getting used to him as a person, a person invading her very private world. She was deciding with the cold, reasoning side of her mind whether to trust herself to him. She was no longer the light, jovial companion. He could see a real struggle going on. "And you would be in charge?" she asked again.

"Yes, I would be in charge."

"Until I learned to play ..."

He smiled the boyish, amused smile and leaned against the pillar of her bed crossing his arms. "Until you learn to play."

She picked up the silver goblet and took a long drink, looking at him over the rim, sizing him up. He could tell she was seeing him not as a fearful monster but as the man she had been falling in love with since the first moment she saw him in the garden at Jericho. She set the goblet down and turned to him smiling, her arms outstretched. "All right. I'll play and you can be in charge, but only while the moon is out."

"It's agreed, my love," he said taking her in his arms and holding her for a moment while he marveled at how fragile she was and how lovely the fragrance of her hair. Then in one swift, sure movement he picked her up and started for his bed.

"Your bed?" she asked. "Not mine?"

"It's my bed when I'm in charge."

"And when I learn to be in charge it will be mine?" He stopped and looked down at her; she was soft and yielding, no longer frightened and aloof. "Of course when you're in charge, you choose."

* * *

The next morning she lay in his arms running one finger across his eyebrows and around his well-shaped beard, and looking at him with soft, loving eyes. "I've decided to let you be in charge, but just at night when the moon is up."

He pulled her closer to him and kissed her eagerly until she laughed and pulled away. "And what is the grand prize that I'm to win?" she asked.

He was immediately sobered, and when he spoke it was with an emotion she hadn't seen before. She thought she detected tears in his eyes. "The prize is our son. You'll have a son. He'll be my favorite son but you'll carry him with you back to your country and he'll always remind you of me. I'll be left with nothing but a memory of great joy."

She sat up and her hands flew to her slender, slightly rounded stomach. "I'll have a son? You're sure?"

He pulled her down to him and held her as though he never wanted her to go. "Yes, you'll have a son. Such loving can only produce a son, and he'll rule justly and wisely when we're both gone."

She was overwhelmed. The thing she wanted most, the impossible desire of her heart was to come about through this man whom she found so utterly irresistible. "But you'll come to visit Sheba?"

"I'd like to think that I could, but in my heart I know it will never happen. But we'll be partners, and our son, when he is old enough, can come and visit me. He must come back to be instructed further in our faith."

"And what if you don't recognize him?"

"Not recognize our son!" He almost laughed, then grew serious. "You're right. He must have proof, not for me but for my subjects. Here's my ring. It's the only thing I own that was my father's other than the crown. I treasure it above all else. The one that holds this ring holds my heart. Take it. Never let it from your sight, and when the time comes, send it back with our son."

She took the ring and held it to the light, then fitted it on each of her fingers. It was obvious they were all too small. It was a large, rather crudely formed setting with a lion on each side of a flat, luminous stone etched with the crossed pyramids that made the six-pointed star. She knew this was the symbol most often used on Israel's banners and hangings and the lions were the symbol of the tribe of Judah.

Solomon lay back among the cushions and watched her. "As he wears this ring," he said, "he'll always remember that he's of the tribe of Judah and his symbol is the king of beasts—the lion."

She leaned back in his arms and turned to look at him. "What sort of man will he be, this son of the leopard queen and the lion of Judah?"

"He'll be a king we can both be proud of. Maybe his kingdom will last longer than mine. I pray that it will."

"We'll call him David in memory of your father."

"In our language David means beloved, and this son will truly be beloved."

* * *

Later that day when the feasting was almost over and many gifts had been exchanged, the queen asked to make an announcement. Solomon was amused and curious, but he quickly gave her permission. She stood up before the happy revelers, and waiting until everyone was quiet, said, "We've opened the treasure houses of Arabia and spread them at your feet. We've brought our gold, our perfume, and our incense. But there is one gift yet to be given—a gift that expresses my own affection for your king. It is a gift too precious to be bought, it is only given to those we choose to honor above all others." With that she called Tamrin to her and ordered him to have the gift brought into the hall.

No one spoke as all eyes turned to the great bronze doors though which Tamrin had disappeared. Suddenly there was the rolling thunder of drums, the high trilling of singers, and the pounding of dancing feet as a glorious procession entered the hall. Women dressed in diaphanous gowns of bright colors with jangling ankle, bracelets, silver armbands, rings, and toe rings sang and beat their small finger drums while others with leopard skins thrown over their shoulders and cinched at the waist carried gold incense burners that quickly filled the room with the fragrance of sandal-wood. Drummers dressed only in leopard skins came next and trumpeters, acrobats, jugglers, and dancers all paraded into the room.

Last of all Tamrin appeared in the door with a white Arabian horse that was simply but elegantly adorned with golden bridle and woven trappings. The way parted before him as he came slowly and majestically toward the throne.

Solomon was deeply moved. He came down the steps of his throne and, ignoring Tamrin, took the bridle and began talking softly and persuasively to the horse. For a moment the horse veered to one side, tossed her head, shook her magnificent mane, and bared her teeth. Tamrin moved as though to help and the queen hurried down the steps, but Solomon continued to talk softly to the horse.

Everyone in the room waited in fearful anticipation of some disaster. They knew how their king had wanted just such a horse, and they all feared this could prove to be an abysmal disappointment if the horse rejected him.

Only Solomon seemed confident. He continued to talk, and very tentatively the horse seemed to be listening. Then to everyone's amazement, Solomon started to back in a circle and the horse followed him. He moved up and down the hall, and the horse moved with him as though there were some special communication only the two of them understood. "See," the people said, "it's true, just as we've heard. The king knows the language of the animals."

From that day on the white Arabian horse and the king were inseparable. A bond developed between them that brought the king much happiness, more happiness than any of the other animals he had adopted over the years. This horse, whose name remained Zad el-Rukab, just as the queen had named her, gained a reputation for flying over the ground with her hoofs barely touching, and for loyalty to her master of an unusual degree.

* * *

The time passed quickly and the day came when the queen had to leave. It had been decided that she would go to Solomon's port of Ezion-Geber and sail in one of his vessels as far as Ethiopia. Here she would go ashore and check the feasibility of actually moving her capital to this coastal site before returning home to Marib. "I would like to move, to start all over again; to found a city on the new principles I've learned and worship the God I now believe in."

Solomon had decided to travel with her down to the Red Sea. He hated saying goodbye and wanted to be with her as long as possible.

They went first to Jericho where they reviewed all that had happened to them since her arrival. They laughed again at Solomon's fear that she might have the feet of a donkey and her wonder at the story of the winds being held in control under his throne. They left regretting that the magical time would soon come to an end.

They traveled to the coastal town of Eloth and then rode the two and a half hours to the island port of Ezion-Geber. The queen was interested in every aspect of this port. "Why is it built on this island?" she asked.

"This used to be called Jezirat Faraun when the pharaohs of Egypt anchored their ships here," Solomon said. "On the landward side of the island there is a natural harbor that shelters any ship from the turbulence of the Red Sea. I paid Hiram the king of Phoenicia twenty thousand kors of wheat and twenty kors of beaten oil for the ten ships he built for me here in this place."

"And he brought the cedars clear from his mountains?"

Solomon nodded. "It took eight hundred camels just to carry the lumber needed for the ships."

They spent a day examining the ship she would sail in. There were orders given and provisions added that would make the trip by sea enjoyable. She had sent her camels with Tamrin and Il Hamd on the long land route back to Marib, packed with precious gifts from the king. The more personal gifts were to go with her by sea.

The island had a wall with towers spaced evenly around it, and there was a fortress in which they were given the royal rooms built by Hiram's men for just such an occasion. From one of the rooms there was a balcony from which they could watch the activity in the sheltered harbor and beyond that view the mountains of the Sinai. From another room on the opposite side there was a similar balcony that looked out to the south from which they could see the vast expanse of sea down which the queen would sail.

"When you leave," Solomon told her, "I'll come to this place and watch your ship until it disappears. It'll be the most difficult thing I've ever done."

Because she couldn't bear to see the pain in his face, she quickly changed the subject. "My love," she said, "I'm about to leave and you've never told me what was of most importance in the world."

"Still at the last you are asking questions." Solomon couldn't help smiling.

"If I am to raise our son, surely I must tell him what his father thought was most important."

"What do you think I'll say is most important?" This was the pattern they had followed. He was always testing her to see what she would say before he shared with her his own concept.

She thought for a moment, then her face brightened and her eyes sparkled. "Of course you'll say great wealth. You have amassed gold and silver and it has permitted you to buy everything for both you and your people. Yes, wealth is most important."

Solomon shook his head. "A man can have great wealth and be a fool and waste it so that he is worse off than a poor man. So I would say wisdom is of utmost importance. Wisdom with understanding."

Bilqis was astounded. "Why wisdom?" she asked.

"A man who has wisdom has everything to make him happy. He will know that his life is short, a fool may rule after him and utterly destroy all that he has so carefully built. He'll begin to look for things that are lasting; things that don't change and don't disappear with this short life."

"I don't understand," she said.

"It's obvious that when I die I'll leave all the fine buildings I've built, all the gold I've collected, the fortune I've amassed, my carefully designed crown, the clothes I take such pride in. I can take none of this."

"There is nothing we can take when we die. This is the ultimate sadness of life."

"Ah, but you are wrong. My father taught me to view things differently. Before I was born there was another child my mother had that died, and when asked why he was no longer mourning, my father said, 'He cannot come back to me but I can go to him.' You see, that is the clue to what is eternal. I will go to my God when I die. He is a spirit and is not left behind in some earthly temple. The people I love are also made of eternal spirit, and they too will be with me there. Everything else will be left here to molder into dust."

Bilqis stared at him with a look of wonder and amazement on her face. "Our love and the child I carry are eternal. Even the temple you have built and your fine palace is as nothing compared to these treasures."

"We must never forget this. We may never see each other again, but our child and our love is something that will last long after everything else is gone."

The next day as her ship moved out into the sea and the sails filled with the southerly wind, the queen stood at the ship's rail. She was watching first the man on the balcony who stood there as long as she could see, and then it was the island she watched until it too disappeared. Something within her, a hardness, a fierce independence was crumbling, breaking apart. She couldn't ever remember feeling such pain. She who had never cried felt tears coursing down her face. It was as though the only thing in the world that really mattered was slowly receding and would soon be gone forever.

Only when the first star of the evening came out was she finally willing to leave the railing, but her eyes were red with weeping and she could not endure speaking to anyone. She had not imagined it would be so painful to love someone. She had never experienced anything that meant more to her than her country and her throne. All of this was new. She wondered if there would ever be an end to this terrible grieving.

It was on the second night a strange healing began to take place. There was something she must remember. Something important. Something he had told her. She struggled to remember just how the words went. "Our child and our love," he had said, "will last long after everything else is gone." She repeated the words over and over again trying to understand just what he'd meant.

The child was born before she finally reached home. It was a boy, and she named him David. As she held him in her arms and crooned to him like any peasant mother, she found that she loved him with such a tender, piercingly fierce love that it astounded her. Finally she understood what Solomon had been trying to tell her. "Of our love we formed an arrow," she said, "an arrow that will shoot into the future where we can never go. Of all the things I've done it alone is lasting and eternal." This child and these words at last brought comfort to the troubled queen.

Epilogue

The queen never returned, and Solomon never saw her again. However, in the country of Ethiopia a young man ruled who proudly recorded that he was the son of the great Solomon and the queen of Sheba. This son, as legend tells us, did make one very memorable trip to Jerusalem.

Perhaps we can catch a glimpse of this young prince as he stands on the quay watching the men load a ship with the gifts he is taking with him. He is excited. This is the first time his mother has allowed him to travel without her. He is going to visit his father in the strange, far-off country to the north.

Undoubtedly both Tamrin the trader and his mother have told him often of her daring trip to visit the king of this country. He has been told of the gifts they exchanged and how his mother had finally given the king a prized, white horse. Then, perhaps, his uncle Rydan would tell how the king had written into the state agreement that his best gift to the queen would be an heir. "And you," he would say, "are that heir."

He had always known that someday he was to set sail for that far-off country to visit his father. He twists the crudely made ring on his finger. It has been his father's and before that his grandfather's. When he was a child his mother had tied it around his neck and then later after he had promised to take care of it, she let him wear it.

Tamrin and a huge retinue of men from his own tribe are to make the trip with him. They are to sail to the port of Ezion Geber where Solomon's garrisons will meet them and escort them across the Sinai to the town of Gaza.

"I'm giving you the city of Gaza, my son," his father had written. "It will be a permanent possession, a resting place before you travel on to see me in Jerusalem." He had seen the scroll and read the words himself. He noticed that in the scroll he had been addressed by his personal name of David and not his kingly title of Menelik I.

The names of places, the writing on the scroll, and the accent of the messengers were all foreign to him. For the first time he felt hesitant about going. After all these years of longing to meet his legendary father he found himself afraid. "What if my father doesn't acknowledge me? What if he is disappointed?"

He could have spared himself the worry. Tradition tells us that before he even arrived in Jerusalem the people mistook him for Solomon. At the court of his father he was immediately recognized and picked out of the milling tribesmen he had come with. "I don't need to see the ring," Solomon said. "Without a doubt you are my son."

It was a joyful reunion. All that Solomon had found lacking in his other sons was abundantly present in this handsome young man. Menelik, like Nathan's son Mattatha, enjoyed studying the law with the priests. He was interested in hearing all that his father had learned about animals and plants and he asked questions about truth and wisdom much as his mother had done.

Though it had been agreed on from the beginning that Menelik had come only on a visit, still Solomon loved him so, and he determined not to part with him. He actually toyed with the idea of replacing Rehoboam with Menelik. Unfortunately, as time passed there were those who grew jealous of Solomon's attention to Menelik, and they plotted against him.

When Solomon realized the ill will toward his favorite son, he reluctantly agreed to let him return to Axum. Before agreeing, however, he extracted from his priests a promise that each would send his eldest son with Menelik back to his country. These young men, who were well versed in the temple rites and rituals, were to take with them replicas of each item in the temple's furnishings. With these they would set up a temple and worship just as they did in Jerusalem.

I like to think that perhaps it was for this son that Solomon collected his proverbs. His bits of wisdom gleaned over the years would be of great help to the young king.

As Solomon watched him go he must have realized that nothing in Jerusalem had changed. Rehoboam would be the next king at his death and undoubtedly Jeroboam would return from Egypt to cause him trouble. He could well believe that just as Ahijah had predicted, ten of the tribes would go to Jeroboam while only Judah and Benjamin would be left to Rehoboam.

What he didn't know was that only five years after his death, the pharaoh, Shishak, would march up and Rehoboam would buy him off with the riches his father had carefully amassed. The three hundred golden shields of the house guards, treasures from the palace, and most of the golden objects from the temple itself were all taken by the greedy pharaoh. Shishak recorded this entire campaign on the south wall of the temple at Karnak, where it can be seen today.

Four hundred years after the Davidic line first came to the throne, the glorious temple Solomon had built was destroyed. The people were taken into captivity and their country became a Babylonian province.

As to Menelik I, the son of the leopard queen and the king who was known as the lion of Judah, he established a kingdom that until the rise of Islam extended over most of Ethiopia and Yemen. He built a beautiful capital at Axum and a port city at Adulis. As we might expect, he is supposed to have built many of the dams that can still be found in the highlands. These dams were used to store water and to irrigate the land during the dry season just as they did in Marib.

In 1904 the tomb of Menelik I was found in a large mausoleum. The coffin contained the body of a king still wearing his golden crown. The crown was carefully removed and has been placed with other crowns of the Ethiopian kings in the famous cathedral of St. Mary of Zion in Axum.

Haile Selassie was the last king to rule in Ethiopia. At his coronation he rode his horse through crowds of excited people up to the gates of Axum. Here, under the sign of the coptic cross, he cut a symbolic cord and, like those many kings before him, declared, "I am the son of David and Solomon, and Ibna Hakim." Ibna Hakim means "son of the wise" and is another name by which Menelik I was known.

Stranger still, in the church of St. Mary of Zion, the ark of the covenant is still supposed to reside.

Solomon had hoped his temple would last down through the ages, or that his line of kings would still rule in Israel. How surprised he would have been to find that the son born of his love for a queen who came seeking truth would have descendants that would rule down to the twentieth century in Ethiopia, a country he never even visited.

Sources

BOOKS

Aharoni, Yohanan and Avi-Yonah, Michael. *The Macmillan Bible Atlas.* New York: Macmillan Publishing Co. Inc., 1977.

Baines, John and Malek, Jaromir. *Atlas of Ancient Egypt.* Littlegate House, Oxford: Oxford Phaidon Press, Ltd., 48, 147.

Baum, James E. *The Unknown Ethiopia.* New York: Grosset & Dunlap, 1927.

Dobelis, Inge N., ed. *Magic and Medicine of Plants.* Pleasantville, N.Y.: Reader's Digest Assn, Inc., 1986.

Doe, Brian. *Southern Arabia.* London: Thames & Hudson, 1971.

El-Qur'an. Aden, South Yemen: Maktaba El-Araby.

Gardner, Joseph L., ed. *Atlas of the Bible: An Illustrated Guide to the Holy Land.* Pleasantville, N.Y.: Readers Digest Assn. Inc., 1981.

Great Events of Bible Times. Garden City, New York: Doubleday & Co., Inc. 1987.

Jenner, Michael. *Yemen Rediscovered.* London: Longman, 1983.

Keller, Werner. *The Bible as History.* New York: William Morrow and Company, 1956.

Lord, Edith. *Queen of Sheba's Heirs.* Washington, D.C.: Acropolis Books 1970.

Muller, Madeleine G., and Muller, J. H. *Harper's Bible Dictionary.* New York: Harper & Row, 1961.

Pankhurst, Sylvia. *Ethiopia, A Cultural History.* Essex, England: Lalibelia House, 1959.

Philby, H. St. John. *The Queen of Sheba.* London: Quartet Books, 1981.

Tarcici, Adnan. *The Queen of Sheba's Land.* Beirut, Lebanon: Nowfel Publishers, n.d.

Tenney, Merrill C., ed. *The Zondervan Pictorial Bible Dictionary.* Grand Rapids, MI: Zondervan, 1974.

Tonkin, Thelma. *Ethiopia With Love.* London: Hodder and Stoughton, 1972.

Westland, Pamela. *Encyclopedia of Spices.* Secaucus, New Jersey: Chartwell Books Inc. 1979.

PERIODICALS

Brisco, Thomas V. "Human Sacrifice in the Ancient Middle East." *Biblical Illustrator* (Summer 1984): 73.

Biblical Archaeology Review (1). Shanks, Hershel, ed. "Nelson Glueck & King Solomon: A Romance That Ended," no. 1 (March 1975): 1–16. (3).

——Singer, Suzanne F. "Winter Palaces in Jericho," no. 2 (June 1977): 1. (5).

——Shiloh, Yigal and Kaplan, Mendel. "Digging in the City of David," no. 4 July–August 1979). (7).

——Flinder, Alexander. "Is This Solomon's Seaport?" no. 4 (July–August 1989): 32–42.

——Hammond, Philip C. "New Light on the Nabataeans," no. 2 (March–April 1981). (10).

——Negev, Avraham. "Understanding the Nabateans," no. 6 (November–December 1988): 27–45. (15).

——Shanks, Hershel. "The City of David after Five Years of Digging," no. 6 (November–December 1985): 22–38. (14).

——Beit-Arieh, Itzhaq. "New Light on the Edomites," no. 2 (March–April 1988). (14).

——Stager, Lawrence E. and Wolff, Samuel R. "Child Sacrifice at Carthage," no. 1 (January–February 1984): 31. (11).

* * *

Look for more captivating biblical stories to come from River North and Roberta Kells Dorr.

river north

FICTION FROM MOODY PUBLISHERS

River North Fiction is here to provide quality fiction that will refresh and encourage you in your daily walk with God. We want to help readers know, love, and serve JESUS through the power of story.

Connect with us at www.rivernorthfiction.com

- Blog
- Newsletter
- Free Giveaways

- Behind the scenes look at writing fiction and publishing
- Book Club

MOODY
PUBLISHERS

www.MoodyPublishers.com